Illusions

ORDER OF THE DRAGON - BOOK I

ALLISON A. ANDREWS

AAW PUBLISHING

For Krystal, Shannon, Melinda and Jammi-Lee, for being my test audience and loving these characters as much as I do.

For my husband, Andrew and my daughter, Evelyn, who were patient while these characters and their story consumed my every waking moment!

Without you all, this wouldn't have been possible.

Contents

Song List

Hold On - Chord Overstreet
Without You - Ursine Vulpinr, Annaca
Ghost Town - Benson Boone
Take On The World - You and Me at Six
On The Rise - Generdyn, Bellsaint
Unsteady - X Ambassadors
Sanctuary - Welshly Arms
Not Your Baby - Cadmium, Jex
I Guess I'm in Love - Clinton Kane
Warriors - League of Legends, 2WEI, Edda Hayes
Survivor - 2 WEI, Edda Hayes
Everybody Wants To Rule The World - Lorde

Prologue

I SAT IN MY car, staring ahead momentarily, my mind racing and my heart beating a hundred miles an hour. These things just did not exist in real life. Yet, here I sat, staring at the scene before me. They moved so quickly, almost as if they were dancing with each other. Yet the end of the dance would culminate in one of their deaths. One protected me from the other, yet I still did not understand why. Why me? Why had I been chosen? Why was I the one who had to discover that the reality that so many others lived with was an illusion? To find out that the actual truth was so terrifying that it made me wish that my ignorance still protected me?

And most importantly... Why was I still sitting in this car when I could be gone by now? Surely normal, sane people did not wait to see who was about to win in a battle to the death when their own death would surely follow...

I guess I should start from the beginning...

Chapter One

"HAPPY BIRTHDAY ISOLDE." My identical twin sister, Aurora, said as she walked into my bedroom, and I woke groggily with a groan. Being reminded that I had just turned a quarter of a century old was not my ideal way to be woken up. I had once vowed that I would refuse to tell people how old I was after I turned twenty-one, and well... Twenty-five felt like a death sentence.

"Hey. Thanks. And happy birthday to you too." I managed to respond through the haze of the hangover that was currently holding me hostage. My head felt as though it had been invaded by a hive of bees, and I looked around, half expecting to see the bus that I was certain had hit me in the middle of the night.

"Big night?" Aurora grinned evilly at me, and I threw a cushion at her from where I had swept it onto the floor next to my bed the night before.

"Maybe just a little. A girl only turns twenty-five once, right?" I reached for the bottle of water that I had remembered putting next to my bed, wishing I had thought to take Panadol before falling asleep. I had long ago learned that alcohol and I were not a good mix, but my best friend Ainslie

Wilson had insisted on taking me out for a girl's night before I turned twenty-five, and it had somehow turned into an alcohol-binging session. I was struggling to remember the activities of the night before, but all I could remember were random images that didn't make much sense to me.

Swearing never to drink again, I crept slowly out of bed, attempting to avoid the rush of blood to my head, and headed for the bathroom. One glimpse at myself in the mirror and I knew I resembled the Bride of Frankenstein. Or maybe the monster himself. Usually, my reflection was one that I was happy with. With green eyes, long dark reddish-brown hair, tanned skin, and a curvy figure, I knew I was attractive, and I normally took great pride in my appearance. However, I appeared to have forgotten to remove my make-up the night before, and my face looked more like the Joker from Batman than my usual clear-skinned, bright-eyed self.

"Wow… babe, you're a mess!" My boyfriend, Will Blake, entered the bathroom behind me and caught a look at my reflection as I gasped at it in horror. He seemed to realise it was the wrong thing to say as I glared at him through eyes that were ringed with smudged mascara.

"You think?! Remind me not to go out with Ainslie for a girl's night ever again," I grumbled as I turned the hot water on and stripped my pyjamas off. Will just shook his head, laughing, as he closed the door behind him, and I stepped under the steaming hot water.

As I washed the makeup off my face, I again struggled to make sense of the images from last night that flashed through my mind. I remembered having dinner with Ainslie, Will, and Ainslie's boyfriend, Alex. Then the rest of the night consisted of flashes of light, dancing, singing into a microphone drunkenly (I seriously hoped that was a nightmare and not something that I had actually done), then being in an alley with a man who seemed familiar to me, before being in the back of a taxi.

It was the image of the man that had me worried the most. What on earth had I been doing in an alley with a guy who wasn't Will? The man's incredibly handsome face was not one that I recognised, yet there was something familiar about him. Like I was meant to know him. And that he knew me very well.

After an eternity in the shower, I stepped out, feeling marginally better, and dried myself off. I wrapped the towel around myself securely and returned to the bedroom I shared with Will. My clothes from the night before were strewn across the room, something that was usually unheard of. Both Aurora and Will constantly joked about my almost manic cleanliness.

"Oh, so you are going to work today?" Will asked, walking up behind me as I reached for the hideous uniform I was forced to wear to my job as a duty manager of Opalescence, a bar in the city. The uniform was for day shifts when the bar was respectable. Night shifts were less formal, and I could wear jeans and a singlet top. Showing the appropriate amount of cleavage, of course. By day, we served alcohol and pub meals to business people attending meetings, and by night, we served alcohol to those same business people, but they were different kinds of meetings they were attending then. Many a clandestine affair had both started and ended at Opalescence.

"Of course I'm going to work... Unless you have a better offer?" I smiled coyly as Will wrapped his arm around my bare waist.

"Oh, I have a better offer." He nuzzled my neck. "Happy birthday, by the way." I allowed myself to briefly close my eyes and lean back into him as he slowly kissed his way down my neck. A brief flicker of déjà vu that was gone too soon made me wish that I could stay standing there for longer.

However, I knew I couldn't afford to miss work, and my boss wouldn't accept a hangover as a good enough excuse to call in sick, especially on my birthday.

"How about we pick this up tonight? I'm working until seven, and then I'm all yours." I gently pulled away from him and he sighed, knowing that there was no use. He was used to spending half of every weekend keeping himself amused. It was part of the reason we had moved in together in the first place.

"Sounds good. Want me to pick you up?" Will went to sit on the edge of the bed as I continued getting ready.

"No, I'll catch the ferry. You can cook dinner, though." I grinned at him, knowing that I would come home to pizza but not caring much. The idea of working with this hangover was scary enough without the thought of coming home to cook dinner.

I eventually made it out the door and drove to the City Cat ferry terminal. Grabbing my handbag, I headed to wait for the ferry, scrolling mindlessly through all my various social media apps while I stood behind several other commuters waiting on the gangway.

Suddenly, out of nowhere, a rush of images hit me, and I must have looked crazy as I struggled to stay upright. I had never experienced anything like this before, almost like psychic visions that you see people having in movies. I thought I must have been losing my mind. Or my imagination was running away with me, which was more than likely.

I was remembering more from my time in the alley with the mystery man, but the images I saw could not be right... He was whispering in my ear, trying to tell me something important. I could hear his voice in my ear, low and urgent, but it was as though the sound was down very low, and his words were nothing more than a low murmur... I could not for the life of me remember anything he said.

I had led what you would call a fairly normal, even boring, existence up until now. My mother swore that I was born mature and grew even wiser than her every day. My father said I had an old soul, that I had lived before. My sisters just thought I was boring and never had any fun. Of the opinions expressed, I was inclined to believe the latter above all the others. I had always done exactly what was expected of me. I had graduated high school with good grades, went to university, had a good job, and was in a relationship with the perfect guy... The only rebellious thing I ever did was to drop out of uni to travel to the UK and work. And that only ended up lasting four months because I missed Will too much, so I'd come back home and worked for a few years before going back to uni to finish my degree. So, that didn't explain the bizarre images in my mind right now.

I shook my head to clear it as I looked around to find myself already sitting on the City Cat, halfway to the city, the river winding away in front of me...

How on earth did that happen?

My apparent sleepwalking puzzled me as my mobile buzzed in my handbag. I pulled it out absentmindedly and read the text message from Ainslie, wishing me a happy birthday. I hadn't even thought about the fact that it was my birthday since I'd left home, and I suddenly realised that I had not received any presents yet. I was instantly ashamed that the thought had entered my mind. That was not what birthdays were about... Well, it shouldn't be what birthdays were about, at the very least.

But something had to make up for the fact that I was ageing, without my consent, I might add. Presents were just compensation for the ageing process once you turned twenty, and the next milestone birthday was thirty... Or even worse... Fifty. I shuddered at that thought.

I was pulled from my musings as a nearby tour guide started pointing out places of interest around us, and I found myself listening in with a small smile.

"So, welcome to Brisbane, Queensland's thriving capital city. It's the third biggest city in Australia, and it was built on either side of the river we are now on, the very originally named Brisbane River, which winds from beautiful Moreton Bay behind us, right up into the mountains you can see over there." She pointed with her little stick topped with a flag, and all the tourists nodded and smiled. "This river is a big part of the lives of all who live here, and we even have a festival once a year that is all about the river called the River Festival. We do love coming up with original-sounding names here, as you can tell." She tittered, and the tourists all laughed politely. I covered my snort with a cough.

"Brisbane's inhabitants are split between north-siders and south-siders, depending on which side of the river you hail from. We just got on at Bulimba, which is one of our inner city suburbs on the south side." I popped my headphones on to sit back and enjoy the ride along the river.

I always loved seeing people visit Brisbane and had heard the spiel given many times by different tour guides when they brought their groups on the ferry. Although I'd travelled some, I still loved my hometown. After heading to London when I was twenty, I knew how lucky I was to live in Australia, with our fantastic weather and laid-back attitude to life. I still enjoyed my time away, but I'd never been so happy to return to the sunshine state and the country of 'She'll be right, mate'. Even on a mid-winter day, all that was required was a singlet top and a warm jacket. Sure, we complained of being cold, but we really had nothing to complain about. And with how hot it was today, in the height of summer, I would have happily taken the winter chill over the heat that had me sweating whilst I sat at the back of the ferry.

Moving to slide my phone back into my handbag, I saw a flash of something on the inside of my wrist, something golden, and I turned my arm over to look, but there was nothing there.

Vowing never to drink again, as it now seemed to mean I was seeing things, I closed my eyes and attempted to clear my mind of visions and other weird occurrences before I had to start an eight-hour shift, helping other people become intoxicated instead.

Chapter Two

I ARRIVED HOME THAT night, pulled my car into the visitor space next to our townhouse and climbed out of the car, digging around in my handbag to find my house key. As I unlocked the front door, I was surprised to find all the lights out, as Will's car was still in the driveway.

Moving through the house, turning on lights as I went, I called out to Will without any response. I knew that Aurora wasn't at home, as she and her boyfriend, Jacob, were out celebrating Aurora's birthday together, but Will had messaged me ten minutes ago to see how much later I would be, so his absence now was strange. Coming to the top of the stairs, I could see a flickering light shining through the crack at the bottom of our bedroom door, and I moved to open it a little uncertainly, apprehensive of what I might find on the other side. My hand was still on the door handle, and it took me a moment to register what I was seeing before I let out a gasp at the scene before me.

The room was lit entirely by tea-light candles placed all around the room, with rose petals scattered all over the place. And there, lying on the bed on his side, propped up on one elbow, was Will, nervously playing with what looked like a ring box.

The look on my face must have been priceless as I gaped at him in shock. I raised a shaking hand to my mouth, watching as he rose to his feet and moved to stand in front of me, silently dropping to one knee and holding the ring box open in front of me.

"Isolde Smith... I love you more than I ever thought it was possible to love someone. Would you do me the honour of becoming my wife?" His voice was thick with emotion that he struggled to hide, and I was momentarily struck by how handsome he was, with his brown hair cut short and his perfect sun-kissed skin. Wearing a fitted t-shirt and jeans, I could appreciate the effect that regular hours in the gym and running had on his body.

Swaying in place for a moment, my heart swelled, and I had to remind myself to breathe. After another stunned moment of silence, I dropped my handbag and flung myself at him as he rose to meet me. I kissed him hard, unable to think straight. We had talked about getting married for a while, but I had no idea he had been planning this. I felt as though the breath had been knocked out of me.

"Is that a yes?" He asked with a grin as he stepped back to look at me. I smiled at him, rapidly blinking to keep the happy tears from escaping my eyes, and simply nodded, unable to speak. I couldn't imagine marrying anyone else. With a small laugh, he lifted me off the ground and swung me around for a moment before setting me back down and kissing me softly. We looked down together as he slid the most perfect ring onto my finger.

"I had this designed months ago. I hope you like it?" He asked nervously as I stared at the elegant ring that now sat on my left ring finger. Vintage inspired, with a large square diamond set in a white gold band, it was surrounded by multiple little diamonds and garnets, my birthstone.

"It's gorgeous! I couldn't have chosen better if I tried." I held my hand out before me, transfixed, as I turned my hand this way and that, the diamonds catching the light of the candles nearest to me. I could stare at it all night.

"That's fantastic... Now go get ready 'cause we're going to your parents for dinner." He smacked me playfully on the butt, and I was momentarily knocked out of my happy place, looking up into Will's smirking face in surprise.

"What? You propose to me, then drag me off to my parent's house to have dinner... What's so romantic about that?" I asked, attempting to keep the disappointment out of my voice. I thought a romantic dinner at home followed by a mind-blowing love-making session was in order, not a forced visit to my parent's house.

"Sorry, babe, but they rang today to confirm that we were going there for dinner for your birthday. Did you maybe forget to mention something about that after you last spoke to your mother?" I wracked my brain, trying to remember the details of my previous conversation with my mother last week. She may have mentioned something, but I couldn't remember saying yes. Knowing my mother, that didn't matter.

"Surely, when you told them you were proposing, Mum would have understood?" Even saying the words, I knew that wasn't likely, and Will laughed as he shook his head.

"Have you met your mother? I'm surprised she didn't insist that she was sitting in the room as it happened. This was the compromise, propose first on my own, then hand you over to them all." Will's eyes twinkled as he grinned with a shrug, and I sighed, knowing full well that there was no point in trying to get out of it.

"Fine." I pouted, and after a few more kisses of joy, I headed into the bathroom to get ready for a visit to my family.

As I stood in the shower, I paused to think about what had just happened. I was now engaged. I had a fiance... Perhaps even harder to grasp was that *I* was someone's fiancee. I remembered the first time Will had ever called me his girlfriend, back when we were nineteen, and I felt the same tingle of excitement run up my spine at the thought. At the time, I had already been referring to him as my boyfriend to my friends, but we had never actually used those words in front of one another, and I was so excited when he was the first one to say it. I was sure I would feel the same excitement when I heard him use the word fiancee for the first time. I tried hard not to even think about what my reaction would be the first time he used the word wife... It was all a lot for a girl to take in on her twenty-fifth birthday... However, it was something I could get used to.

We arrived at my parent's house, and I knew instantly that Mum had told my sisters. Aurora and I were the youngest and second set of twins in the family. My five other sisters, Briseis, Dido, Guinevere, and fraternal twins, Selena and Aphrodite were all gathered in the lounge room of my parent's house as Will and I walked through the front door. My mother had a thing for mythological names, probably to compensate for our rather standard last name. There was a look of bittersweet happiness on my twin's face, which I assumed was because this was just another step towards adulthood that we had to take together.

Everyone held their collective breaths, and my sisters all sat on the edges of their seats, each trying to get a glimpse of my left hand. With a grin, I held my hand up and was immediately set upon by six screeching women who ranged in age from twenty-five to thirty-two. The chaos was interrupted as my mother and father entered the room, followed closely by five children, my nieces and nephew, who had been in the kitchen hounding my mother about dinner. My sisters' collective partners were already out on the back patio, and Will quickly made his escape to join them, closely followed by my father after he gave me a congratulatory hug.

"So, how long has everyone known about this?" I eventually got the chance to ask as they all sat back down again, and I joined Aurora on the floor.

As the women of my family all answered at once, I marvelled at my luck to have such a close family. My parents had both come from big families and had wanted a tribe of their own. My mother was the youngest of ten, with three older brothers and six older sisters, and my father was the youngest of twelve, with six older brothers and five older sisters. When they started their own family, they continued to try for a boy but eventually gave up with the arrival of a second set of twin girls. My dad had to settle for seven tomboys instead. We had all enjoyed camping and fishing as children, and we had still maintained our strong family bond. We were all just lucky that the partners we had each found were happy to be with women whose family was their world.

I listened absently as Aurora began telling us about Will's plan to have her out of the house so he could propose tonight, as my youngest and favourite niece, Annelise, crawled into my lap. She was Briseis' daughter, and I had recently been named her godmother, something that I was immensely proud of. I played with her curls, seeing another flash of gold on the inside of my wrist. However, as soon as I looked down at my wrist properly, it was gone again. Refusing to give any more brain space to strange occurrences, I put it down to a trick of the light. I sighed contentedly. I hoped my life would always be this way, surrounded by family and loved by a man who would never leave me...

As I lay asleep in Will's arms later that night, I was pulled into a vivid dream.

"Isolde, you have to be careful. It's starting." I ran to keep up with the man in front of me as he signalled for me to follow him. He was at least a head taller than me, and I raced to try and keep up with him through the fog swirling around us.

"What's starting? Why do I need to be careful?" I had to yell as he was getting further and further ahead of me, slowly melting away into the fog with each step until all I could make out was a shadow.

I could hear the faintest laugh that slowly began to get louder behind me. I turned in a half circle as the laugh took on a sinister tone, filling the space all around me. My heart started to race with fear, and I clapped my hands over my ears and fell to my knees as the laughter began to echo inside my head, making my ears ring.

It ended abruptly, and now the sound of my breathing echoed through the fog.

"Get up! We need to get out of here!" As I tried to get back on my feet, the man appeared at my side and took hold of my arm. I kept a close eye on him as he surveyed our surroundings with a great deal of anxiety. I was struck by his intensely handsome features; his dark brown hair, chiselled jawline, and sun-kissed skin left me in awe. He stood tall and had a well-defined physique, with his muscles showing through his shirt sleeves. However, what truly caught my attention were his eyes; they were a striking shade of blue that seemed almost unreal.

A shadow crept closer behind him, bringing my focus back to the situation we were in, and I let out a piercing scream as the laughter resumed, even louder than before. Squinting through the thick fog, I could only make out the silhouette of a man, but his piercing blue eyes shone through.

"Isolde." It was almost as though the shadows sang my name, and a chill ran through me. "We will find you, Isolde. He can't keep you from us forever, Isolde." Never had the sound of my name been so terrifying. The voice that spoke sounded ancient and sinister, and I began to shake.

The man in front of me whirled to face the shadowy figure behind him, just as it was joined by another with the same eyes, another laugh joining the one that was already deafening me. I couldn't make out if this figure was a male or female.

My companion urged me to run, yelling the word as he charged into the fog to face the shadowy figures. I strained to see through the haze, but all I could discern were muffled sounds of battle. Suddenly, a woman's voice whispered urgently in my ear. "It's not time yet, Isolde. You need to wake up!"

I sat up with a start, my breathing ragged, as the darkness of my bedroom replaced the images from my dream.

"Babe? What's wrong?" Will's voice cut through the darkness, groggy, and I could tell that I'd woken him up.

"Sorry baby… Just a weird dream… Go back to sleep." His breathing evened out again, and I envied his ability to fall asleep so quickly. I gently pushed back the covers and climbed out of bed, going into the adjoining bathroom to get a drink of water.

After a quick glance at myself in the mirror, I refused to look at my reflection, not wanting to see the paleness of my skin and dark circles under my eyes. That dream had done a number on me, and my hand shook slightly as I turned on the tap to fill my glass.

As my grasp on reality slowly returned, I was puzzled at what I'd just seen. The man who had been protecting me in the dream was the same man from my sketchy memories from the night before. There was something eerily familiar about him. But it was the two shadowy figures that concerned me the most. Even now, I could hear that laugh ringing in my ears, and another shiver ran through me. There was something very sinister about that laugh. And what did that voice mean about finding me? Whatever it was, I was certain I didn't want the owner of that laugh to ever find me.

But it was just a dream, right?

Chapter Three

OUR ENGAGEMENT PARTY WAS the weekend before I returned to university for my final semester. My parents had offered to host it for us, as our townhouse wasn't big enough for all of our family and friends to gather.

After Will proposed, the weeks had flown by in a flurry of engagement invitations and wedding preparations. We agreed that a spring wedding in September would be perfect, but we had limited time to organise everything. Thankfully, my bridesmaids, Ainslie and Aurora, were incredibly supportive and enthusiastic about the dress designs and colours I had chosen. Throughout the entire process, Will was an amazing fiance. He made sure to be involved in every step of the planning, and we ultimately decided on a garden wedding at his grandparents' property in the Gold Coast Hinterland. The location was not only breathtakingly beautiful but also cost-effective. I kept waiting for something to go wrong, but everything was turning out perfectly.

We spent the day rushing around madly with my sisters and parents, making all the final arrangements, and when the first of the guests arrived, I was still upstairs in my old bedroom, putting the finishing touches on my outfit. Will entered the room behind me and stood looking at me as I turned to face him and struck a pose.

"How do I look?" I asked as he walked forward, wrapping me in his arms, the love in his eyes threatening to make me cry and ruin my makeup.

"Like the woman that I can't wait to marry in eight months," he said huskily, kissing me on the forehead. I hugged him tightly, wishing that I didn't have to go down and play hostess. I rose onto my tip toes to kiss him softly, and he wove his fingers through my hair in the way he knew I loved. I deepened the kiss, pressing my body closer, and his other hand slid down my back before coming to rest on my hip. I felt his grip tighten as I wrapped a leg around him, and I could feel him begin to harden against my abdomen as he started kissing down my neck. I did nothing to stop the moan escaping my lips as I arched my back and ground myself against him, causing him to emit a low groan.

"Damn, Isolde, whatever is going on with your libido lately, I'm loving it." His words were muffled against my neck as he reached between us.

Just as he was about to slide his fingers beneath the band of my underwear, my father called my name from downstairs, announcing the arrival of our first guest. Will sighed as I reluctantly pulled away, and we shared a look confirming that we would pick this up later. I had long since discovered that the members of my family were fantastic at killing the mood.

Hours later, the party was in full swing, and I entered the kitchen to organise another platter of food, happy to have a second to myself. I hadn't slept well for weeks, and it was beginning to take its toll on me. There was nothing I wanted more right now than to curl up beside Will and fall into a dreamless sleep.

I took a moment to close my eyes and leaned against the pantry door, allowing myself to think of the nightmares that had been plaguing me since my birthday. Always the same, and yet they made no sense to me at all. Images of violence and creatures that were human in appearance, but their faces were cruel, their eye teeth replaced by fangs.

Will told me that I had taken to talking in my sleep, something that I had never done before, and the lack of sleep was affecting him too. Two mornings ago, I had awoken to discover that he had moved to the couch in the middle of the night to sleep without being awoken by my cries of "No, please don't!" He was concerned that it was because of all the stress of the wedding and returning to uni, but I could only hope it was that simple. Something about the dreams made me think that the stress of my everyday life had nothing to do with it at all. I was still seeing flashes of something gold on the inside of my right wrist. It was like when you see a movement in the corner of your eye, but it's gone when you look right at it. Maybe I was just losing the plot.

"Babe, you okay?" Ainslie interrupted my musings as she came in search of me, looking to help with the food.

"Yeah, I'm okay. Just tired." I gave my best friend of fifteen years a quick hug before busying myself with the food platters. Ainslie hesitated as she looked at me for a moment, before starting to cut up more cheese and cabana. I could see her looking at me every few minutes as we chatted about superficial things, the concern on her face obvious.

The doorbell rang and I left Ainslie with the food to see who it was. I opened the front door and smiled at my fathers' brother, James, and his wife, Sophia, my favourite uncle and aunt.

"Hey guys, we were wondering where you were! Now the party can really get started." I kissed them both on the cheek and took their jackets.

As I turned to close the door behind them, the hairs on the back of my neck suddenly stood on end, and I froze, looking out into the darkness. Although I could see no reason for my sudden anxiousness, something kept me from moving. I knew, without a doubt, that something was watching me from the darkness. Something with ice blue eyes.

"Isolde? What's wrong, honey? Is someone else coming in?" Sophia came to stand beside me for a moment, looking outside as well. I forced myself to smile and shut the door firmly, locking the deadbolt.

"No, no one's there. I just saw the neighbour's dog, that's all." I sucked at lying, and my aunt and uncle looked at me with a fleeting look of concern before I hurried them out to the backyard. We had strung fairy lights through the trees and along the fence to make it more inviting for people to sit outside, as the house was just too hot with this many people to be inside. My aunt commented how beautiful it all looked, and I answered automatically, my mind still on the presence that I had felt outside.

I wished that I could talk to someone about it, but something was stopping me. I had no idea why I felt that I couldn't tell anyone, but nothing about the situation made any sense to me at all. I looked over to where Will and Aurora stood away from the others. From the look on Will's face, Aurora was saying something that was concerning to him, and he looked up, noticing me watching them. After a beat, he smiled at me, and Aurora followed his gaze. She hesitated briefly before smiling as well. I couldn't help wondering if they were talking about me, as neither of their smiles seemed to meet their eyes. Probably discussing what the hell was going on with me...

Somehow, I managed to make it through the rest of the engagement party without any more incidents. I was even game enough to bravely say good-bye to each of the guests, walking them to their cars with Will at my side. I no longer felt the presence that I had felt before, though I could sense that someone was still out in the darkness, watching me. I didn't know whether that was more or less alarming. Not only was someone watching me in the dark, but there appeared to be more than one person out there.

After all the guests had left, we got to work tidying everything up with the help of both our families. This was the worst part about having a party at home... the dreaded cleanup.

"Isolde, is everything alright? You've been spaced out all night." Aurora came up beside me, shaking me out of my reverie, as I stood with a garbage bag in my hand, staring off into space.

"Yeah, just tired." I went back to collecting rubbish, though my twin continued to look worried.

"Will said you've been having nightmares. Are you sure nothing's worrying you?" I could see that Aurora wasn't going to let it go, but there wasn't anything that I could think of to tell her. Everything in me wanted to tell her what I had been feeling. I desperately wanted to share the details of my weird dreams about the blue-eyed men, but from the time that this all started, the instinct not to share the horrors with anyone else had stopped me from saying anything to my loved ones. People would think that I was going insane... And who was to say that I wasn't?

I looked at my twin and smiled. "I guess I'm just stressed, consumed with wedding plans and so on."

I resumed collecting rubbish, hoping that my words were enough to stop her from asking any more questions. Soon after, Aurora wandered away to busy herself with stacking chairs.

Why was it so important for me not to tell anyone? I never kept secrets from my sister or Will, yet now, here I was, lying to both of them, pretending to be fine when my head felt like it was running around in circles trying to work out this mystery. Who were the two terrifying men in my dreams? Why was my mystery man protecting me from them? All of these questions were constantly plaguing me, and I had no answers.

I had a strong feeling that something had shifted within me, and I couldn't shake the sense that something bad was on the horizon.... That particular thought was not helping me sleep at night, even without the nightmares.

The following Monday, I caught the City Cat to university, ready to begin the final semester of my degree. I didn't have any idea what I would end up doing, but I had always had a keen interest in the lives of those in the past, so had majored in European History. It was probably a good thing that Will earned good money as a property developer, as I wasn't likely to be rolling in money any time soon.

I stared out the window as the City Cat flew along the river. I enjoyed people watching, observing as the tourists snapped photos of the massive houses along the river, gazed up at the Story Bridge and pointed to the various landmarks along the way. This sure beat catching the train or the bus, and I smiled, letting the wind whip my hair around my face as we sped along the river. Leaning my head back against the headrest, I closed my eyes and finally experienced the much-needed sense of peace and tranquillity that I had been yearning for over the past few weeks.

My first lecture for the day was Witchcraft and Demonology, a subject that I had been looking forward to studying ever since I had started my degree. I'd deliberately left it to my last semester so that I had at least one subject that didn't stress me out to the point of crying, as had been the case with one of my third-year subjects the semester before.

I took my laptop out and turned it on, looking around to see if anyone I knew was in this class as well. I spotted a few familiar faces and smiled at acquaintances that I had made over the past few years. I had just started to return my attention to my computer when I recognised someone, and I froze, as it was someone that could not possibly be there.

It can't be him, surely.

I had been seeing this mystery man in my dreams for weeks now. The only face that was clear amongst all the madness. However, I still had no idea who he was, and now he had appeared in the flesh. Gorgeous as ever, he walked up the stairs to the back of the lecture theatre and looked completely at ease.

I must be hallucinating. Or am I still dreaming?

It would be a nice change to my nightmares of late, but I knew, even as I pinched myself, that this was not a dream. I stared in wonder, shocked to discover that this man existed and was no longer a figment of my imagination. Maybe I had noticed him at some point over the past couple of years, and my subconscious was putting his face on my mystery man. However, if that was the case, I was certain I would have remembered this guy before now. He looked like someone I would normally only see in a magazine. Because people this stunning did not exist without airbrushing and makeup. While Will was attractive, this man was on a whole different level.

He took a seat at the very back of the room, and it wasn't until he gazed directly at me that I realised that I was completely turned around in my seat, staring at him. I wanted to turn away, but his eyes held me, transfixed. We gazed at each other for what could have been an eternity.

Everything about him pulled me in, and although we were separated by several rows of other people, it felt like we were the only ones in the room. He felt dangerous, yet I knew, without a doubt, that I would be completely safe with him.

It wasn't until the lecturer started speaking that I turned back to face the front of the room, embarrassed at how long I had been staring. I shook my head to attempt to remove all distractions from my mind, wanting to take everything in. When I looked down at my keyboard, I saw a hint of gold on the inside of my wrist once again. But this time, it didn't disappear straight away, and I got a proper glimpse of what had been slowly driving me a little mad. If someone had asked me what it was, I wouldn't have been able to describe it, but it was as though a golden tattoo of something was there, just beneath my skin.

The person beside me cleared their throat loudly, and I jumped, having momentarily forgotten where I was. When I glanced back down, my wrist was bare once again.

I managed to take lecture notes, but knowing that the person who could potentially answer all of my questions was sitting only a few rows behind me was enough to distract even the most dedicated of students. I had to fight the urge to turn around on more than one occasion, especially as I could feel his eyes on me. It was at that moment that something occurred to me.

His eyes.

In my dreams, his eyes were blue. But now they were brown... The eyes of my mystery man were so distinct that there was no way I could have imagined them. They were the most piercing blue I'd ever seen before; there was just something about them. Those same eyes were on the other two figures in my dreams, and yet the mystery man's eyes had a quality to them. I did not fear his eyes as I did the eyes of the other two. Although he sat a few rows behind me, I would have been able to see those eyes from a mile away. It couldn't be him... and yet, everything else about him was the same...

As the lecture ended, I gathered my belongings as quickly as I could, but I didn't see him leave, even though I had kept my eyes on the door the whole time. One of my friends came over to talk to me, but I craned my neck to look around her, trying to work out where he'd gone. It was as if he had vanished. One more thing to add to the mystery.

Just what I need, another thing to obsess over.

I spent the rest of the day looking for him in my other class and all over the campus, but I never saw him again. I wished that I could call Aurora or even Ainslie and talk to them about this, but they would wonder why I was obsessing over some guy when I was getting married to the perfect man.

Maybe that was the key to all of this!

Perhaps I was subconsciously scared to get married, and I was making up all these crazy things as a way to let my fears out. I was sure that was what a psychologist would say, like the words of the one I saw briefly when

I was young. I hadn't thought about that period of my life in such a long time, but I realised now with a start that the reason I had been taken to see a psychologist at the time was that I was having weird dreams... I was told by my family that I had woken them on several occasions, screaming in terror, but I was never able to remember them when I awoke.

They had started not long after a childhood friend of both mine and Aurora's, Bianca, had mysteriously disappeared one day when we were six. No one had ever found her, but Aurora and I were the last people to see her. I shivered at this memory, and I realised then that I needed to stop thinking about all of these things and just let them go, but I didn't know how to. It was consuming me, and it was starting to worry the people that I loved.

As I sat on the City Cat on the way home that evening, I made the decision that I was going to let it go. I was going to stop imagining that someone was watching me in the dark, and I would find some way to help stop the nightmares. I had no idea how I was going to accomplish these things, but I needed to try. Otherwise, my life would begin to unravel, and I could not have that happen.

Chapter Four

AFTER MAKING THAT DECISION to push my issues aside, I was able to make a conscious effort to return to normal. Although I did still have the nightmares, they were not as constant, and after almost six weeks, they occurred only once or twice a week. I avoided seeking faces in a crowd for fear that I would start seeing the face of my mystery man everywhere. I had managed to get day shifts at work for a few weeks, and I used assignments as excuses not to go out, avoiding leaving the house after dark... And for now, I was breathing again...

I finally started to resemble my former self again. Will's sleeping patterns had now returned to normal, as I no longer kept him awake every night because of my nightmares. I still had not been able to rid myself of the constant sensation of being watched. It wasn't always a sinister feeling, but even when I felt protected, there was still the knowledge that someone was watching me from the darkness at night. And I was still seeing flashes of gold on the inside of my wrist occasionally when I moved my arm.

It was our sixth anniversary, and Will was determined to take me out to dinner to celebrate. I had just completed my final mid-semester exams with flying colours and was able to take a brief reprieve from my hectic study schedule.

As I dressed to go out, I ignored the anxiety I was feeling about leaving the house at night, and I allowed myself to daydream, recalling that night six years ago when our relationship had finally changed. I'd had a crush on him for years, all through high school, and on that fateful April day, a group of us had gone out for an evening of fun. We'd somehow separated from the others and ended up wandering through South Bank Parklands. Stopping to admire the view of the city, I'd turned to say something to him as we found a bench to sit on. Something in the way he was looking at me caused me to stop and take a breath. It was as if he'd just suddenly realised that I was no longer the little girl in pigtails that I'd been all those years ago.

He had cupped my face gently in one hand, looked at me for a moment, and then kissed me softly. After what felt like an eternity, he looked at me again and said, 'I just wanted to know what it would be like to kiss you."

"And what was it like?" I'd managed to whisper, unable to believe that this was happening.

"Like something that I could get used to," he'd whispered back, and we had continued to kiss until our group of friends happened upon us again.

They'd all been taking bets as to how long it would be before Will finally woke up to the fact that I was there, and none of them was even the slightest bit surprised.

We started dating after that, even though I had plans to head to the UK in six months. Will was adamant that I shouldn't give up those plans for him. We did take a break from our relationship while I was away, but we kept in touch, and neither of us dated anyone else in the months I was gone. We knew we had something special, and I was more than happy to step into his waiting arms when I got off the plane.

We had been together ever since, and I thanked my lucky stars every day that Will had finally seen me.

Will had the night all planned out. He'd told me to wear something comfortable but dressy, so I wore my favourite dress, which happened to be one of Will's favourites as well. I was reminded of this when he looked at me appreciatively as I walked out of the bathroom, commenting that maybe we should just stay in instead. I smiled at him coyly, and it took quite a lot of effort on both our parts to walk out the door instead of stripping that dress off right then and there.

The night was young, and I climbed into Will's new work car, curious about where he was taking me, as he had been adamant about keeping it a surprise. He drove into Fortitude Valley, holding my hand the whole time, looking at me every chance he got.

As soon as Will pulled into the car park, I knew exactly where he was taking me. It was a restaurant that relied solely on word of mouth for advertising and was tucked away in an unnamed building. I had been there several years ago for a friend's birthday and had fallen madly in love with it. There were no chairs, just pillows on the floor on either side of a low table, and each group of diners were curtained off to give the illusion of privacy, although you could hear everything that happened around you. It was dimly lit and intimate, and it was exactly how I wanted to celebrate our anniversary.

I turned to Will as we waited to be seated, kissing him softly in the hallway that resembled a rainforest.

"Thank you for being so good to me. I don't think I could have ever asked for anyone more perfect to fall in love with."

"And here I was thinking that I was the one who'd won the prize. I have never been happier in my whole life than when I'm with you." He took my hand and squeezed it as the waitress led us to our curtained-off area, tucked away in the back corner. We sat side by side, our fingers entwined as we talked. Still waiting for the waitress to return, I excused myself to go to the ladies and made my way through the maze of curtains.

After washing my hands, I redid my lipstick, and I caught yet another glimpse of the mark on my wrist. I ignored it, choosing to forget about visions and weird marks. I knew that my state of bliss was evident on my face, and I was happy it was there for the entire world to see. This was exactly how a woman in love was supposed to look.

I returned to the table, and Will pulled me back down to sit close beside him, putting an arm around me and running his fingers down my arm slowly.

"I ordered you a Pina Colada." He leaned in and nuzzled my neck. I felt a shiver run through me at the feeling of his breath on my skin, and he let out a low chuckle.

"I've been thinking about this for weeks, especially with how easy it's been to make you come lately," he whispered in my ear as he ran a hand up my leg, slowly slipping it under my dress. He trailed light kisses slowly down my neck before returning to claim my mouth as his hand began working its way under the lace band of my underwear, causing me to gasp against his lips.

"I do love the privacy in this place. Almost as much as I love the sight of you in that dress." I was too turned on to utter a response, and I reached my hand up to tangle my fingers in his hair, pulling him closer and kissing him back hungrily. Being so sensitive to his touch came in handy, and within minutes, I was moaning against his mouth, coming as he worked his hand expertly between my legs.

Will moved back a fraction and smirked. "I knew I'd love that. Watching you come undone and knowing anyone could walk in at any moment." I looked at him with a smile, trying to regain my breath. The excitement of what we had just done swirled within me, and I was more than aware of how flushed I was. I went to respond to him, but at that moment, the waitress appeared with our drinks.

"Ready to order?" She handed us our drinks, and Will grinned at me before glancing up at her as I worked to get myself under control. I noticed that I was holding the menu upside down, and I felt Will fighting not to laugh beside me as he answered her.

"We'll just need another few minutes."

After a few hours that flew by too quickly, Will asked for our bill and we left the restaurant. As we walked back to the car, the unsettling feeling of being watched overwhelmed me and I stopped for a moment to look behind us. I'd had a few cocktails and the world had taken on the slightly fuzzy look that it got after consuming a few too many alcoholic beverages. There was no one else around, and I didn't know if this should relieve or scare me. Will turned to look as well, before looking down at me, concerned.

"What's wrong?" There was an edge to his voice, and I forced myself to look up at him with a smile.

"Nothing. I just thought I heard something. Guess I was just imagining it." But as I breathed these words of comfort, Will was knocked off his feet with such force that his hand was ripped from mine.

I screamed as a dark shape landed on top of him, moving with such speed that all I could make out was a blur of motion, as Will cried out in pain. I rushed forward to rip him free but froze as the thing that was holding him down turned and snarled at me. It was a man, of that much I could see, but he looked feral. His face was twisted in rage, but what scared me most were his eyes. They were piercing blue.

I didn't know what to do other than continue to scream, trying to pull him away, wanting to help Will but unable to rip the creature from him. It continued to attack Will in a frenzy, and his screams mingled with my own.

The creature (surely it couldn't be a man) moved with such frightening speed that I could barely make out its movements as it slashed at Will, and not just with its hands, but with teeth that almost looked like fangs. He threw me off him and I landed on the ground with a thud.

Rising to my feet, I rushed forward again, finally managing to shove the creature from Will's now silent form lying on the ground. As it wheeled to turn its fury on me, another blur of motion knocked it to the ground, and I fell to my knees beside Will, lifting his head into my lap. Blood gushed from the wounds all over his face, neck and chest.

So much blood.

I was completely ignorant of the fight that was happening behind me until the noise stopped. I looked up and locked eyes with my rescuer, only to realise that I already knew who it would be. The eyes of my mystery man, the same piercing blue from my dreams, were looking at me with utter devastation as I continued to rock Will in my arms, begging him to open his eyes.

"Please, baby, come on! Don't you dare leave me!" I begged him with everything in me, and still, he did not move. I turned to look up at my rescuer again, as he stood motionless, staring down at Will's still form.

"Please, help me! I don't know what to do!" I sobbed imploringly, and he hesitantly took a step forward. As he did so, two police officers tore around the corner, having been alerted by my screams. With a fleeting glance at me once more, the mystery man disappeared so quickly it was as if he had never been there.

The officers arrived at my side and began asking me questions, but all I could do was ask them for help repeatedly, unable to comprehend anything beyond the fact that Will still had not opened his eyes. One officer managed to lead me away, but I refused to look away from where her co-worker attempted to revive Will.

An ambulance arrived moments later, and the two paramedics set to work on my fiance as the police officers again attempted to question me. I managed to tell them vaguely what had happened, that a crazed man had attacked us, but that another man had arrived and fought him off. I couldn't tell them if a weapon had been used because I had no memory of seeing one. I was sure that the man had used his bare hands. And possibly his teeth. It was all a blur of screams and snarls.

They loaded Will into the ambulance, and we raced to the hospital with the siren wailing...

At 9:43pm, he was pronounced dead on arrival.

Chapter Five

I COULDN'T BREATHE. THIS could not be happening. I must be in one of my nightmares again. I felt as though I was floating, and I wished that I could wake up. I sat motionless on the hospital bed, being treated for shock, unable to take in anything that was happening around me.

I did manage to look up when my parents flew into the room, anguish and grief written all over their faces as my mother took me in her arms, crying and rocking me. It was then that it hit me, and I began to shake uncontrollably. I realised that I was not just shaking, as I started heaving with great, racking sobs. My father hugged both my mother and me, unable to handle my grief, wanting to take my pain away as all fathers are supposed to. But how do you save your child from the pain of losing the love of their life?

Sunlight streamed through the window, and I awoke slowly, reaching for Will as I did every morning. Only the bed was empty beside me. I opened my eyes slowly and was confused to find myself in my bedroom at my parent's house.

What am I doing here? And where is Will?

Slowly, my mind drifted back to the events of the night before, and I lay in agony, feeling as though my heart had been ripped from my chest. I lay like this for what may have been minutes or hours until my mother came into the room to check on me.

"Honey? Are you awake?" I couldn't answer as my throat was raw from crying, and I just stared at the ceiling. Aurora entered the room after my mother, her face tear-stained. I didn't react as she lay down beside me, but once she wrapped her arms around me, the tears began to flow again, and I buried my face into her chest as she rocked me, crying just as hard as I was.

My mother sat on the edge of the bed, smoothing my hair in a way that only a mother can, unsure of what else she could do for me. Our family had never been touched by a tragedy such as this, and none of us knew how to get through it. But eventually, my sobs died down, and I fell asleep again, welcoming the deep, black void of nothingness because there was nothing left for me when I was awake.

The following days were a blur. Will's family and mine gathered in silence. No one could find the words to express how we were feeling, least of all me. I hadn't spoken since the hospital, not even to Aurora. Will's sister handled the funeral arrangements, as I was no use to anyone, and Will's mother was in a similar state. Will's father just sat stiffly with his arm around his wife, his eyes staring into a far-off place, no doubt a place where his son still lived and where there was no talk of muggings and death.

The police had arrived the day after the attack to get my statement, but my mother had asked them to wait for when I was ready, explaining that I could barely speak, let alone think, about the events of that night.

However, all I did was think about that night. I played the scene over and over in my head, day and night, trying to work out what I could have done. My sisters were taking turns sitting with Aurora and me, as I could barely handle having her out of my sight for longer than it took for either of us to go to the bathroom. I wished that it had been me that the creature had gone for. But then, Will would be here, experiencing the pain that I was in, and I couldn't wish that on him. Surely, death would be easier than the thought of a future in which the love of your life no longer existed?

If only I had been able to pull the thing off of him. If only I had not paused to look back, we would have seen what was in front of us. If only my mystery rescuer had arrived earlier, he could have stopped the creature before it even crossed our path.

If only, if only, if only...

The day of the funeral dawned bright and sunny, and I lay in bed cursing the world. Had I led too blessed a life up until now? Had the Fates decided that I needed to have a bucket full of trauma to make up for years of unknown bliss? If that was the case, couldn't they have given me some sort of warning so that I could have appreciated everything more? I looked back over the years with Will and felt so much agony at all the moments that I took for granted. No one expects the love of their life to die. It was just too much to deal with.

"Isolde? Are you awake?" Aurora entered the darkened room, two steaming mugs in her hands, letting the sunlight from the hallway spill in behind her. As far as I was concerned, the sunlight was taunting me. Just reminding me that I had been living a carefree life, and now I was paying for it.

Putting the cups on the bedside table, Aurora crawled into the bed next to me and put her arms around me. We had both been staying at our parents' house since Will had died, with Jacob dropping into the townhouse to get us anything we needed. I just couldn't face the house yet. It was too painful. I felt as though I had no more tears left to cry, and I was sure that everyone around me was worried about my numbness. I was just too exhausted from the lack of sleep, the constant thinking and worrying.

"Are you going to be okay today?" Aurora was still pushing me to talk, whereas everyone else had given up. I was grateful not to have to answer questions with the others, but Aurora had been persistent. I turned to face her and studied her face for a moment.

"Aura, I don't think I'm ever going to be okay again." My voice was croaky from lack of use, but Aurora just looked relieved that my silence seemed to have been broken finally.

The funeral was moving, as funerals are meant to be, but I had little memory of it by that evening. The night of the funeral felt as though the end of my life with Will was now finalised. He was buried now, so I was meant to start moving forward again. Of course, no one was going to say that to me, and maybe they didn't even feel that way. Perhaps it was just me projecting my own feelings onto the situation, but I couldn't help the way I was feeling. Aurora kept hovering, and my parents never let me out of their sight, but I was starting to feel claustrophobic in my old bedroom. It was time to return to my home. To begin to pick up the pieces of my former self.

It was late in the night when I pulled up in front of the house, which no longer felt as welcoming as it used to. Now it was just a painful reminder of what would no longer be. I would have to sell it. There was no way I could afford to live here without Will's income to pay the mortgage, and the memories that it held were too painful to endure.

I sat in my car, staring at the front door for what felt like hours, when a movement in my rear-view mirror jerked me from my reverie. Before I had a chance to do anything more than squint at the reflection in the mirror, the driver's side door was flung open, and I was pulled roughly from the car.

"You shouldn't be here. It isn't safe." A body pressed me firmly against the rear passenger door, and I gasped as I looked up into the face of the man who had jerked me from the car. With a faint trace of an Irish accent, all I could do was stare into the eyes of my mystery man. I hadn't been this close to him in our previous physical interactions, but I remembered now just how tall he was, as I had to crane my neck to look up at him when we stood this close together. Eventually, I found my voice as he looked around, obviously searching for the danger he was talking about.

"Well, I would say that's obvious, seeing as you've just taken it upon yourself to rip me out of my otherwise safe car." He looked back at me briefly as I spoke before continuing to scan the area, barely acknowledging my words. I was starting to get annoyed, a feeling that I should be grateful for, as it was the first emotion I'd felt since Will's death that had managed to make its way through my mind-numbing grief.

"I want some answers right now. Who the hell are you?" I pushed him away from me and glared at him. He still refused to look at me for longer than a second, constantly watching for the apparent danger that had led him to drag me from my car. After another moment of silence, I couldn't take the frustration anymore, and I pushed past him, pulling my house keys from my handbag.

"Fine, if you want to continue this whole mystery man routine, I'm going inside." A split second after the words were out of my mouth, I was promptly knocked to the ground, the wind knocked out of me, and a body lay heavily across me, holding me down. At first, I thought it was *mystery man*, as I had started referring to him in my head until I realised that my attacker had come from beside me, not from behind.

In the time it took me to come to this realisation, the weight on top of me was gone, and the sound of fighting broke out behind me. I scrambled to my feet and plastered myself to the side of my car once again, transfixed by what was happening in front of me. It couldn't possibly be true.

The person who had knocked me to the ground was Will.

"Stop it!" I found my voice as the two of them traded kicks and blows so fluidly it was as if they were dancing. Will had always been active, but I had no idea where he had developed these skills from. Momentarily distracted by the sound of my voice, Will stopped for a moment, and I took a step towards him. But one powerful kick from my mystery man sent Will flying across the front lawn. The force with which he had kicked Will had lifted him off his feet and sent him flying at least twenty feet, something that no normal human being could do.

I gaped in shock at the scene before me as the man spun on the spot and shoved me into the back seat of my car, taking my keys from me before diving into the driver's seat and tearing out of my driveway, hitting the central locking at the same time. All of this occurred in a split second, and we were already halfway down the street before I realised what was happening. I slammed my hand against the door, knowing it was useless, and I was not suicidal enough to leap from a car that was tearing along suburban streets at such a terrifying speed.

"What the hell is going on?! We have to go back. That was Will!" I knew I had finally reached hysteria.

"I'll explain everything once you are safe!" A glance at me in the rear-view mirror was all I got. I was still unable to process what I had just witnessed. How could my dead fiance be in my front yard, performing these fantastic martial arts moves that he could only have fantasised about doing when he was alive? Why was a stranger rescuing me from him? I had far too many questions, and I was not prepared to wait until I was 'safe' - a situation which I doubted that I would agree with - as I had no idea who this man was, and both times I'd been alone with him in the past week had been at the scene of some violent attack.

"Start talking right now, or I will ring for help faster than you can drive, so help me God. I am beyond my limit right now!" I said through clenched teeth, with my fists balled into tight fists at my side, though whether this was from anger or fear, I couldn't tell; the adrenaline felt the same. The car began to slow to a more agreeable speed, and for the first time, he looked me directly in the eye, though it was via the rear-view mirror.

"My name is Liam."

Finally!

"Alright, Liam. What the fuck is going on?" My voice was thick, and I had reached the point where my usual filter on swearing was lifted. I would have preferred to have had this conversation face to face, as I felt myself starting to tear up. I hated that my body reacted to sadness and anger in the same way by causing me to cry.

Almost as if he could read my mind, Liam pulled the car to a stop next to a playground. He unlocked my door and took my hand to help me out of the car, which struck me as very courteous, especially for someone who had just, in effect, kidnapped me and stolen my car. He led me to a picnic table and sat facing me. He was still not entirely relaxed, but at least he was now able to look me in the eye, something he hadn't done before.

"Okay, here's the truth. Your fiance was killed by a vampire." He stated this so seriously that I may have believed him if it wasn't so ridiculous.

"Aha... A vampire... Right... And what are you, some sort of vampire slayer? I've seen that show too... What else have you got?" My disbelief was more than evident in my sarcastic response, but he just continued speaking as though I hadn't interrupted.

"Will is now a vampire himself. A vampire that is intent on turning you into one as well. And it is my job to keep that from happening. He was never meant to be turned; that wouldn't have been Adam's plan, but unfortunately, he had not fed in a while, and he got sloppy. He should have decapitated Will to keep him from turning, but you stopped that from happening." He went to continue, but this was enough for me.

"*Excuse me*? He *should* have decapitated my fiance?! He killed him. He didn't need to pull his fucking body apart!" Disgusted, I started to rise to my feet, intent on storming off, but Liam reached up and pulled me back down.

"I know this all sounds crazy. I remember my reaction when I was first told of all of this, but I cannot sugarcoat this for you." His gaze held mine, and I found it impossible to look away. "Your life has changed now in more ways than you know. Adam had a goal that night. He was meant to get you instead, to turn you into a vampire like him. He failed, but in turning Will, he has recruited the perfect foot soldier to do it for him. Will still retains his love for you, but his love is now an obsession, and he will stop at nothing until he has you." He was so serious. Whether real or imagined, he believed everything he was telling me.

In my mind, I went over everything he had just told me. Could this all have been some massive practical joke that they had cooked up together? If I hadn't known Will so well and known he would never put me through this sort of grief, I might have believed that over this crazy story, I was being told. However, there was something about Liam that made me think that he was telling me the truth.

"Wait... why did this... Adam... Why did he want to turn me into a vampire?" I couldn't believe I was talking about vampires in all seriousness.

Liam took a deep breath.

"Because of the prophecy. You're the one that is meant to bring peace and stop them. He was trying to stop that from happening." I couldn't help but gape at him now. He had truly lost his mind somewhere along the way. Vampires, prophecies... It was as if I had stepped straight onto the set of some seriously lame horror movie. This guy was one of those people who wrote fan fiction in their spare time, convinced that the dark was out to get him. And here I was, all alone in the dark with him.

He must have realised that my mood had changed and shook his head.

"I know this is all hard to believe. However, some part of you knows that I am telling the truth. I know that you have begun to see things. It all started the night we first met. The night before your twenty-fifth birthday." In all the craziness of the past week, I had forgotten about the alley in my flashes, instead focusing only on Liam's involvement in Will's death.

"I know you don't remember anything from that night, but I told you then that the danger was coming. And I know you have been sensing a presence in the dark. I know you've been having the nightmares." How the hell did this guy know all of this? Was he a stalker, on top of being seriously delusional?

"Did you drug me that night? Is that why I can't remember anything except blurred images?" I went with the only logical explanation for this weirdness, but he just shook his head.

"No. You cannot remember anything because the first day or so when the change sets in is incredibly disorientating. Throw in the amount of alcohol you'd had that night, and I'm surprised you remember anything at all, to be perfectly honest." That last part was said with underlying judgement, and I raised an eyebrow at him, but he didn't look away. It felt eerily like I was being told off by my father. Although admittedly, he was much closer to my age than my father, and I found him disturbingly attractive, even with everything that had been going on lately.

"The change? What change?" He'd made it sound like I was starting menopause.

"Your psychic ability." Right, that was it. This guy was insane.

"My psychic ability? Okay, seriously, Liam, if that's even your real name, you're fucking nuts." Again, I went to get up, but this time when he pulled me back down, he held me in place. The strength in just one hand was enough to render me motionless, even without losing myself to his unblinking gaze.

"I know that you think this is all crazy. If we had time to waste on trying to ease you into this, then I would be happy to do so, but there is not enough time for that. You need to understand the danger that you are in. I have been placed in your life to keep you from being turned into one of them, and I need you to be aware of what is going on." He moved his hand away, perhaps sensing that I wasn't going to run off yet again. "You cannot be making stupid mistakes like the one you made tonight." I glared at him, offended. He continued talking, not looking the slightest bit concerned. "You cannot go back to that house at night. It was the home you shared with Will, and he can get in there without an invitation. Your sister cannot return there either. Jacob has been safe up until now because Will only awakened tonight. You can return during the daylight to pack up your things. You will be safe with your parents because you never shared a home with Will there." None of this made sense. I was struggling to take everything he was saying in, and I shook my head.

"Liam, you haven't told me how you know anything about any of this. Who are you?" He looked at me for the longest time. Eventually, he took my right hand and turned it over, palm facing upwards. He traced a finger over my wrist before looking up at me again.

"You're not ready to know that yet."

Chapter Six

I WOKE THE NEXT morning, convinced that the night before had just been another one of my dreams. Until I saw the bruise on my arm from where I had fallen when Will knocked me to the ground. Liam had driven me back to my parents' house in silence and had no doubt maintained his vigil outside in the dark somewhere. I couldn't take any of it in. I didn't want to accept what I had seen. Will, the love of my life, had attacked me, intent on killing me. It just could not have happened. I had to have made it all up as a way of dealing with my grief. Right?

Wrong... I could feel Liam's eyes on me all day. Finally having confirmation that someone was always watching me didn't make me feel any better, and when a real estate agent just happened to call me to discuss selling the house, I wondered at the timing, the convenience of the phone call. I noticed my knuckles turning white as I gripped the phone, as the woman prattled on, her voice echoing through my bedroom as I stared down at the phone in my hand.

"Can we meet at the house tomorrow?" I had barely heard her speaking, but I found myself saying yes, without really understanding what I was agreeing to.

"You're going to organise to sell the Townhouse already?" Aurora had been listening in from the bedroom door, having heard the phone ring, and looked taken aback. She sat down on my bed, pulling her legs up and wrapping her arms around them to hug them close. "Are you sure about this? It doesn't seem like the right time to be making such huge decisions, Is." I shook my head.

"It's just a conversation... I don't have to decide straight away, I guess. But we can't afford to stay there without Will's income; you know that." I swallowed hard, my eyes welling up. I could feel the panic beginning to rise, as once again, the idea of trying to navigate through life without Will overwhelmed me. Never mind the fact that I'd seen him walking around the night before. My hands started shaking, and Aurora got to her feet, moving to stand in front of me as she took my hands in her own. She held my gaze as she squeezed my fingers.

"Hey, we'll figure this out, okay? You're not alone in this. Just breathe." She guided me through some deep breaths, and I squeezed her fingers back.

"I'm okay. Thanks." She pulled me into a hug, and I relaxed into her arms for a moment before stepping back. "I think I need a bit more sleep."

Aurora nodded, although she hesitated at the door, turning back to watch me as I climbed back under the covers, suddenly so very, very tired.

The next morning, I drove back to the townhouse earlier than the others, determined to face it on my own, before I was joined by my parents and sister to meet with the real estate agent. I parked in the driveway and made my way to the front door, head down as I dug through my bag to find my house keys. But once I reached the front door, I came to an abrupt halt, noticing that the door was already open a crack. Surely Jacob hadn't forgotten to lock up when he'd last been here?

I hadn't gotten close enough to the door the night I'd last been here to notice if the door was open then, but I was remembering Liam's words of caution. That a vampire could enter a house they used to reside in without invitation. I stepped forward cautiously and pushed the door open, not yet crossing the threshold. I could feel my heart thumping loudly in my chest, the adrenaline beginning to kick in, as I slowly eased my way into the house, scanning the downstairs area. I could see the whole first floor from here, and nothing appeared to be out of place. Moving as silently as I could, I slowly made my way upstairs, and by the time I reached the top of the staircase, the sound of my heart beating rapidly was deafening in my ears. Aurora's bedroom door was open, as was Will's office and the main bathroom, and I could see that all were empty. That just left our bedroom, across the landing, with the door closed.

I swallowed hard as I stood in front of the closed door, trying not to think about the last time I'd come home to a seemingly empty house to find a surprise proposal behind this door. Now was not the time to crumple into a heap. I slowly turned the door handle and let the door swing open. The room was empty, and I could see that our bathroom was also empty through the walk-in robe. I let out the breath I'd been holding, feeling the tension leave my body. I surveyed the room, and for a moment, I felt relieved until my eyes fell on the bed, and I noticed the bunch of flowers lying there, next to a note. I stood staring at it for a moment, positive that I did not want to read it.

A few thunderous heartbeats later, I finally moved closer, walking around the bed and gingerly lifted the letter with a shaking hand.

> *Roses are Red,*
> *Violets are Blue.*
> *We're meant to be forever,*
> *I'm coming for you.*

I could feel tears beginning to sting my eyes as I read the words written in Will's distinctive handwriting. My hand shook uncontrollably, and I let the letter fall to the ground as I stepped back and slid down the wall on my side of the bed, staring at the flowers. They were an elaborate arrangement with two large white lilies at the centre. Will had been buying me white lilies for six years.

I had no idea how long I sat there, but I was jerked out of my living nightmare by the sound of my parents and sister entering the front door, calling out to me. I shot to my feet, snatching the letter off the ground and shoving it into my handbag. I couldn't bring myself to touch the flowers as I fled back downstairs. I would never be able to feel safe in that room again.

That afternoon, my family and I set about the task of packing up the house and making it ready for the real estate agents to show people through. The woman that had contacted me the day before had wandered through the house with dollar signs in her eyes. She gleefully informed me that a townhouse in the heart of Bulimba would have no problems at all selling for the asking price, not even noticing as I had gripped my father's arm.

"It really would be best to pack up the house and get it staged. It makes it easier for the buyers who come through for the inspections to imagine themselves here and the lives they want to lead. We'd target young couples starting out. This is the perfect starter home in this suburb. I've got a few interested parties looking already that a home like this would appeal to. It will sell quickly; I can almost promise you that."

But what about the life I had meant to start in my home?

Aurora had had a word with the woman after this, asking if she could kindly curb her enthusiasm in light of the terrible circumstances that caused me to sell my home in the first place. She'd had the sense to look ashamed after that but still advised us to stay with our parents so that we would not be constantly cleaning.

As I battled the overwhelming prospect of packing up the life that Will and I had been building together so soon after his death, I wondered if Liam had had anything to do with the real estate agent's last request. It did seem a little odd, as most people remained living in their homes whilst they were on the market. It just seemed too neat and tidy. I brushed the thought aside, as there was no way Liam could have influenced some random woman before I even knew I was going to be putting the house on the market.

Although who knew? I knew nothing about 'mystery man', as I was still in the habit of calling him. Maybe he had some mind control powers. I mean, I had just discovered that vampires were real, so why not people with supernatural powers as well?

My family had noticed the change in my mood over the few days that it took to pack up the house. I was no longer silent, no longer the walking zombie that I had become in the days that followed Will's death. Yet there was something manic in my turn of personality, according to my ever-perceptive twin sister. Aside from several breakdowns when packing up our belongings, I kept looking over my shoulder as though expecting someone to be there. Of course, only I knew that this was with good reason. They couldn't understand why I refused to allow anyone in the house after the sun went down, forcing everyone to leave as soon as I noticed the sunlight fading away, no matter if they were in the middle of packing a box. No one was game enough to argue with me, though, putting it down to post-traumatic stress after the attack.

I was more than willing to let them believe this, as the letters that awaited my arrival each morning were hard to ignore, each one more ominous than the last, and accompanied by increasingly creepier gifts. The letter today had been in the form of yet another poem.

Roses are Red,

Violets are Blue.

You can't live without me,

You know that it's true.

It had been placed on the kitchen bench next to a dead bird, the neck twisted at a sickening angle that was almost certainly broken. It had taken all my resolve not to throw up. I had managed to dump the bird in the wheelie bin before Aurora and Jacob had come inside, the letter joining the others, each one a crumpled ball inside my handbag. Painful reminders of what Will had become and that I was no longer safe within the walls of the home we had shared together.

"Alright, that's it. What's going on?!" Aurora demanded as she dumped the last load of boxes onto the back of Jacob's ute. I had been once again scanning the front yard. I was ever watchful, and it was driving my sister crazy. Jacob had the sense to busy himself with doing one final sweep of the house, leaving me to come up with a reason for my actions. Thankfully, I had a pretty good one, even though it was not the main reason.

'Well, let's think about this for a moment. A week and a half ago, I watched as my fiance was attacked by some psycho who ripped him apart in a dark alley... Don't you think that's enough of a reason for me to be just the slightest bit freaked out?!" Although I knew Aurora didn't deserve it, all my frustration and confusion from the past few weeks was now focused on her. A part of me was angry that she didn't just guess what was going on so that she could know what I was going through, frustrated that she had not worked it out. I knew I was being stupid, that there was no way any normal, sane person could guess what I was going through, even my identical twin. However, they always say you hurt the ones you love... and my secret had gotten Will killed; the one person I loved more than anything, and anyone in the world was gone, and now I knew that it was because of me.

Without realising it, I found myself curled up on the ground beside the ute, shaking with silent sobs, as my sister held me in her arms, unable to fix my problems or understand what was going on. And I could never let her know.

Jacob and Aurora eventually drove back to our parent's house, leaving me to follow behind in my car. But I didn't immediately leave. I let myself back inside one last time, moving silently around the house. My steps echoed through the empty rooms, once so full of life and love. We had lived here for three years, and it was full of so many memories. We had planned to start a family here one day when we were ready, and to see the rooms now empty was yet another painful reminder that our life together was now over.

The hardest part of these last few days, aside from the very unwelcome poems and gifts, had been packing up Will's belongings. After an unsuccessful attempt to pack up his clothes and his office that led to one of my worst breakdowns, I eventually asked one of my sisters to do it, and those boxes had been taken to his parent's house the day before, to sit in the garage until we were all ready to go through them. I had no idea if I would ever be ready for that moment.

Chapter Seven

THAT NIGHT I SAT staring out my bedroom window at my parents' house, unwilling to unpack the boxes that were scattered around the room. I refused to get settled here, as I knew I could only handle a few weeks in my parents' house. They had said that they wanted Aurora and me to stay, but we had both agreed that we needed to find our own place to rent as soon as possible. I refused to be one of those boomerang children, coming home every time something went wrong. Granted, usually, the things that were wrong were trivial things, like running out of money or having issues with roommates, nothing quite as drastic as a dead fiance, but still, I did not want to fall into that category.

I was so lost in thought that I didn't notice someone staring back at me through the window until they moved. I jumped, startled out of my dark thoughts, and caught my breath as Liam tapped on the window. I moved to open it, wondering why he did not just come to the front door rather than climb up to a second-story window.

"Hello." His voice was quiet as he sat on the outer side of the windowsill, resting his feet on one of the large branches of the tree he had just climbed up.

"Do you want t-" Liam cut me off before I could finish inviting him in, raising his hands in protest, almost in fear.

"Don't invite anyone you don't know in... Or anyone that you have not seen in a while. I will just stay out here for now. It's better this way, trust me." I raised my eyebrows.

"Trust you? Why should I do that? You've got me jumping at shadows and fearing the dark!" It felt good to have someone to blame for all the crap going on in my life. Liam just shrugged, which infuriated me more.

"You know what's in the dark now; you should be afraid." His simple response caused me to growl under my breath, knowing he was right but liking nothing about it. He ignored my obvious hostility and continued like there had not been days between our last talk and this one.

"Are you ready to hear the truth now?" Why was he asking me this? He was the one who told me I wasn't ready!

I said as much, but he waved it aside.

"There are still a lot of things you're not ready to know about yet. I meant about what's out there in the dark." I paused to think about this for a moment.

"I guess even if I'm not ready, I still need to know what's out there. Especially since the dark seems fixated on me for some reason." I shuddered involuntarily at the memory of Will's unwelcome gifts.

"It's a long story." Liam settled himself more comfortably, leaning back against the window frame so that I could see him side-on, and crossed his arms.

"If it starts with once upon a time, I'm pushing you off the roof," I said as I sat back down on my bed, pulling my pillow to me and hugging it to my chest like a security blanket. Liam huffed a laugh that didn't reach his eyes as he turned to look at me.

"Well, it certainly doesn't end in - and they all lived happily ever after." I shivered at that; I did *not* need reminding that the world was no longer a happy place.

"Five hundred years ago, there were two brothers. Their father was the master of a small estate in Ireland, and the eldest brother was set to inherit the estate upon their father's death, leaving the youngest with no inheritance, as was the case in those days. The youngest brother had joined the priesthood, and both were happy with their lot in life." Liam no longer looked at me as he told the story, instead staring off into the dark as if watching the story unfold before his eyes.

"However, one day, the eldest brother went missing. After a year of searching, their father lost hope, and upon his death, the estate fell to the youngest brother. He didn't want the position, as he was happy in the cloisters of the church and did not much like the idea of leaving to take a wife." He flashed a look at me before turning away, continuing to speak with his arms still crossed firmly over his chest.

"But he did his duty and went to his father's home. When he took up his role, he also inherited the secrets that his father had kept from him. His father had died several days short of his twenty-fifth birthday, and that was when the nightmares started. The younger brother did not know what they meant and believed it was just the grief of losing his father and his brother so close together." He turned to look at me properly again and held my gaze as he continued. I stared at him, giving him my full attention, unable to pull myself away from the haunted look in his blue eyes.

"However, his mother came to him and told him of his true birthright. She'd had five sons before the births of his brother and himself, though none had survived infancy. This made him the seventh son, like his father before him, who had lost six older brothers before becoming the master of the estate. This made the young man the seventh son of a seventh son.

"Upon his birth, his parents had been approached by a stranger, a woman. She had told them that he was destined to be part of an order of men and women, each destined to protect humanity from the realm of the supernatural. They called themselves The Order of the Dragon." I felt my eyebrows raise at this but didn't dare interrupt as Liam went on.

"The young man was thrown by this, unable to understand what this meant. But on the night that his mother told him of his supposed destiny, his brother reappeared in the company of a stranger. At first, the younger brother was overjoyed that his brother had returned, but as the night wore on, he noticed differences between the person his brother used to be and the man before him. Upon closer inspection, he noted, with fear, that there was cruelty about him. He would not tell them where he had been, but he watched his younger brother and mother hungrily, as though waiting to pounce." Liam cleared his throat now, emotion beginning to show.

"And then he did. He allowed the stranger to attack their mother, holding his younger brother down and forcing him to watch as the stranger drained the life from her, an unwilling witness to the murder of the last remaining member of their family. Once he'd finished, the stranger turned to him, moving to bite him as he had done their mother after putting him through the trauma of watching him remove her head from her body.

"However, before he could bite him, the house was suddenly under siege as the tenants of the estate attacked. The servants of the home had recognised what the older brother and his companion were and sounded the alarm. Vampires." He stared at his hands as he took a breath, steadying himself before he continued. I remained still, processing everything as best I could.

"The younger brother managed to flee separately, as he feared the mob would come after him as well, as he was covered in his mother's blood. Eventually, he found an abandoned church. It was within those crumbling walls that he crossed the path of another vampire. He managed to escape the clutches of two vampires, only to meet another and succumb to their bite. For seven days, he remained, until he awoke the final night, and the change was complete." A long pause followed as Liam gathered his thoughts some more. The story was taking its toll on him, but he continued.

"However, he was something different to his brother. Though he, too, had become a vampire, his personality was unchanged. He was still the man that he had been before. Although, he now had a strength that he did not previously have. While he now craved blood, he was able to quench his intense thirst with the blood of animals.

"As he remained in the church, he began to sense the presence of others nearby, and he eventually came out of his hiding place. And that was when they found him, the members of the Order that his mother had been telling him about." Liam looked at me once again that piercing gaze holding me transfixed once more.

"They had come in search of him, each using their unique gifts to seek him out. Although they knew what he had become, they also knew that there was something different about him. He had both the powers of a vampire as well as the gifts that he was born to, making him more powerful than either side. As he learned more about his powers, along with those of his brother, he realised that his brother appeared to have powers that were unheard of in other nightwalkers. Because of this, the brothers were evenly matched and battled against each other for centuries.

"Although the members of the Order aged slower than normal humans, they are not immortal, and soon there were only a handful of people who remained as families grew smaller and less likely to have as many children. The Order held some hope, however, in a prophecy of a young woman who would have powers even greater than both the brothers, a young woman who would defeat the darkness finally. She was the seventh daughter of both a seventh daughter and a seventh son, and her powers would have no bounds." He fell silent finally, his story now finished.

I looked down at my lap, noting that I had almost ripped my pillow in half as I had pulled and scrunched at it throughout his long tale. Realisation dawned on me. Something I'd never really thought about before. My mother was the seventh daughter in her family, and my father was the seventh son in his. And I was their seventh daughter.

How had I never put this together before?

"Are you trying to tell me that this... this prophecy... it's supposed to be about me?" I whispered, unable to speak any louder. I think my voice had run away, and I wished the rest of me could have done the same. This was all too much to take in.

"It's not supposed to be about you, Isolde; it is about you. You are the one we have been waiting for, knowing that you would finally end this war." Liam watched me closely as I took this in.

"And this is why you've been following me? Why you were at my university that day?" For once, it was Liam's turn to look confused.

"What do you mean? You've only ever seen me the night before your birthday... and then, when Will..." He didn't finish his sentence, but the memory of that night came flooding back, and I let it go for the time being.

"Does this mean that you are one of them? The Order?" I had guessed this much anyway but wanted to hear it said aloud. Liam nodded.

"And so are you. Even if the prophecy had not been about you, you would have been one of us. You still would have had gifts, but the powers you have are so much more than gifts. Eventually, you will see a tattoo show up on the inside of your right wrist. A golden dragon. It's a symbol to show that you will remove the darkness from the world." I started, looking down at my wrist, which presently was bare, with no sign of the gold I had still noticed from time to time.

"When you say powers, what exactly am I meant to be able to do? So, I can sense a presence in the dark? Most women can do that." Aside from the nightmares, I could think of nothing else. And the nightmares didn't feel like power, more like a curse.

"The reason you aren't aware of them is because you haven't been introduced into this world yet. That is why Adam was trying to get to you first.

"You see, depending on which of the bloodlines a vampire belongs to, if a person is turned by them, they will either be evil or... well, not good, but on the side of good..."

I must have looked confused because Liam suddenly shook his head.

"Sorry, I hadn't told you about that part yet. There are two different vampire bloodlines. When the youngest brother came to hide in the church, another vampire was already there. The blood memories that flooded through him as he lay there for seven days were not those of an evil race but of those who fought against them, who did not need to feed on the blood of men. The two bloodlines began before Christ. We do not know if those who began the war are even still walking this earth." He rubbed his neck as though he felt the bite at his own throat.

"So, when a human is changing, they are flooded with the blood memories of those who turned them?" I was trying to put it all together, and Liam nodded.

"It is through those memories that they become either a nightwalker or one who can walk in the light, what we call daywalkers. Although they do not usually fight with the Protectors, they are usually always there somewhere. It is how our side has managed to hold out for this long. But with our numbers now dwindling so low, it's only a matter of time before there are no Protectors left, just the two bloodlines once more."

"What is a Protector?" I was confused, trying to keep track of all these different names being thrown around.

"The Members of the Order call themselves the Protectors. Protecting humanity from the realm of the supernatural."

Good lord... this is crazy! I must have spoken the words out loud, as Liam laughed softly, though there was no humour behind it.

"That was along my line of thinking when this was all told to me. The night that I was told about the Order, I thought that the world had gone mad."

"So, there are two different breeds of vampires? And the good ones can walk in the daylight?" I still couldn't grasp all of this.

"The nightwalkers are the ones we fight against; they can only feed off the blood of humans and can't consume human food. They retain only the worst of their human personalities, although they seem to be able to continue to love. Still, it is obsessive love, as I explained to you that night about Will." Liam's eyes flicked over my face as tears welled in my eyes. I swallowed and nodded, motioning for him to continue, as the memory of the notes from Will made it hard to breathe.

"The daywalkers are a little different. They still require blood to survive, but they can survive on animal blood, and they still consume food. They aren't entirely good, as they can be cruel and less in touch with their feelings than humans. They often appear devoid of emotion, but it's more that they don't feel the same way about things that humans do, as they find most human problems trivial. But they are at war with the nightwalkers and have been since before anyone that I know can remember. We'll be able to explain more tomorrow when you meet the others." I shook my head at these last words.

"No, tomorrow I go back to uni and work. Tomorrow, I start going back to normal again. This is all some sort of crazy nightmare that I'm now going to wake up from." Liam looked at me sympathetically.

"Isolde... this is the real world... the rest of it is the dream..." I felt a tear roll down my face. No, I stubbornly thought to myself, I would not be brought into this. I needed normal right now.

There was a knock on my door, and I turned as Aurora entered the room backwards, her arms laden with boxes. I jumped up to block the window, but Liam was already gone, so fast that I thought he had fallen. There was no thud or groan, and if Aurora noticed anything unusual, she didn't show it as she placed the boxes under the very window where Liam had just sat. She didn't notice that my entire world was completely different now. After she left again, I sat down on the bed and stared intently at my wrist, willing myself to see the flash of gold that I had seen so many times. Nothing appeared.

Thoughts swirled in my head. He had to be wrong. Surely, the stories weren't about me. I was too normal. Boring even! Until now, everything had been stock standard in my life. Leave school, go to university, get a job, meet a guy, travel, and get engaged. Nowhere in my plan had there ever been the words "save the world"! I was not an activist. I never took any interest in world peace; I ran away from all the different activist groups that set up shop around campus at uni... There had to have been some mistake.

However, as these thoughts were going through my head, something happened. Faintly at first, a symbol began to appear on my wrist. It started as a flash of gold, nothing more. Then it grew brighter. Eventually, it was as though someone had come along with a pen and drawn a symbol in gold ink and then turned a light on. It was so bright.

But it was not the dragon that Liam said members of the Order had on their wrists. It was a rising sun.

A symbol to show that you will remove the darkness from the world. Sunlight eliminates the darkness.

I had no idea where that thought had come from, and the appearance of the tattoo did not make me feel any better. In fact, it scared the crap out of me!

Chapter Eight

AFTER BREAKFAST THE NEXT morning, I resolutely placed my laptop in my backpack and packed my uniform into a separate bag. I pulled on a jumper, ensuring that the tattoo was covered by the sleeve, as it was now fully formed and hadn't faded since last night. At least it had stopped glowing, though. I was adamant I was going to uni first, then straight to work. That was until I went out to my car to discover Liam already sitting in the driver's seat.

"No," I said firmly, refusing to accept that this was how it was. Liam ignored me and reached across, opening the passenger door and waiting for me to get in. He looked ahead as though he were a parent waiting for a belligerent teenager to do as they were told. I went around and threw myself in the car, tears of anger and frustration rolling down my face, once again feeling as though I had no control over my own life. I didn't even realise that I hadn't shut the door until it slammed shut on its own, and I stared at it in shock.

"Yes, that was you," Liam said as he started the engine and began to drive. He headed towards the city, and I wondered, with a curiosity that I refused to show, where we were going.

Twenty minutes later, when he pulled up in front of a very old and run-down home in New Farm, I began to wonder again if this wasn't all some sort of joke until I stepped through the front door and realised that the outside was all just an illusion.

"It's a glamour," Liam explained, seeing my look of shock as I took in my surroundings. On the outside, the house looked to be a simple three-bedroom old Queenslander, which was in a complete state of disrepair. Once through the doors, though, I entered a... Grand Manor. There must have been over twenty rooms, and I was guessing that the other homes around this one were all one glamour to hide this same building.

"Why didn't you guys just get office space?" I couldn't understand why they needed to go to this sort of trouble just for their headquarters.

"We not only work here; this is also our home as well. As long as we call it home, no nightwalker can cross this threshold. And because of the glamour, if one of us is turned, we can't find it again. It's part of the magic." More surprises.

"Magic is real too?!" *When would the craziness stop?*

A soft laugh from above made me jump, and I looked to see a breathtakingly beautiful woman peering down at me from the landing on the second floor. Her long black hair rippled behind her as she descended the grand staircase with agile grace. I took in her simple jeans and singlet top, her casual attire seeming out of place with her stunning features. She would have looked more at home in a ball gown. If I were to try to guess her age, I'd say somewhere in her mid-thirties, but she seemed almost ageless.

"Welcome, Isolde. We have been expecting you. I see that Liam still has not divulged everything yet." She shot Liam a look over my shoulder, her green eyes filled with understanding, before continuing. "It is all a bit much to take in at once. I wish someone had told me in stages." She came forward and took my hand gently, giving it a squeeze.

"I'm Patrice. Before long, you will learn everything, and it will all stop being such a shock." I seriously doubted this part but allowed myself to be towed through several rooms, each filled with fancy antiques, reminding me of the palaces I had visited in Europe. We came to a stop finally, coming to a room that seemed completely out of place in this grand old building. It looked like it belonged in a James Bond movie, filled with computer monitors and gadgets as far as the eye could see. In the centre of the room stood a massive round table with several people sitting around it of various ages. As we entered the room, a sudden silence descended, and I found myself feeling uneasy due to the various looks I was getting. These looks ranged from mild curiosity to full-blown admiration, but one woman around my age seemed to be strongly disapproving. Someone in this room did *not* want me there, but Lord only knew why.

"Everyone, as you all know, this is Isolde. Isolde, meet... well... everyone." Patrice waved her hand toward those seated at the table as Liam walked around the other side. He took a seat beside the woman who did not so much as look at me now, busying herself with scanning the screen of the laptop in front of her. I nodded at the group and allowed Patrice to lead me to an empty chair directly across the opulent table from Liam. The silence continued for a moment until a middle-aged man on my left reached out to shake my hand.

"It's nice to see you again, Isolde. I'm Gerard." I looked at him closely, trying to place where I knew him from.

"Wait a minute... Mr O'Connell? You look the same!" Realising that the man beside me was, in fact, the same man who had taught me in grade two, I looked around the table once more, looking at the others properly for the first time. I recognised more familiar faces, noting people who had been scattered throughout my past, and not a single one of them appeared to have aged a day since I had last seen them. They all smiled back.

"We've been protecting you since you were first born, Isolde." The last sentence was spoken in a familiar Spanish accent, and I looked over to see Katyana, from my brief stay in London, smiling at me from where she sat at a computer across the room.

"But... you're the same age as me..." I was confused at the sight of Katyana, with whom I had shared a bedroom in a share house in London. We had spent many a drunken night at the Walkabout Pub near our house as I drowned my homesick sorrows. Seeing her here, now, was very surreal.

"I'm forty-five, actually."

I remembered now about what Liam had said, that they aged differently to normal people, and I wondered briefly how old Liam was. I also found myself scanning the people around me, wondering if one of them was the vampire, the younger brother from Liam's story last night. A few men here could have fit the description, so I was left wondering.

Everyone looks so human.

We had come in during the middle of a meeting, and they all continued the discussion we had walked into, deferring to Patrice now that she had joined them. I tried to follow along with what was being discussed, but I found myself just looking around at the people at the table. I didn't know how to feel about all of these revelations, and I almost felt violated by how much they all knew about me. It was like finding out I was on some sort of reality TV show that I hadn't auditioned for. Some of them treated me as though I was the Messiah, the second coming, which I found very uncomfortable, whereas others, like Patrice, Katyana and Liam, treated me as though I was one of them, on the same level as them. The woman next to Liam seemed to perceive me as a threat to whatever was happening between them as she moved closer to him without even glancing at me. Her name, as she was introduced to me, was Alana, and she was from the US, somewhere in the south, judging by her accent. I realised I'd have to set the record straight with her, as I had no intention of having anything romantic happen between Liam and myself. Will wasn't even cold in his grave yet! Then I realised with a jolt that he never would be either.

After the meeting, Patrice took me on a tour through the lower levels of the Manor and gave me more details about the Order.

"This location is one of about a hundred others like it around the world. This one was set up around the time of your birth." She threw me a sad smile over her shoulder as she lead me into the kitchen. "Vampire activity in Brisbane wasn't much of a problem until then."

Fantastic, more deaths on my hands.

Liam joined me as I sat on a seat at the bench and watched Patrice move around the kitchen, making lunch for us both. He remained silent as Patrice handed me a sandwich, moving to sit on my other side as she ate her own. I wasn't quite sure what to make of all of this, simply taking a bite of the sandwich and looking around the room quietly, although I could feel Liam watching me closely.

Afterwards, Patrice led me upstairs, and I realised that I had misjudged the size of the Manor. It was far bigger than I first thought. There were at least thirty bedrooms, branching off several hallways, each one with its own bathroom and designed to be inhabited by a member of the Order. Most appeared to be filled with personal items, although I was unsure how many members of the worldwide order resided here full-time.

"This is your room... should you wish to stay here," Patrice said, showing me a room at the end of one of the many halls. She smiled as I opened my mouth to protest.

"It will be yours no matter what, even if you do not choose to live here." Liam had followed behind us, and Patrice left us alone to see to other affairs. During the meeting, I learned that she was one of the elders and the leader of this particular chapter of the Order. As I stood in the middle of 'my' room, an overwhelming sensation threatened to take hold of me again, and I swayed on my feet.

"Here, sit down." Liam guided me to a soft armchair, which I gratefully sank into.

"I keep waiting for someone to yell cut or something, to discover that I've walked onto the set of a movie..." I looked around in wonder, trying not to fall in love with the room that I was in.

"Where do you think people got the ideas for those sorts of movies from? Our presence is not as secret as we would like to believe it is, although it does have its advantages. Your reaction mirrors exactly how the rest of the world would be if they found out it was all real." Liam sat on the bed, facing me. He was, quite possibly, the most beautiful man I had ever seen. I blushed a little at that thought, unable to hold his gaze for long as he smiled a slow, easy smile.

Suddenly I was overwhelmed with the need to sleep; the weight of it all was just too much for my brain to deal with. Liam saw the shift in my energy, possibly noting the fact that I was about to pass out because within seconds, I was curled up on the bed and Liam was quietly letting himself out of the room, having placed a blanket over me. I felt myself being pulled into a deep sleep, everything that I had learned in the past week flooding through my mind, making its way into my dreams.

When I awoke, I couldn't remember anything from those dreams, but I realised, with an empty feeling in the pit of my stomach, that I wasn't going to be able to run away from this. I felt a single tear slide down my cheek, and I rolled over, wiping it away, to discover Patrice sitting in the armchair that I had vacated earlier, a steaming mug sitting next to her as she read from an incredibly old-looking book.

"Hi." I yawned as I sat up, and Patrice looked up with a smile, closing her book and handing me the mug, which turned out to be filled with chamomile tea.

"Liam said you'd probably need someone to talk to once you'd woken up." She said this as she moved to sit on the edge of the bed. I felt a connection with Patrice, almost as if she was another mother whom I had known all my life. I pulled my legs up underneath me, giving her more space.

"So, is Liam my very own guardian angel or something? He keeps showing up at exactly the right moment to save me." I left out that he couldn't save my fiancé. A bit too bitter, and it was not Liam's fault.

"It's one of Liam's gifts. He can tune into any one of us, and he can also see into our thoughts if he wishes." I must have looked taken aback at this because Patrice patted my legs reassuringly. "Don't worry; it's not something that he enjoys doing often, and he tends to be able to switch it off, only using it when necessary. Unfortunately, with your circumstances lately, it's been necessary for him to see your whereabouts quite a lot." This did not make me feel much better, remembering the thought I'd had about how attractive he was when we were talking earlier, but it brought me to the subject that had been bothering me since last night.

"What gifts or powers am I meant to have? Because I don't think I'm going to be shooting laser beams out of my eyes any time soon." Patrice smiled at this, seeing through my bravado.

"We don't know. They will present themselves in time. However, Liam told me about the car door this morning, so we can assume that you have some telekinetic abilities." She gave my leg another reassuring pat. "We will work on those in time. But the prophecy does say that your powers will know no bounds, so I know we can expect great things from you." As she leaned forward to push a strand of my hair behind my ear, I closed my eyes for a moment, trying not to wallow in self-pity. I wasn't sure how I would cope with the weight of all these expectations on me.

"I know it feels like a lot now, but you're surrounded by people who know exactly what you're going through. Who have all experienced something similar. If you need to talk, any one of us will be here for you." As she left the room, I bit back on the words that I wanted to say. How many of these people had mysterious prophecies about them? How many of them were expected to be the answer to ending a war they knew nothing about?

That afternoon, I walked through the ground floor rooms of the Manor, talking to some of the others and watching as they went about their tasks.

I didn't feel as though I was a part of this... couldn't feel like I belonged. Or, more accurately, wouldn't allow myself to feel like I belonged. This was not my world. I just wanted normalcy again. I just wanted to finish my university degree and start piecing my life back together. I did not want to belong to a secret world that I could not even tell my loved ones about.

Then I found the training room. I watched as Alana and Liam sparred with one another, trading punches and amazing kicks, and realised that this was something that I did want to learn. Something to channel my anger and frustration through. As I stood watching, Liam stepped up his attack on Alana, who had previously had the upper hand. She threw all her weight into her next punch, which Liam blocked with his right forearm, before ducking low and sweeping her feet out from underneath her with his foot, stopping to kneel on one knee beside her as she lay winded on her back. Leaning a forearm on his knee, he looked over at me as I stood at the door. Noticing that Liam's attention was elsewhere, Alana arched her neck and looked up over her head. Even across the room, I could see her eyes roll before she sprung to her feet in a move that I could have only dreamed of doing one day.

"I should have guessed." She spat the words over her shoulder as she walked out through the door on the opposite side of the room. I tried not to take her attitude personally, but as I could see no reason for it, this was incredibly hard to do. Liam could see how her rudeness threw me, shrugging with an exasperated look.

"Sorry about Alana. She is jealous for several different reasons, which I will tell you about another time. She is a nice person, though." Liam began putting away the weights that lay scattered around the room.

"Yeah... I guess I'll just have to take your word for it, Liam." I leaned against the frame of the door, hesitant to enter the room, even though I was itching to get my hands on the punching bag that was hanging in the corner.

"How was your sleep? Feel better?"

"Not even remotely. Until I wake up from this nightmare, I don't think sleep is going to be much of a relief." I tried to hide the resentment I felt from him, but he sensed it, nonetheless. I remembered what Patrice said about him being able to hear our thoughts, and I heard him sigh as he came to stand in front of me before lifting my chin so that I was forced to look directly into his eyes. I knew I should be uncomfortable at the familiarity he had with me, but something about it just felt normal. The only normal thing about my life right now.

"Isolde. I know that right now, this all seems crazy. That your world is shattering apart, and there doesn't seem to be any way to fix it. However, eventually, the hurt fades. The memories that you and Will shared will always be there. But you are going to be around for a very long time. And the destiny ahead of you is so much more than this. All of this." I looked up at Liam with tears of anger in my eyes.

"You have no idea what this feels like, Liam! I lost the love of my life only two weeks ago, and since then, I've discovered that he is a vampire who is on a mission to turn me into a vampire as well, all because of some crazy ass destiny that I am supposed to have. Not to mention the fact that I have been keeping secrets and lying to my twin sister, the one person in the whole world who knows everything about me!" I was getting angrier with every word that I spoke, and Liam seized me by the shoulders, turned me around and marched me over to the punching bag.

"All that anger you're feeling? That's good. Anger is the first step to take in dealing with all of this; it is about time you got past denial. Now take your anger out on that." He pointed at the punching bag as he handed me a pair of boxing gloves. I couldn't believe the nerve of this guy. It was him that I felt like punching, not the bag, but after seeing his skills before, I knew I was no match for him.

So, I punched the bag. I punched with such force that it caused the bag to fly back. Thankfully, Liam caught it before it could swing back and hit me. I gaped at it for a second before hitting it again... and again... I felt the past three months' worth of fear, confusion, grief and anger flowing through me into the bag as I pounded with all my might. I even threw in a few kicks for good measure. I didn't know when the tears started to flow, but suddenly I was shaking uncontrollably as fat tears rolled down my cheeks by the bucket load. I stopped punching and slowly melted to the ground, no longer able to stand under the force of the emotions that had slammed into me.

I felt Liam's arms come around me, and he rocked me gently as I sobbed my heart out. I rested my head against his shoulder as my sobs quietened, and I continued to cry silently now, no longer mad at him but unable to look at him either.

"Believe me, Isolde. I understand your pain more than you know."

Chapter Nine

"ISOLDE? DID YOU HEAR me?" I looked over at my mother, noticing her concerned face, as we sat across from each other the next morning, eating breakfast.

"Sorry, Mum. What'd you say?" She continued to look at me for a few more moments before speaking again.

"I said, what time is your meeting with the solicitor?" I chewed my mouthful of cereal slowly, swallowing before responding.

"In an hour and a half." I was dreading this meeting, knowing it was one more step closer to the end of my life with Will. I was due to be meeting with the solicitor who was in charge of his estate, along with his parents and sister. After yesterday's events, and knowing everything I did now about what was really out in the world, the last thing I wanted was to be sitting in a room with Will's family and having to lie to them.

"Dad said he'll be back in time to take you." My mother watched as I got up and put my empty bowl in the dishwasher. I nodded silently and headed up to my room to get ready. I'd asked my father to come along, as I honestly wasn't sure how much I would take in, and I figured someone had better be there who could make sense of it all for me.

After a shower and putting on make-up for the first time in weeks, I stood in front of the mirror on my bedroom door and stared at my reflection. I barely even recognised the woman staring back at me. My face was pale, even with makeup on, and my hair hung limply down my back. I couldn't even remember the last time I'd washed it, and I wound it into a bun on top of my head to hide the oiliness.

Get it together, Isolde.

I pulled on a pair of jeans and a singlet top, before throwing a cardigan on over the top.

This is as good as it's going to get.

I went and sat in the armchair next to my window, staring outside. Yesterday, I'd been able to function, but today was a different story. All I wanted to do was crawl back between my sheets and sleep until the grief and darkness had lifted, and I could breathe once more. Was this what my life would be like from now on? A constant, aching black hole that consumed my waking hours, and nightmares about the monster that Will had become when I slept?

"Peanut? You ready to go?" My father stood at my door, and I felt my heart break a little at the sadness on his face. I wondered how long he'd been standing there, but I could tell it had been long enough to see his youngest daughter lost in a world of despair. I tried to smile, but I knew it wasn't doing much to relieve him, as he squeezed my arm when I walked past him, leading the way out to his car. This was going to be a long day.

Several hours later, I was back at home, still reeling from the meeting with the solicitor. Will's family had been just as depressed as I was about being there, but his parents were aware of the information that was shared prior to the meeting, so it was just a formality for them. Will had gone with them only six months ago to get all of his affairs in order, around the time that he'd picked up the ring. Ready to start our lives together.

It turned out, even at the age of twenty-five, Will had begun to amass a large investment portfolio, including properties and shares. Worth several million already. His parents were pretty well off, but I had never known just how much money they all had. And now, everything that had been Will's belonged to me, his sole beneficiary. He'd left some personal items for his parents and sister, but everything else was to be left for me and any children we may have. Since we hadn't managed to get to the baby-making part of Will's life plan, the reality that I was now a multi-millionaire at the age of twenty-five whilst still a university student was a lot to process.

"Will had planned to tell you all of this on your wedding night. A bit of a wedding gift, I guess. He was so excited about the life he was building for you both, Isolde." His father's voice was shaking with emotion as he'd given me a tight hug at the end of the meeting. I'd just stared at him in shock. Finding out that Will owned the townhouse outright, having paid off the mortgage last year, had been the biggest shock though. When we'd arrived home and Aurora overheard my father telling my mother everything, the first thing she'd done was come running upstairs to find me.

"So, you won't be selling anymore, right?" It took me a moment to work out what my twin was referring to. Then I felt fear grip my belly and I shook my head frantically.

"No, Aura, I'm still selling the Townhouse." I couldn't tell her the main reason why, but I honestly didn't know that I wanted to keep it, even without the issue of Will being able to get in and murder us all in our sleep. "There are too many memories in that house. I can't bear being there anymore."

Aurora studied my face briefly. "But, you might change your mind. We shouldn't rush into anything."

"There's no we in this decision, Aurora. It's my choice, and I'm selling it." I didn't mean to sound as harsh as I did, but I was tired and it had been a very emotional day. Aurora looked stunned for a moment before her face closed off. I knew that look well. My sister had always been the more dominant of the two of us, and she didn't like it when I stood up to her.

"Sorry Aurora. I just... I won't change my mind about it, okay?" She nodded stiffly at me after a moment, and I could tell this wasn't going to be the last I heard of it.

"We'll talk about it later, I guess. When you're ready to decide what we should do." The tone in her voice indicated that once I was no longer considered to be in a delicate state, my sister was going to tell me exactly how she felt about the fact that all the decisions were up to me right now. I could only hope that my parents could talk her out of whatever mood she ended up in later tonight, cause I was tapped out. And, I had somewhere to be.

"Can't I just burn the house down?" Liam looked at me thoughtfully, as I ranted later that evening, sitting across the table from him in the study that was off his room at the Manor. We were meant to be going through mind-clearing techniques in an attempt to unlock my abilities, but I could tell that shutting my brain off was going to be difficult when I had so many problems rolling around inside my head. One would think that becoming a multi-millionaire in one day was a good thing, but it was just giving me one more thing to stress about now.

"I think we should avoid committing arson just to keep your sister from arguing with you about selling the house, Isolde." He smirked a little, as I flopped back in my chair and sighed. It was the first time I'd seen him out of black clothes, and I found myself taking note of the fit of his white long-sleeve shirt that clung to his impressive biceps. He cleared his throat, and I shook myself out of my distracted state.

"It would be so much easier than dealing with Aurora when she gets like this. She does not do well with being told no." He laughed a little, and I raised an eyebrow.

"I'm very aware of how strong-willed your sister is." That was true. As he'd been tasked with guarding me for my entire life up until now, I had no doubt that he had witnessed many of the moments in our lives where Aurora had tried to get me to do what she wanted.

"Then you know I'm right." Liam just shook his head, still smirking.

"Be that as it may, I think burning the house down is a bit extreme. In our experience with the nightwalkers, once the target of their obsession has moved out of the home that they were in together, they don't tend to return. There shouldn't be any need to burn it down, no matter how much easier it would be for you when it comes to Aurora." His statement made me think of a question that had been burning in the back of my mind.

"So, does the Order just rock up to people's houses when their loved ones are turned into nightwalkers and just say 'FYI, ya gotta move cause your husband is a vampire now, oh, and truth bomb, he's gonna murder you now unless you get outta this house?'." My words were glib, but I did want to know how that all worked, as they'd told me they also had to keep the Order a secret from the rest of the world. Liam laughed a little before answering.

"It's not quite like that, but we do influence the family to move in our own way. Magic is obviously used to help persuade them that it's suddenly a really good time to sell up and move far away, start a new life and so on. We are also fortunate that, as more people are getting cremated these days, we don't have quite as many people turning as we used to. Nightwalkers tend to also be quite brutal in their feeding habits, so they don't turn as many people as you'd think." Well, that all made sense, and was also slightly terrifying. I regarded Liam for a moment, as I processed what he'd just said.

"Well, I guess that works. It's still amazing that no one has worked out that vampires are real and are shouting about it all over the internet."

"Modern technology has brought with it a lot of challenges for us, that's true. But, the few who have learned the truth and started broadcasting it everywhere have mostly been written off as crazy. The tin foil hat wearers, for instance." That was easy to believe. I was suddenly forced to question everything I'd believed about the crazy people yelling about conspiracies on the internet. I was now part of an organisation that was a conspiracy-theorists wet dream.

"So, what do I do about Aurora then?"

"You could just tell her no." He stated it so simply, and now it was my turn to laugh, though it didn't have much humour behind it.

"Sure. You make that sound so easy."

"In my experience, it becomes easier when you stop trying to keep everyone else happy and just start to focus on what you need instead." I regarded him thoughtfully for a moment.

"You're right, I guess. But, when does that ability kick in? Cause that's not something that too many people my age have been successful at, in my experience." I was hoping he'd reveal how old he was, but he just shook his head with a smile.

"When you realise that the only person in the world who can make you happy is yourself, Isolde." I stared at him, as his words struck down deep within me. And the meaning behind it.

After the longest time, I cleared my throat, needing to get this training session back on track.

"So, what do I need to do to clear my mind?" He nodded over to the corner behind me, and I turned to look. I'd not noticed when I first came into the room, but he had a little meditation corner set up. There were cushions on the floor, on either side of a low table, with 3 candles on it.

"Take a seat over there." He got up and went to switch off the lights as I took a seat on the cushion closest to the wall. The room fell into darkness, lit only by the flickering candles, and I was suddenly struck by the intimacy of the situation. Liam hesitated for a moment, before coming closer.

"I find it easiest to switch off from all the chaos in this house when I come to this spot and focus on the flame. I've been using these techniques for a while now, whenever things get too noisy in my head, to try and bring myself some peace." He sat down with surprising grace for someone so tall. But then, this man could make fighting look like a dance, so I shouldn't be surprised by anything he did.

"So, do I close my eyes, or…"

"Focus all your concentration on the centre candle." I followed his direction, lowering my eyes from his face to gaze at the tallest candle in the middle, noticing how everything else around me became darker as I stared into the bright flame. "I have always found staring into a flame to be calming. I believe it has the same effect on you, from my observations over the years."

There was truth to his words. I had always found myself drawn to flames when given the opportunity. When camping, I always gravitated towards the campfire and had spent many an evening staring into the flickering flames, entranced. Moments when I thought I had been alone and unnoticed.

"Now focus on your breathing. Narrow your consciousness down to only the flame and your breaths." His voice had taken on a calming tone, and I focused on willing my thoughts to drift away, slowing my breathing. I continued, losing count of how many breaths I'd taken, forgetting where I was, and everything going on in the world around me, and just gazed into the flame. I felt a calm descend upon me, and everything else ceased to exist, there was only my breathing and the flame, which seemed to be growing bigger the longer I stared at it. I was no longer aware of where Liam was in the room, where I was, or even who I was at that exact moment.

The sound of a door slamming startled me, and I jumped as the flame leapt up in a ball into the air, the candle falling with a thud. Liam jumped to his feet as the flame hung suspended in the air, my gaze seemingly holding it there. I could feel his shock without looking at him, knowing that my face must have a similar expression. Slowly, he reached down to pick up the candle, raising it so that the small ball of fire attached to the wick once more. I let out the breath I had been holding as he lowered it back to the table, grateful that I hadn't managed to set fire to the Manor on my first night of working on my powers. He watched me intently, as I continued to stare at the candle in shock.

"Well... that was interesting."

I'll say...

An hour later, I let myself out of Liam's suite, having fallen back into my mind-clearing exercise with no more incidents. Liam said he needed a bit of sleep before I left and he was on guard duty again, so I decided to find Patrice to discuss when we would start my magic lessons. As I shut the door behind me, I turned to find Alana standing a few feet away, the expression on her face showing her surprise at seeing me there. Her eyes narrowed as if she'd just realised whose room I had come out of. Before I could say anything, she turned on her heel and stormed back around the corner. I shook my head. I had a strange feeling that this woman and I were never going to be friends, especially if she thought I was moving in on the man that she clearly had feelings for. I had no idea what the relationship between herself and Liam was, but I had no intention of getting caught in the middle of it all and feeding into the little melodrama that they had going on. I had far more important things to worry about.

Finding Patrice in the kitchen yet again, I accepted the bowl of noodles that she handed me, as she seemed determined to keep feeding me any time she saw me.

"How was your session with Liam?"

"Interesting." I wasn't quite sure how to describe to her what had happened with the flame, so I thought I'd leave it up to Liam to tell her. He probably understood what had happened far better than I did anyway.

"When should we start working on my magic lessons? You mentioned yesterday that I'd need to start working on a few things?" I was realising now that I was eager to throw myself into anything to distract me from the grief I was still dealing with. Patrice smiled sadly, and I knew she'd worked that out too.

"How about we just get you through your last exams, first? Don't you have an assignment due next week?"

Honestly, was there anything about my life that these people didn't know?

"Yeah. I was going to ask for an extension though. I haven't opened a book in three weeks." Because that's how long it had been since my fiance had been brutally murdered before my eyes and turned into a vampire. Surely, that would be enough to get my lecturer and tutor to give me a compassionate extension... I just needed like a few months... I didn't think I'd get quite that long though.

"How about we go into the library now for a few hours, and Katyana and I can help?" With the exception of Alana, everyone had made me feel so welcome, and I felt my throat constrict with emotion a little. Maybe they didn't quite understand the pressure they were putting on me with this whole prophecy deal, but they were at least attempting to help me feel like I belonged here. I nodded, and once we finished eating, I followed Patrice into the library and we got down to the task of getting me through the final few weeks of my academic life.

I returned to my parent's home in the early hours of the morning, allowing Liam to drive me home so that he could take up his vigil outside. It had felt strange knowing that I was going to sleep while he just sat out in the dark, but he assured me that he was more than used to it. I knew that was true, given that he'd had more than twenty-five years of experience now. I still hadn't learned who the daywalker was amongst the Order, but I felt like standing guard in the dark for hours and hours was more of a job for him, rather than Liam.

After several fitful hours of sleep where my dreams were once again plagued by mysterious figures with blue eyes and sinister laughs that made my ears feel like they were bleeding, I dragged myself out of bed and went in search of my sister. As it was a weekend, I knew I'd find her in bed still. Jacob was at work, so I knew she'd be alone, and I let myself in, sneaking into bed beside her. Although our interaction the day before had been strained, I didn't like fighting with my sister, and I just needed to get things sorted with her.

Aurora rolled over and looked at me, slowly waking up.

"Hey." I pushed a strand of hair out of her face, and she blinked at me slowly.

"Hey. You okay?" Lately, it had been her climbing into my bed, not the other way around.

"Sort of. Are we okay?" I sounded so needy, but with my sister, I didn't care. It was the one relationship where I had always felt completely honest. At least, until this year, when everything started to turn to shit. I couldn't shake the feeling that my dishonesty was a large part of why everything had turned awful. But it wasn't like I could tell her. The Order had been very firm about that, and really, I wasn't sure that she would believe me anyway. She'd definitely be marching me off to the mental health ward, thinking that I'd finally lost it.

"Of course we're okay. I'm just worried about you, babe. You're making so many snap decisions lately, and I'm worried that one day you're going to wake up after the grief has lessened, and suddenly you regret all these changes." She reached over and pulled me to her, and I snuggled into her arms, grateful for the contact.

"I know... I guess I just need you to trust that I know what I'm doing. Can you try and understand that?"

"Okay... But what are we going to do about finding somewhere to live? Because as much as I love Mum and Dad, I can't take much more of the constant parental interaction." I could relate. Our parents had been hovering a lot since we moved back in, and the attention was starting to become grating.

"How about we start looking for somewhere to rent together? We don't need to buy this time. You and Jacob will want your own place one day, I'm sure?" Aurora hesitated for a moment, and for a split second, I wondered if everything was okay with their relationship. She eventually nodded though.

"Yeah, you're right. That's a good idea. Let's start looking today, okay?" And just like that, we had a plan, and I hadn't had to get into an argument with my sister. Or burn my old house down.

Chapter Ten

THE FOLLOWING FORTNIGHT, I finally got around to speaking to my boss.

"We'll miss you around here, Isolde. I'm so sorry about everything that happened. Will was a good man." Danielle gave me a hug as I stood up after having dropped the bomb that I wasn't going to be coming back. I fought to keep the tears at bay. I had always known this was a temporary job, but we had been like a little family here, and they had all known Will. I hadn't seen any of them since the funeral, but they had all been texting constantly. I really needed to start to do a better job of keeping in contact with everyone, but had been struggling to respond to messages ever since Will's death.

"Thanks, Danielle. I'm going to miss you all too. But with everything that has happened, I just need a fresh start." She nodded in understanding.

"Do you know what you're going to do?"

"Yeah, I've got a job lined up. I'll be starting once I finish my exams in two weeks. It's a research assistant position. Might as well put that university degree to use." I figured this was the closest I'd get to telling people the truth, and I wasn't technically lying. The Order did pay their members, and quite well, I might add. And I was researching... I was just leaving out the ass-kicking aspect of my new position.

Aurora was growing increasingly suspicious and regularly questioned my whereabouts over the following weeks. With my time constantly taken up by the Order in the months since Will's death, I wasn't actively searching for a new home, causing frustration for Aurora. Adjusting to more change was something I wasn't ready to handle yet. I hadn't told her that I wasn't returning to work, so I was able to use that as an excuse for the most part. However, that didn't explain my change in attitude and the fact that I was slimming down rapidly due to my daily workouts with Liam. Both my twin and I had curvy builds, but all the exercise combined with forgetting to eat a lot had meant I'd become quite thin at an alarming rate.

Though others seemed hesitant to comment, it was something that had concerned Patrice greatly, as she informed me when she pulled me aside one Saturday morning as I walked through the front door.

"Isolde, I'm worried about you," she stated simply as she lead me by the hand into the kitchen.

"Why?" I had thought I'd been doing well, not falling into a grieving heap every hour, as I had been doing up until around a month earlier. I had been burying myself in my studies, training with Liam and taking tentative steps towards learning about my, as yet elusive, powers... I thought I'd been doing a great job of pretending.

But apparently not. This was made quite clear as Patrice put a plate full of bacon, eggs and hash browns down in an empty spot at the large bench.

Liam was already there, having headed straight to the kitchen when we arrived together. He was sitting at the long table with Alana, Katyana and another man by the name of Sam, whom I had only met for the first time the week before. Sam was English and looked to be around thirty, though I was fast learning that looks meant nothing when it came to age with these people. I had found out that Patrice was two hundred years old the week before, something I was still reeling from. The idea that I was now going to live such a long life was incredibly overwhelming.

"You are becoming far too thin, and I rarely see you eat." Patrice served herself the same food, glancing at my plate with a look that told me to sit my butt in the chair and eat my breakfast. I wondered briefly if I would be allowed to leave the table if I left so much as a piece of rind on my plate. Alana was watching this exchange with a smirk, and I felt something in me snap.

"What is your problem, Alana?!" My words were harsh, and she looked shocked for a moment before her eyes narrowed. I had so far just avoided her and not reacted to any of her little snippy comments, but I was tired. She opened her mouth to retort now, but Liam cut her off.

"Leave it." She closed her mouth again, still glaring at me, which I found even more frustrating. I could see that whatever the problem was, I was not going to find out any time soon, so I ate my breakfast in a quiet rage, seething at everyone, including Sam and Katyana, who had sat with their heads down through the entire non-conversation, obviously knowing more than they were willing to admit.

After I begrudgingly finished my breakfast, I went into the library and started studying where I had left off the night before. I'd sat my last exam two weeks ago, and now that I was finished with uni, I was going through the histories of the Protectors, trying to learn all I could about what exactly their part was in this war. I had started from the beginning, as I figured it would be best to know everything. I read back over my notes from the night before, figuring my half-asleep brain needed a refresher.

The history of the Order goes back as far as Ancient Greece, but the written histories only started from around the first century AD. The Order of the Dragon didn't exist as we know it until that time.

Before then, each of the seventh sons or daughters simply fought against the dark as individuals. As the Roman Empire expanded its borders, the Order slowly formed. With members coming from different civilisations to band together in secret, they were united in their intent to keep the presence of vampires a secret from the rest of humanity. This allowed them the ability to live under the illusion that they were the superior race on Earth.

When the Roman Empire began to fall, and society became more superstitious, it had been harder to keep the war contained, and that was when the Order formed in the way it was now known, with elders and the use of magic.

I had somehow managed to condense over two thousand years of history into three paragraphs. I wasn't entirely sure if that was a positive thing or just showed how much more I had left to read. I pulled out the book that I'd been reading last night and opened it up to where I'd left my place marker. After half an hour of study, I felt someone's eyes boring into the back of my head, and I didn't need to turn around to know that I wasn't the only one still pissed about the hostility in the kitchen.

"Fuck off, Alana." I knew that she would hear me, but I found I just didn't care. For the past two months, all that she had done was treat me with disdain, as if my presence was an insult to her personally.

"Whatever, Isolde. You want to know what my problem is with you?" I turned as her voice rang out across the quiet room, ready for the fight that had been brewing for weeks.

"Sure. Enlighten me. Why are you such a bitch?" She glared at me, still leaning against the door frame.

"You have no idea, do you? You haven't got a clue."

"No, I bloody well don't. All I know is that since I first met you, you have been nothing but a snooty bitch to me when I've done nothing to deserve it." She scoffed at this. I resisted the urge to throw the incredibly heavy – and ancient - text that I was holding at her. I figured that the others would probably see this as an insult to the book, though.

"You've had it so easy. Your life has been so blessed. Do you have any idea what it has been like having to keep you safe these past twenty-five years? You've just had everything handed to you." I had no idea what this woman was babbling about, but I was not going to listen to another moment of this crap as Alana came further into the room, her hands balled into fists at her side.

"Excuse me?!" I was on my feet now, turning to face her as my own hands clenched into fists at my sides. "Blessed?! Not even eight weeks ago, I witnessed the love of my life get ripped apart by a vampire and then found out that he is now one himself. Not to mention the fact that it is on me to stop some vampire war that I know nothing about. So, you can stick your blessed life comment up-"

"Oh, poor you, you watched your fiance die? I watched my entire fucking family die. I didn't have anyone to protect me. I didn't get treated like cotton wool when I turned twenty-five and had all of this thrust upon me." I was beginning to see that nothing I said to this woman would make her happy as she came to stand right in front of me. Now I was becoming royally pissed off.

"So, your life sucked? That is *not* my fault. Nor did I ask to be treated like cotton wool, as you so nicely put it. You clearly have some issues that you need to deal with on your own, and you can quit taking them out on me because I didn't fucking ask for any of this to happen to me, in case you forgot." Once I started swearing, I often had an issue with stopping, but at this moment, I didn't feel like being polite.

"That, right there." She pointed a finger in my face, and I smacked it away, seething. "That is your problem. You keep whining about how you didn't ask for this. Toughen up, princess, and get over it-" Alana's tirade was cut off by the sound of Liam clearing his throat as he leaned against the door frame, just as she had done moments ago.

"We can hear the pair of you from upstairs," Liam said quietly, looking at Alana meaningfully. She just shrugged and spun on one heel, pushing past him as she marched out of the room in a way that clearly said this was not over. As far as I was concerned, it was. She was just a bitch, plain and simple.

"It's not as simple as that," Liam commented, and at first, I thought I must have spoken aloud, but I remembered what Patrice had said about his powers.

"I thought you didn't like to use your mind-reading abilities." I flopped back down, wanting to just be left alone. For his part, Liam ignored this last thought and came over to sit across from me at the desk.

"I didn't particularly need to use them; it was written all over your face. And yes, Alana does have issues, which she shouldn't be taking out on you." I realised he was dressed for sleep in a pair of grey sweatpants and a white long-sleeve shirt. Our argument must have brought him from his bed. I knew he tended to sleep during the day for a few hours, having spent his nights ensuring my safety.

"Look, she told me about her family. And I get it, her life sucked, but I don't see how that has got anything to do with me." Liam sighed, rubbing his face as I glowered at him.

"It's not just that. Her family was killed when she was a child in a house fire, and she was the sole survivor. Her extended family was fractured, and she spent her childhood going from foster home to foster home, and it was not the most pleasant childhood, as you can well imagine." I nodded, though I still saw no reason why her childhood gave her any right to be such a bitch to me. Liam continued on, his expression showing that he'd heard my train of thought.

"When she first showed up on our radar, she was twenty, and the elders had originally thought, incorrectly, that it was her that the prophecy was about, as her mother had been a seventh daughter, and we believed her father had been a seventh son. For the few years after she turned twenty-five, she was trained much as you are being trained now.

"Then you were born. And we realised that we'd got it wrong. When the elders looked back over her family history, it turned out there had been a stillborn older brother before her father, the birth was never registered, though, and her father hadn't known of him. Therefore, for a few short years, Alana had gone from feeling like nothing to believing that she had this destiny. To be told that the same destiny was not hers but was the birthright of this young woman who had everything in life that she'd never had... Can you see where this is going?" I could, and although I pitied her, which I was sure she would be thrilled about, I found that I was angry as well.

"She wants this destiny? She can have it for all I care!" I was beginning to feel like a petulant child, but I was beyond caring.

"Unfortunately, it doesn't work that way, as you know." The way that he spoke to me, like a parent, was beginning to grate on me, but I gritted my teeth, as there was still another question that I felt needed answering.

"There is more to it than that, though, isn't there? She seems to think that I'm out to steal you away from her or something to that effect... Doesn't she?" I looked him directly in the eye and was amused to see him squirm a little uncomfortably at the question.

"She is jealous of the fact that we spend so much time together, as she has made it clear to me, on several occasions over the years, that she wished to have a relationship with me. She is under the impression that you and I have developed feelings for each other." I rolled my eyes, though I ignored the fact that I was pleased that he didn't appear to return her feelings, telling myself it was because I believed that he was too good for her.

"Does the fact that I was engaged to be married until three months ago even factor into her way of looking at things?" Liam smiled a little.

"No, unfortunately, it doesn't. Anyway, that is why Alana is, rightly or wrongly, treating you the way that she is. Now, why don't we head to the gym to work off some of that anger you've still got stored up? Seeing as I'm clearly not going to be able to get any sleep while you're this angry and screaming every thought in your head." He got to his feet, putting a hand out towards me. I took it and stood, looking up at him.

"I thought you could block out our thoughts?"

"I usually can. But with your thoughts, Isolde... I seem to have trouble tuning you out." He held my gaze for a moment before turning and leading the way out of the room. I could see that the conversation was now over, but I didn't feel any better for it and just wished that Alana would get over her issues and realise that if it were up to me, I would give up my destiny in a heartbeat if it meant that I could go back in time and still be a happily engaged woman, preparing to marry the love of my life. I didn't understand why she would think something was happening between Liam and I, anyway. I treated him no differently than I did anyone else in the house, and I couldn't see anything different in how Liam treated me compared to the others... I mean, sure, he looked out for me, but that was his job, right? I guess we all had a few issues to deal with...

That afternoon, Aurora and I went to have a look at a few houses together, finally taking a step up from scrolling through the rental listings online. After looking at the first three houses, I was starting to feel a little disheartened, as the homes that were in our price range weren't what we had hoped. We stopped into the real estate agent who had handled the sale of the townhouse, thinking that they may have apartments for us to at least look at.

"Hello, girls. I heard you're house hunting?" It was the same shameless woman who had sold the townhouse for me. I'd hoped never to have to deal with her again after the settlement went through a few weeks ago, and I was almost tempted to ask for another estate agent, but she had already started talking.

Don't they usually have different people who handled the rental side to the sales side of the business?

"I have the perfect place for you. It's just a few streets away..." She continued prattling off info about the house, and Aurora and I wrote down the address, saying we would meet her there in ten minutes, as it was currently empty.

"I doubt this place is going to be any good, Is. I mean, is a house in Bulimba really going to be in our price range? It's probably just an old shack." I nodded in agreement as Aurora tried to find the house listing on her phone while sitting in the passenger seat.

I followed the directions the GPS lady gave me in her prim and proper voice, and moments later, Aurora and I got out of the car, gaping at the house in front of us. This couldn't be it, surely? The address we wrote down must have been wrong...

On the outside, the house ticked all of our boxes. It had a small front yard with a simple garden and a beautiful big frangipani tree that was still in flower, unheard of in late June.

We stepped through the gate and met the estate agent at the door.

"Megan, are you sure we can afford this place?" I was certain she had made a mistake. She probably hadn't been listening properly. I looked around the wide verandah, wishing that I could afford an old Queenslander like this. It had been renovated to pristine condition. Through the window, I could see polished floorboards.

"It's under the amount you told me." Aurora and I must have had identical looks of disbelief on our faces as Megan nodded vehemently as she continued. "Yeah, the landlord was adamant about how much to list it for. Only just went on the market today. Come on. We'll have a look inside." Aurora and I exchanged excited looks and clung to each other, both trying not to get our hopes up.

But upon stepping through the door, I knew immediately that we'd found our new home. With its polished wooden floors and high ceilings, the four-bedroom house was exactly what I had always imagined living in. The location was perfect, only three streets away from the river. I could easily walk to and from the ferry if I wanted to. Two of the large bedrooms had adjoining bathrooms, which meant I wouldn't have to share with Aurora and Jacob... I forced aside the tightening feeling in my chest and tried not to imagine growing old here with Will and instead pictured the home that Aurora and I could make for ourselves... It was bittersweet, but I knew we had to make this place ours. The twinkle in my sister's eye confirmed my feelings, and we did our best not to do a happy dance right in the middle of the lounge room.

After having dragged both of our parents all over the house and signing all the paperwork at the real estate agents to get the ball rolling Aurora and I could do nothing else but talk excitedly about our new home. My father was convinced that at that price, there must be something wrong with it, but I refused to let myself be concerned. It was the first time since Will's murder that I had felt any kind of excitement. It felt good to feel something other than grief, anger, frustration or the debilitating numbness that I was so familiar with.

I made myself a simple dinner that night, enjoying having the house to myself for the first time since we'd moved back in, as everyone else was out for various reasons. After indulging in a lovely, relaxing bath, I entered my bedroom that evening and immediately brought Ainslie's number up on the messages app on my phone. I was excited to share some great news with her, having dropped off the radar with her lately. I hadn't been in touch with any of my friends much since Will's death, and I knew I needed to start to reach out more.

A movement out of the corner of my eye made me look up and promptly stopped texting. Sitting on my window ledge, just as Liam had done several weeks earlier, was Will.

Chapter Eleven

I DROPPED THE PHONE and stood motionless, staring at Will, who leaned casually against the window frame, as though sneaking up the sides of houses and terrorising women in their bedrooms was something that he did every day... Which, for all I knew, could be true these days.

It had been seven weeks since I had seen him, although I had felt his presence in the dark outside of the house, a constant reminder of what he had become. But the creature sitting on my window looked exactly like my Will, the man that I had loved for the greater part of my life.

He smiled his breathtakingly beautiful smile that had always been able to make me melt at the knees.

"Hey, beautiful." God, his voice. I hadn't heard it since that fateful night, which felt like a lifetime ago, but was only three short months.

Every part of me wanted to run into his arms and hold him so tight that he could never disappear again. Every part except the pit of my stomach, which was screaming at me to run back out the door.

"What... No hug? Is that any way to greet your dead fiance?" I backed up a step, although I knew he could not come into the room.

"What are you doing here?" I finally found my voice, though it sounded alien to me, robotic even.

"I came to see you. I miss you." This was near impossible. Although I knew what he was, what he'd become, he didn't look like the demonic creature that had attacked me in my front yard. Why did he have to be so beautiful, so perfect... so Will? I took a deep breath and stepped back again, now standing in the doorway of my bedroom, still staring at the man at my window.

"Leave now. I know what you are, and you are not welcome here." As I said this, I sent a silent plea to Liam, hoping against all hope that he was listening from somewhere nearby. I hadn't spoken to anyone from the Order since this morning, but I knew Liam was usually the one on the nighttime watch when I wasn't at the Manor.

"Now, now. Someone has been telling you stories, haven't they? Telling you that I'm one of the bad guys." Will shook his head, the condescension in his voice making me want to throw something at him, but I was still frozen where I stood. "Did you ever stop to think that maybe your precious Protectors are the bad guys? What sort of person spends their entire lives stalking someone?" I raised an eyebrow at this last question.

"Yes, who would spend their entire lives stalking someone? Tell me, Will, what is it you have been doing every single night since you woke up? Leaving me threatening notes and dead animals? Staring up at my bedroom window, by any chance? Or hiding in the shadows, waiting for me to be alone? I've felt your presence, Will, so don't try to deny you've been the one doing the stalking."

"I won't deny that I've been watching you, Isolde. You're the love of my life, and it breaks my heart to see you with him." Will spat out the word 'him' as though it was a bad taste in his mouth. For a moment, I wondered who he was talking about, but then I realised he must be referring to Liam.

I didn't know how to respond to this and just stared at Will, praying that Liam would appear soon and this torture would be over.

"You know what he is, don't you?" Will continued to taunt me, but this question threw me.

"He's one of the Protectors. Like me." I shrugged as though this statement meant nothing.

"He's nothing like you or any of the others." Will was enjoying this; I could see it in his ice-blue eyes. Eyes that were so similar to Liam's, now that I thought about it.

I refused to let him get to me, although I knew where he was going with his goading remarks, and I didn't like it.

"Don't you want to know what I'm talking about? The Isolde that I knew would have been bursting at the seams with curiosity." Something in me flickered, a memory, though it was gone before I could recall it.

"The Isolde that you knew is gone. She disappeared the night you died." Although I said this with a hardness that I truly wished I felt, inside, I was falling apart.

As I struggled to pull myself together, Will continued to grin at me cruelly. It was a smile that I would never have thought possible on his face. He truly had become a stranger to me.

"You can't fool me, Isolde. You forget I know you better than anyone, probably even better than you know yourself." How true this statement once was.

As I struggled for a comeback to this last remark, Will suddenly disappeared from the window. I heard a loud crash and the sounds of struggle, though I was too afraid to go near the still-open window. I could hear the sounds of fists hitting flesh, and every part of me wished that I could see what was going on, that I could see who had come to my rescue. My instincts, however, told me that it was Liam. With the racket they were making, for the first time, since I'd learned the truth, I was grateful that my family was out after dark.

After what felt like an eternity, the sounds of fighting disappeared, and I stood motionless in my bedroom doorway, preparing to flee the room if necessary. When Liam appeared soundlessly at my window, I let out the breath that I had been holding and moved to sit down on the bed, my legs unable to hold me up anymore.

"Are you alright?" Liam made no move to come through the window, taking Will's place on the window ledge, and my suspicions of his true nature were doubled. Seeing him sitting where Will had sat only moments ago did not help my feelings of unease, and he watched me warily.

"Not even the smallest bit. He's going to keep coming back, isn't he? I'm never going to feel safe again." I wrapped my arms around myself, feeling as though I needed to protect myself from some unseen danger. I missed the feeling of protective arms around me, of someone else shielding me from the world's dangers. The realisation that I was now alone in a cold and dangerous world was crashing down on me. I didn't realise I was hyperventilating until I looked in the mirror and saw my reflection. Liam could do nothing from his vigil at my window, and I realised that he was the one who would be there to protect me, no matter who or what he was.

"Come in." I managed to breathe these words out in between my gasps for air, and after a moment's hesitation, Liam climbed through the window and was at my side, his arms enfolding me as I continued to sob silently.

"You're not alone, Isolde." Liam held me close, stroking my hair in a way that made me feel safe, something that Will had done only a few short months ago when I awoke in terror. Something that my mother used to do when I awoke from my nightmares as a child. Nightmares about creatures in the dark, with piercing blue eyes, terrorising my dreams. As I rested my head against his shoulder, tears streaming down my face, the memories of all my nightmares over the years came flooding back to me. With startling realisation, I understood now that Liam had been in the dark, watching me my whole life, and entering my dreams, almost as though his presence in my mind drove out the terrifying creatures that lurked in the dark.

I pulled away and looked up at him through my tear-filled eyes. He reached to wipe a tear away, and I clasped his hand in my own.

"You've been in my dreams all my life, haven't you?" Liam touched my face again with his free hand, wiping away another tear that slid slowly down my face.

"I've been watching over you since you were born, Isolde. I have protected you from your nightmares as much as I could over the years, though I could not do it after you turned twenty-five. Those nightmares are part of the process that you need to go through to deal with what your life now involves. The ones you had as a child, though, I could protect you from those." We sat so close that I felt as though I was falling into his eyes. I had known that part of his mind-reading abilities meant he was able to communicate telepathically to a degree, but I had never put the connection together. Something had changed between us in that instant of realisation, and I was petrified of what I was feeling.

"You're the younger brother, aren't you? The daywalker?" I had to know, though I didn't know what I would do with this information once it was confirmed. It was probably better for me not to know, but I couldn't bear being treated so delicately anymore. I needed to know everything. Liam just looked at me sadly for a moment before nodding. I let out another long breath, feeling as though I was deflating.

"Why didn't anyone tell me?" I was tired of all the secrets and lies, of being treated as though there were things I wasn't allowed to be told. Liam let go of me and stood up. I thought he was going to leave, but he just moved to the door, closing it so that the light that had previously flooded into the room from the hall was reduced to a sliver under the door. I should have been afraid, but I had come to trust Liam so much with my safety that it did not occur to me to be scared. I just wanted answers.

"In life, I was Liam O'Brien. These days, my last name has disappeared, as has the love I once held for my brother. I am simply Liam. However, yes, I am the younger brother. When I said I understood more than you could know, I meant it. I know how it feels to have my whole life ripped apart and have all of this thrust upon me. " The sadness in his eyes was heartbreaking. "And the reason that no one told you was that I asked them not to. I wasn't ready to have you look at me with the same fear that you hold for Will and Adam." Liam didn't return to sit on the bed, instead sitting on the window frame again, as though waiting for me to tell him to leave.

"Liam, the number of times that you've come to my aid in the past three months alone, and yet you still thought I'd view you as a monster?" I tried not to be offended at this thought, and Liam smiled, relaxing a little. I moved to his side, peering out the window to reassure myself that Will had truly left, before leaning against the window, my arm lightly touching his.

"I guess I keep forgetting how incredibly well-adjusted you are. Although you thought that we were all mad and that this was some nightmare, you've accepted it, taken it all in, and just got on with it." I thought he might have been thinking of someone else; there was no way anyone could have believed that I was well-adjusted. I had certainly declared that all of them were insane and needed to visit the mental ward on several occasions. Liam smiled, and I knew he must have heard my train of thought, which raised another question.

"Patrice told me you hate to use your mind-reading ability... Yet you always seem to know what I am thinking, and you said that you had trouble blocking me out... Why is that?" Liam looked at me for a moment before answering.

"I guess because I've been so attuned to you for so long that when it comes to your thoughts, I have a lot of trouble blocking them out... Does it bother you?" Now it was my turn to be silent for a moment, gathering my thoughts.

"I don't think it bothers me... It certainly comes in handy, like tonight, having you be able to hear me... I guess it's just a little scary having someone else up here beside me." I tapped my temple, and Liam smiled again. I enjoyed seeing him smile, something that felt so rare with the life we both lived. Looking into his eyes, I realised I should have put the connection together before now with his incredibly distinct eyes.

"How come when I saw you at Uni that day, your eyes were brown? It was only that one time; every other time, your eyes have been the colour they are now." That really should have been the giveaway for me. His eyes, the startling, amazing blue that on Will, terrified me, but on Liam, it looked right. Liam looked at me in confusion.

"That's the second time you've mentioned seeing me at your university, yet I swear, you have only ever seen me twice in your life, prior to the night outside the townhouse."

"But... I saw you; we were looking straight at each other?!" Why was he not admitting it? For his part, Liam looked alarmed, though still confused, and it made me wonder if I'd just imagined him that day. Maybe that was why he had disappeared so quickly...

After a long moment, I noticed that I was leaning close to him, closer than was necessary. Both our hands at our sides on the window ledge, our fingers lightly brushed against each other's, and I felt a thrill run up my spine, which took me by surprise. He noticed at the same time, and I stepped back, pushing my hair back from my face in a way I hoped looked natural.

"Oh, I have good news, Aurora and I found a house. We signed the lease this afternoon."

It felt strange to be discussing something from my normal life with Liam, the centre of my very not-normal life, but I needed normal right now.

Liam smiled at me, and I marvelled that I had managed to get three smiles from him in the space of ten minutes.

"I know... It's one of our safe houses." And just like that, my news didn't feel so exciting anymore. I felt myself deflate once again, and I moved to flop down on the bed.

"Of course it is! I guess I shouldn't be surprised. I knew it was too good to be true... Why exactly did everyone bother with the charade?" Staring up at the ceiling, I was annoyed, and Liam knew it.

"Because they knew how important it was for you to retain some semblance of your former life."

"Then why tell me the truth now?" I was confused as to why he was giving up the truth so easily.

"Two reasons... One, I won't lie. I see no point to it, and two, I believe that you need to face up to reality and accept that this is your destiny, and I refuse to play games." I was momentarily stunned before the anger set in. Liam could tell that the warm fuzzy feelings I'd had moments earlier had fled the room as I pulled my knees into my chest and crossed my arms over them.

"I think I want to be alone now." Liam simply nodded and was out the window in one fluid movement, which annoyed me even more. These people had been in my life in one way or another since I was born, and it aggravated me that, though they had all watched me grow up, they still treated me as though I was a petulant child who needed to be coddled... All of them except for Liam, who was the only one who successfully made me feel like one...

The next morning, I arrived at the Manor in the same mood that I had been in when I went to sleep. Cranky.

"Good morning, Isolde. I heard about your late-night visitor." Patrice sat down next to me as I stared at the pile of books before me, struggling to remember where I was up to.

"Who? Liam?" I wasn't paying attention, but Patrice looked surprised.

"Will." She said with raised eyebrows.

"Right, him. Sorry, I'm just a little distracted, I guess." Patrice was at a momentary loss for words. I had just brushed aside the fact that I had seen my dead fiance appear at my window and taunt me for pleasure. I was crankier than I thought.

"Liam also told me you now know the truth of who he is..." Patrice was not going to leave me alone, even though it was clear I was not the best communicator at the moment.

"Yeah." I shrugged, not sure what I was expected to say about it.

"Do you want to talk about it?"

"Not really. I'm in a bad mood right now. I'm probably best left alone." I knew I was being rude, but I just didn't have it in me to care at the moment.

"Okay. I'll leave you to it then." Patrice nodded at me, and I had the sense to hope that she was not offended by my attitude. She left the room, and I found myself staring at the page, reading the same words repeatedly.

After twenty minutes of this, I gave up, shoving the books away from me. I left them piled on the table and headed for the training room, figuring I could put all of my stored-up anger to good use and pummel the crap out of the punching bag. I stopped at the door as I saw Liam doing exactly what I had planned to do. I turned to leave again.

"We might as well do some training while you're this worked up," Liam didn't stop what he was doing as he spoke, and I briefly pictured myself punching him, no doubt amusing him even further.

"Fine." I headed to the changing rooms and changed into my workout clothes, the whole time seething at him.

I came out to find him doing push-ups, continuing to ignore me until I was ready. I took a few practice swings at one of the punching bags to warm up. When we started practising together, I found myself channelling everything I had been feeling, about Will, Liam and everyone else, into my attempts to kick Liam's ass. I wasn't even thinking about what moves to make or when to block, I simply acted on instinct. I threw a punch with my right fist, which he blocked expertly, but failed to see the kick that I followed it with. I connected with his head for a brief second, but he was gone in an instant, appearing behind me. He pulled my other hand up behind me in a vice-like grip, letting me know I had lost that round.

He let me go, and I turned to face him again, not even pausing between attacks. Liam could tell I meant business, and we each threw more energy into sparring than we had ever done together before. It seemed I wasn't the only one with issues right now.

Moments later, he had me pinned against the wall, both of my hands held over my head with one of his own. We were both breathing heavily at this point, and our faces were so close that I could look nowhere but into his eyes, which were boring into mine with a fierceness that I knew was reflected in my own. I didn't know what to make of it all, but I found my gaze drifting down to his lips, which threw me off balance.

What the hell is going on?

We stood staring at each other for what felt like an eternity, the tension palpable between us. Even as our breathing started to steady, neither of us moved, each waiting for the other to make the first move. Eventually, he released my hands and moved away, grabbing a bottle of water from the fridge and tossing me another. He left the room without a look back, leaving me standing alone, wondering what had just happened.

Over the next few weeks, I found myself surrounded by moving boxes yet again. I'd avoided being at the Manor as much as I could, still fuming at Liam and also incredibly confused by whatever had been happening between us.

Early on the day of the move, I shuffled into the kitchen as my mother was boiling the kettle, six mugs sitting on the breakfast bar with coffee in them.

"Who else is coming over?" For a brief moment, I worried that she was accidentally making one for Will out of habit, as she had done the day Aurora and I finished moving back in.

"Your friend Liam got here about twenty minutes ago. I must say, I'm relieved we've got another strong, young back to help out. I was worried that your father would be trying to do too much to help Jacob." I was too stunned by what she said to be insulted that she felt that Aurora and I needed men to help us.

"I'm sorry, who's here?" I was convinced I had heard her wrong. There was no way Liam would be here to help me with my sad attempt to grasp some semblance of my past. I was still a little bitter.

"Your friend from uni... I'm sure he said his name was Liam, but maybe I was wrong. He said he was here to help you move..." Mum looked uncertain for a moment, but I quickly nodded like I knew exactly what she was talking about.

"No, that's right, I just wasn't expecting him so early..." I went outside, still convinced that she had made a mistake. But there he was, sitting on our back patio, eating toast with my father, Jacob and Aurora, looking like he belonged there. I stopped in my tracks and stared at him.

"What are you doing here?" I asked, not realising how rude I sounded until my father looked at me with raised eyebrows. For his part, Liam just smiled his heart-melting smile, the one that I saw so rarely...

Wait, where had that thought come from?

Thankfully, he gave no indication that he had heard me, and it seemed to be one of those rare moments when Liam was able to tune me out while I continued to stare at him.

"I know I'm here early, but I was up, so I figured I might as well get over here to help out as soon as I could." He was a far better actor than I would have expected. Given that, I knew he'd been outside all night.

"Right..." I went back inside to help my mother with the coffee and to escape the weirdness, Aurora following closely behind me.

"So, who is Liam?" I could hear in her tone that she wasn't happy. I figured there could be any number of reasons why, namely that she had never heard mention of this guy who had just shown up out of the blue to help us move. But I didn't have the energy to think about it. I was already exhausted, and I hadn't lifted a single piece of furniture yet.

"Just a friend from uni. I was complaining about moving, and he offered to help, no big deal. I didn't think he'd show up, to be honest, which was why I was surprised to see him here." I thought I did pretty well, though I was becoming concerned at the ease with which I was lying to my sister.

"I didn't realise you were in touch with any uni friends still." She wasn't going to let this go.

"A few... but Liam and I work together now, too, at my research job." And the lies just kept easily rolling off my tongue.

For her part, Aurora continued to look suspicious but, thankfully, let it drop. Although we had never lied to each other, Aurora was usually one to push you to tell her something even if you didn't want to, so I was both relieved and a little sad that she didn't push me further.

Everything in me wanted to tell her about the craziness that was now my life, but I couldn't, and it was killing me. I was tired of lying. Tired of grieving. Tired of my life spiralling out of control... However, there was nothing I could do about it. So, I just ate my cereal in silence and watched as Liam got on way too well with my family.

Once all of the boxes and furniture were loaded into the cars, I slid into the passenger seat of my car as Liam got behind the wheel, assuming the role of the driver yet again. I hadn't driven the car once when we'd been together, something that I had let happen far easier than I would have expected.

We hadn't had a moment alone together since breakfast, and I wanted some answers. My jaw was sore from clenching it all morning as he chatted easily with my father and made plans to fill an extra slot in Jacob's social soccer team next weekend whilst one of his teammates were out of town.

"Right, spill. What's going on? Is there danger looming? Some new, unforeseen evil I'm being protected from?" I should not have been so snappy with him, but moving never brought out the best in me, and I was still smarting from his comments about dealing with my destiny. We had not talked much since the weirdness that had occurred at the Manor, and I had gotten the impression he had been avoiding being alone with me. Not that I'd been going out of my way to spend time with him either, as I sorted through my mixed feelings that were developing and that I refused to fully acknowledge.

"Nope, no evil, just helping a friend move." Liam pulled out of the driveway, and I looked at him closely as he kept his eyes on the road.

"I didn't know we were friends. I just figured I was someone you had to keep safe." I was being brutal now, and Liam sighed, looking over at me finally.

"Of course we're friends. What else would we be?" I wasn't quite sure how to respond to that question, so I just turned to stare out the window, pondering why on earth Liam was here, in my car, helping me move.

"Because I felt bad about what I said." I started, realising that Liam was in my head again.

"Why do you care?" I knew I sounded like a bitch, but I didn't care.

"Because although I said you need to deal with your destiny, I also forgot that I didn't deal with all of this so well in the beginning, either. I had it thrust upon me. The night I was told about the Order was also the night I became a vampire, and I didn't get a chance to deal with it like everyone else, as a human." I kept forgetting about his vampire side, having always seen him as a human with the same limitations as myself. But there was more to him than I realised.

"I guess I am pushing it all aside, but I had my future taken away from me, the future that I dreamt of for myself my whole life, to be married to Will, to have his children... All of that was within my grasp, and I had it all stolen from me in such a brutal way. It's going to take me a long time to deal with it. This life to me feels like a punishment," I whispered the final sentence, not wanting to admit to Liam that every moment I was around him reminded me that Will was no longer alive, at least not in the capacity he was meant to be. Liam took my hand in his as he continued to drive without really looking at the road.

"I do understand. Although I may not be able to relate to that particular part, I do understand all of it. I also know how much it kills you not to be able to talk to Aurora about all of this. My brother and I have been at war for so long that I sometimes forget that he is my brother." His jaw clenched, and he looked back at the road for a moment as if looking at me made it harder to acknowledge. He returned his gaze to me as he spoke again.

"Then I come face to face with him, and it starts all over again. The pain, the guilt that I could not have saved him... Missing the once unbreakable bond... Believe me; I understand that." Liam looked intently into my eyes, which should have scared me, given that he was driving my car, and yet we somehow arrived at the house in one piece. We remained in the car, continuing to look at each other for a few heartbeats more than necessary. I watched him breathe for a moment when something occurred to me.

"You breathe..." I looked at him curiously, and he nodded.

"Daywalkers are basically living vampires. We can eat food, although we still need blood. Our hearts still beat as well." I was surprised by this, and without thinking, I raised my hand to his chest to feel his heart beating against the thin shirt he wore beneath his hooded jumper. I stared at his chest for a few beats first before looking up and finding his gaze on my face as he moved to cover my hand gently with his own, holding it in place.

In the space of one five-minute car drive, everything between us had shifted, and I knew he felt it too. I felt my breath hitch as his eyes lowered to my lips.

We were shaken from our reverie as a car door shut outside, and I looked up to see Katyana and Sam walking over from where they'd parked one of the Order's cars across the road. I looked back at Liam in surprise as he moved his hand away.

"We figured the more, the merrier." He shrugged with a half smile before climbing out of the car. I did the same, and we were joined by the others as Liam opened the boot.

"Put us to work, lady." Katyana smiled at me, and I wondered if either she or Sam had noticed what had just happened between myself and Liam in the car. It didn't appear so, as they started helping Liam unpack boxes. I shook my head and went to join them.

Chapter Twelve

T HE NEXT MORNING, I awoke abruptly, ripped from sleep by the sound of the doorbell ringing. Disorientated, I groaned and rolled out of bed. I winced as my feet hit the cold floorboards and slipped into my fluffy bunny slippers before leaving the room. Grumbling about how early it was, having been up until the early hours unpacking, I opened the front door and was surprised to see Liam, Katyana and Celeste standing there. I was awake enough to take note that Liam was holding a tray of coffee cups.

"What are you guys doing here?" I realised too late how rude that sounded as I stepped aside and let them walk through.

"Well, we figured we'd help you get settled," Celeste said, handing me a bunch of flowers with a big smile. Surprised, I watched as Liam walked into the kitchen and set the tray of coffees down. I noted that there were six as Aurora and Jacob came out of their room, looking as exhausted as I felt. Knowing that the others had bought coffee for everyone made me think my sister might be more welcoming than she had been yesterday with Liam.

"Hi, I'm Celeste." Celeste put her hand out towards my sister, who looked at her briefly before throwing me a look over her shoulder.

"Let me guess, more uni friends that you've never mentioned before?"

Guess I was wrong about the being more welcoming part.

I wondered when my sister had become so prickly towards strangers, but at least she shook Celeste's hand. Celeste, for her part, ignored my sister's rudeness and introduced herself to Jacob, who was much more polite and gladly accepted the coffee that Liam handed him.

"We know how much moving sucks, so we figured we'd come help unpack. Anything to help you guys out after the past few months." Celeste deftly avoided the mention of uni, which I was grateful for, as I didn't want to tell any more outright lies to my sister if I could avoid it.

I watched everyone chat for a bit before heading into my room to get changed out of my pyjamas, suddenly aware that I was still dressed in my fuzzy pink pants and singlet top sans bra.

When I came back out, Celeste and Katyana were joking around with Liam in the kitchen as the three of them set about unpacking all the glasses and plates. I noticed that Aurora was on board with accepting the help that was offered after all, as she'd obviously assigned them the task before she and Jacob headed back into their room.

I found myself watching them for a while, smiling at how they all interacted together, a brother with his two younger sisters.

"Seriously, Liam, why would you put the dinner plates in the same cupboard as the saucepans?" Celeste asked with mock disgust, and Liam threw his hands up in surrender.

"In his defence, he had servants the last time he had to deal with such mundane tasks." Katyana teased, and Liam scowled.

"Hey, that's not true. I've helped with plenty of the Orders relocations."

"Yeah, but when was the last time you were in the kitchen without Patrice?" I spoke up, and he turned to give me an incredulous look as the others laughed, loving that I'd involved myself in the teasing.

"Traitors, both of you." He pointed at the others, and Katyana threw a tea towel at him.

It was at that moment that I realised that these people were now my family too. The past few months, I had kept to myself most of the time when around the others, so wrapped up in my grief that I hadn't once noticed how often they all tried to reach out. The only person who had so far been able to get past my wall had been Liam, and I felt bad about that now. These were good people.

At lunchtime, we were joined by Sam and Celeste's husband, Daniel, another member of the Order, and before long, I was joking along with them as we ate the pizza that the men had brought with them, determined to let them all see how appreciative I was for the unspoken offer of friendship. They all smiled back at me with ease. To them, I had always been a part of the family.

When they were all ready to leave later that afternoon, I walked them to the door. Liam let the others go on ahead before turning back to me as I stood waiting to wave them off.

"I'll come pick you up tonight, okay?" He was standing so close, and it felt so natural when he pushed a strand of hair back over my ear. I was due to start magic lessons in earnest tonight with Katyana and Patrice, and they'd explained that it could be quite physically and mentally draining. Aware that I wasn't ready to stay in the Manor yet, Liam had offered to collect me when Katyana had mentioned it again earlier, and I was grateful once again that he could read my mind, saving me from having to admit out loud that I wasn't ready to give up my freedom and stay in the room that had been set aside for me at the Manor. Even if it was the most beautiful room I'd ever been in, and had been laid out especially for me.

I only noticed the intimacy of how we stood as I heard Aurora clear her throat, having come to stand just behind me. I wasn't sure what look she had given Liam, but I noticed a flash of annoyance in his eyes as he stepped away, walking to where Sam and Katyana stood waiting by the car he'd driven over earlier. I turned to face my sister as I closed the door once they'd all driven off. Aurora shot me a judgemental look before she walked away again, and I sighed as I headed into my bedroom to continue unpacking, alone once again.

I avoided my sister for the rest of the day as I set my room up how I wanted it. It felt so strange to have a room that was entirely my own once again. Aside from the brief time back at my parent's house these past four months, I had shared a bedroom with either Aurora or Will. Even during my brief time in London, I had shared with Katyana and another German student. To have a space that was only filled with my things felt weird to me. And lonely.

When I knew Liam was on his way to come and get me, I had a quick shower and made sure I was waiting outside to avoid having another awkward exchange with Aurora, and I knew that Liam took note of this as he pulled up beside me.

"Thanks for picking me up." I buckled myself in as he pulled away from the curb and turned the car around to head back to the Manor.

"No problem. It gives me a chance to catch up on some sleep anyway while you're with the others." He kept his eyes on the road this time as he drove, and I tried not to think about that too much, although I couldn't help wondering if he was distancing himself a little after the stand-off with Aurora earlier. I wasn't sure if I should be concerned that I was hoping that wasn't the case, having grown used to the moments between us when he reached out to touch me. And I enjoyed them. Best to just push those thoughts out of my mind entirely when I knew he could hear what I was thinking.

I was grateful that he didn't comment at all, but he did reach over and take my hand, squeezing my fingers briefly without looking over. That was comforting at least. I squeezed back and turned to look out the window, continuing to hold his hand. I'd just ignore that too. I was good at ignoring the things that were hard to accept, and I wasn't ready to acknowledge the feelings swirling around inside me yet.

Once we arrived at the Manor, Liam left me to head off in search of Patrice and Katyana while he had a few hours of sleep. The benefit of being a daywalker was that he didn't need as much sleep as a human did, but with the odd hours he had to keep when guarding me, he was using any chance he was able to get what few hours of sleep that he could. I tried not to think about how much easier it would be for him if I just caved and moved in here.

I found Patrice in her office, sitting across from Damon, one of the other elders who had recently arrived from London. So far, I wasn't quite sure what to make of him. He was quite standoffish and barely spoke to anyone except Patrice and occasionally Liam. But I had found him watching me with keen interest several times now, and something about it made me feel uncomfortable. It was different to how the others watched me when they were ready to offer me support and reach out a hand of friendship, except for Alana, who I just tried to avoid completely.

When I'd noticed Damon had been watching me, it had been as though he was assessing me. And had so far been unimpressed with what he'd seen. It was quite disconcerting, and I didn't like it. I hadn't signed up to be scrutinised by a grumpy old man. Although he looked like he was maybe in his mid-forties, being an elder, I had to assume he was at least two hundred or so years old.

Patrice and Damon both looked up at me quickly as I knocked on the open door frame.

"Patrice? Sorry to interrupt. Katyana mentioned today that you wanted to start my magic lessons properly tonight. Something about the moon phase?" Patrice looked briefly at Damon as she nodded.

"Yes, it's a full moon tonight." I wasn't sure if that was directed at me or Damon, but as I had no idea what that meant, I left it to Damon to respond.

"Ah, of course."

Well, that was useless to me.

Patrice smiled when she noted the blank look on my face and rose to her feet as she waved Damon out of the room, dismissing him.

"A full moon is when magic is at its strongest, Isolde. So we should be able to perform a few spells with you tonight. And we may be able to get a read on how strong your power truly is." Right, well, no pressure then. I wasn't feeling particularly confident in these abilities that everyone kept expecting from me, as aside from the fire incident with Liam and the occasional floating object, my powers had been pretty elusive.

I followed Patrice as she led the way out of her office and into the room across the hall that I hadn't yet entered, knowing that it was one of her private areas in the house. The interior of the room was devoid of windows and modern technology, situated in the heart of the Manor. To compensate for the lack of light, an array of unlit candles of different hues and sizes were placed on every surface. The only furnishings present were a low table similar to the one in Liam's study and a collection of large cushions for seating. The room had a ledge running around it, with evenly-spaced candles placed along it. Patrice summoned Katyana from the kitchen, and the three of us took our seats on the cushions.

"So, I'm going to show you how to channel the power of the full moon through you. Essentially, your body will become a conduit for that power, and it will allow you to tap into your inner strength." I blinked at Patrice's bold statement.

"Oookay..." I wasn't confident about this.

"Just follow my lead and repeat what I say." She began a slow chant, using a language I didn't recognise, and Katyana nodded at me enthusiastically, encouraging me to repeat the words. I closed my eyes, the same as Patrice and began to chant the words along with her. I lost track of anything else in the room, and it wasn't until a few minutes later that I realised that Patrice was no longer chanting with me. I opened my eyes, not sure what I was going to see, but nothing appeared to have changed. Katyana and Patrice exchanged a confused look.

"What exactly were you expecting to happen?" I was disappointed that nothing had happened, but I also wasn't entirely sure that I trusted Patrice at this moment when it seemed like she had no idea what to expect.

"It was a spell to light the candles." That would have been really nice to know beforehand. Given our location in the centre of the manor, I didn't know how I felt about setting fire to this many candles without having any real idea how to control the power.

We continued trying for another hour, and by the end, all that happened was that I had broken out in a sweat and had a headache from straining so hard. Patrice looked quite disheartened as she returned to her office to do some more research, and I tried not to feel like I'd disappointed her.

"Hey, don't worry about it, Isolde. You've had a lot going on. We'll work out what the source of your power is eventually." Katyana gave me a quick squeeze before she left as well, as Sam was waiting for her to go on patrol with him. Trying to push aside how dejected I was feeling, I trudged up to the room that I so rarely entered. My bedroom.

Someone had set up a space in the corner for me, similar to the one that Liam had in his study for mind-clearing. I sat on one of the cushions and used the lighter on the table to light the candles, beginning to take myself through the process that Liam had taught me. Of everything I'd learned so far, this was something I had found the most beneficial, and I used it regularly whenever I had begun to feel overwhelmed by this life I now led.

After a long time, perhaps hours even, my mind began to clear out all the thoughts swirling around, and I felt calmer as I continued to stare at the middle flame. I was startled by a knock on the door. Just like the first time, the flame from the middle candle leapt into the air, this time joined by the flames from the other two, and they hung in the air before me as Liam came into the room. He stayed where he was in the doorway, realising he'd interrupted me, and watched as I gazed intently at the three balls of light. I had no idea what I was doing, but the flames seemed to be growing bigger now, and I concentrated on the one in the middle. I willed it to begin moving around the other two in a small circle, and I felt a smile break out on my face as it worked. Becoming more confident now, I then split my focus and encouraged the second and third balls of light to follow the first, and eventually, we both watched as the three flames whirled in a slow circle in front of me.

"Try and see if you can guide them back to the candle wicks one at a time," Liam suggested quietly, and I did as he said. I concentrated on keeping the other two circling while I led the first back down to the candle successfully. Once I did the first one, the other two followed suit easily, and I grinned up at Liam proudly.

"Was that what Patrice was teaching you tonight?" Liam asked, coming further into the room now, taking a seat in the armchair near the window. I shook my head.

"No. She was trying to teach me to do a spell to light candles, not control flame."

"Did it work?" Liam watched me curiously as my disappointment from earlier returned, and I shook my head again.

"No. I couldn't get it to work, although we tried for over an hour. She seemed really disappointed." Liam looked thoughtful now and looked at the candles burning in front of me for a moment. He stood up from the chair and came closer, taking a seat on the cushion opposite from where I sat. He leaned forward and blew out the candles, and the room was engulfed in darkness.

"Try again now." I could make out his face in the moonlight from the window as my eyes adjusted to the lower light. I didn't particularly want him to witness my failure, but something about the earnest expression on his face made me try again. I closed my eyes as I began chanting once more. Nothing happened.

I looked at Liam, expecting to see the same disappointment I'd witnessed earlier from Patrice, but he was just studying the candle closely.

"Try it without the chant."

"What, just think about it lighting up?" That seemed like a crazy idea. If I couldn't make it work with the chant, I seriously doubted I could get it to work without it.

"Just humour me, Isolde."

"Get out of my head, Liam," I grumbled, and he chuckled.

"Stop pouting and just try it." I huffed, and after pouting for another moment, I looked down at the outline of the candle from where I could see it in the moonlight. Taking a deep breath, I began staring at it intently.

Light.

Not only did the candle light up, but every single other candle in the room followed suit until the room was aglow. I hadn't realised how many candles were in the room until that moment, and I gaped around in shock before bringing my gaze back to Liam.

"You don't need spells."

Later, as we drove back to my house in silence, I pondered over the events of the evening. When we saw Patrice again before we left, Liam didn't mention a thing to her about what I had just done, and I wondered at the reasoning behind it. I hadn't noticed that we'd pulled to a stop outside my home until Liam cleared his throat.

"You doing okay over there? You haven't said a word out loud since you lit the candles." The fact that he said the words "out loud" confirmed that he had been able to hear my thoughts for the past half an hour and was leaving me to sort through them all in peace.

"Can I trust the Order, Liam?" I figured I'd just ask the question outright, seeing as he already knew what I'd been thinking. To his credit, he didn't answer me straight away. It gave me some relief that he didn't immediately jump to their defence and assure me that my misgivings were unfounded.

"I think we've been waiting so long for the end of this war that some people are rushing into things too quickly, not having any real idea of what to expect from you and your powers. At least, that's what I got from what little I heard before I came and found you."

That was a very diplomatic answer.

"It was, wasn't it?" Liam responded to my thought out loud with a smile, perhaps to remind me that he was always listening. I gave him a small smile back and placed my hand on the door handle.

"Thank you for dropping me home. I'll see you tomorrow." I opened the door, and Liam reached to take my hand before I could climb out of the car.

"Regardless of what happened tonight, Isolde, I can promise you one thing. You can always trust me, okay? I will always be truthful with you." I scanned his face, seeing the sincerity there, and nodded slowly.

"Thanks, Liam." He held my hand for a beat longer before letting it go, and I swear my skin tingled from where we'd touched. I held his gaze for another few breaths before he nodded, and I headed inside, comforted to know that he would be watching over me.

Chapter Thirteen

S EVERAL DAYS LATER, HAVING finally finished unpacking, Liam took me out for dinner to celebrate.

Since he had helped me move, something in our relationship had changed. It wasn't just about the crazy world we lived in anymore; we had begun to form a friendship. It felt good to have male company again. To have someone open my door for me and pull out my chair. Even just having that guiding hand on my lower back as he let me go first. All the little things that I hadn't realised that I craved jumbled in with all the numerous other things that I missed about Will.

I let Liam order the wine as I looked over the menu. He had brought me to an Italian restaurant that was well known for having some of the best pizzas in Brisbane, and there were so many options to choose from.

"I think I'll get the Margherita pizza. Why not go with the classic, right?" I handed the menu to the waiter, and Liam ordered the same. Once the waiter left, I turned back to Liam.

"So why'd you pick this place?" I was interested to get to know Liam outside of all the madness that was our lives in the Order.

"I've just always enjoyed watching the people here. It's always so busy, and people come to celebrate so many different occasions." I could understand that, having always enjoyed the chance to people-watch myself.

Once the waiter returned with our wine, the conversation moved on to Liam's long life, and I was fascinated to hear him talk about all the centuries he had lived through. All the moments in history that he'd witnessed. He had been present at the beheading of Anne Boleyn, watched Elizabeth I's coronation, witnessed the massacre at Culloden, the beheadings of Luis XVI and Marie Antoinette, and watched as numerous plagues tore through Europe. It was all a history student's dream come true to speak to someone who had been there and seen it all.

I found myself leaning closer and closer to him as he told me all the amazing stories, fascinated at the life he had lived. To anyone else around us, we must have looked like young lovers on a romantic date.

When we arrived back at my house, Liam walked me to the door, and for a brief, awkward pause, we looked at each other. We seemed to have finally run out of things to say. Once again, there was tension between the two of us that both excited and scared me at the same time. After a beat too long, he kissed me quickly on the forehead and stepped back as I unlocked the door and waved goodbye, knowing that he would be watching out for me in the dark once more.

"So, where did you guys go tonight?" Aurora asked as I walked into the lounge room, where she and Jacob were unpacking the last of the boxes. There had been an underlying sense of hostility coming off her all week as members of the Order had joined me each day, helping me unpack and bringing me coffee. Even Patrice had come by, the first time I'd seen her leave the manor since I'd met her. Fostering friendships that I had previously been keeping at arm's length.

"He took me out for pizza in Milton. Best pizza I've had away from Italy. I've got to take you there." I pushed my stomach out slightly to show off my food-baby, and Jacob laughed. Aurora shot him a sharp look, and he went back to unpacking with his head down. I loved Jacob, but he really needed to learn to stand up to my very strong-willed sister.

"Was it a date?" She asked bluntly, and I bristled at her tone.

"No. It's not like that with Liam. We're just friends." I tried to keep the hurt from my voice, but I was also annoyed that Aurora seemed unhappy that I was making friends. Then again, Liam had been around a fair bit since we had moved, helping unpack and make the house feel like a home, and no doubt, the tension between us was evident, especially to my hyper-aware twin sister.

"As long as he's on the same page as you. I don't know many guys who would help a girl move all day without expecting something in return." Jacob made a lame excuse about needing a drink and pretty much fled to the kitchen, obviously expecting a fight. However, I wasn't interested in getting into it with Aurora.

"You don't know many decent guys then, Aura." I shook my head at her, refusing to give her the fight she was so clearly pushing for. "I'm off to bed. Good night." I headed to my room and shut the door, leaning back against it. After a moment of staring at the ceiling, I kicked off my shoes and flopped down on my bed, looking around the room. It still felt wrong to be surrounded by things that were only mine. A stab of grief hit me again, and a tear rolled down my face as I wondered if it would ever stop hurting.

A knock on my window made me jump, and I looked up to see Liam standing outside. I opened the window, and he climbed through.

"Is everything okay?" I wiped away the tears that were still in my eyes, not bothering to hide them as I spoke. It's not like Liam couldn't tell what was wrong with me anyway.

"I heard what happened between you and Aurora... just thought I'd see if you were alright." I smiled at him sadly.

"To be honest, no. I hate not being able to tell her what is going on. It would be safer all around if she did know. What's to stop Will going after her?" I sat back down on my bed as Liam moved to take a seat in my favourite armchair, which sat in the corner.

"You know why. I know it's hard to accept, but a large part of our role in the Order is to ensure the general population remains unaware of the existence of vampires. You've read through the histories; you know what happens when people find out." Remembering the stories of mass hysteria and violence, I knew he was right, but that didn't make it any easier to accept. He could sense my frustration. "We do keep an eye on Aurora. Because she is so close to you and lives in the same home, we do watch out for her to make sure that they do not try to get to you through her. So, she is safe."

"But if something happens to her or Jacob, it would be my fault." Liam could see that I wasn't going to feel any better no matter what he said, so he simply moved to sit beside me, putting his arm around me, and I rested my head on his shoulder. After a few minutes, I looked up at him to find him looking down at me, his look of concern mixed with something else. Purely instinctively, I found myself moving closer. Our lips met, and we kissed softly. As the kiss grew, he drew me to him with the arm that had been around me, bringing his other hand up to stroke my cheek. Softly, he brushed a lock of hair away from my face and wove his fingers through the hair at the nape of my neck, drawing me closer until I practically sat in his lap. We continued to kiss for what felt like an eternity until I reluctantly pulled away, and my brain suddenly kicked in.

"I'm sorry. I don't know what I was thinking." His words were shaky as he sat back, putting distance between us as he rubbed his hand over his face, though he didn't move the one that had slid down to my lower back.

"It wasn't just you. We both let it happen." I knew Liam well enough by now to know he would be blaming himself, thinking himself responsible for what had just happened, but I had been just as much a willing participant as he had been. Liam smiled, and I knew he was in my head again.

"It's something we've been dancing around for weeks. But we shouldn't. You're still grieving. And with the lives we lead..." Our legs were still touching, and I found it difficult to concentrate. Because the memory of his lips on mine was far more powerful than I had imagined. He was the first person I had kissed aside from Will my entire life, and to have it seem so normal, so right, confused me more than anything else. Liam was still in my thoughts as he reached over to stroke my cheek again, our eyes locked. We both knew we should say no, but our actions appeared to be out of our control. Before I knew what was happening, we were kissing again. But this time, it was Liam who pulled away, jumping to his feet so quickly it was just a blur of movement, and I almost toppled off the bed.

"I'm sorry." He glanced back briefly before jumping out the window in one swift, fluid motion. For a tiny moment, he looked back at me with sadness in his eyes before disappearing into the darkness. I sat stunned for a few seconds before falling back to lie on the bed again.

"This can't be happening," I muttered to myself, though I knew without a doubt that Liam would have still been within earshot. Neither of us had planned for this complication.

Late the next morning, I arrived at 'mission control', as I had come to dub the Manor, worried about the reception I would receive from Liam after our encounter the night before. I shouldn't have been surprised that he wasn't there, but I felt myself deflate as I realised that I had wanted to see him. Patrice must have noticed my reaction as she told me he was off on another task, having been sent out when he returned at dawn, which I thought was odd, but I figured my safety wasn't Liam's only responsibility. She gave me a knowing, sad smile as I took my seat at the breakfast table across from Alana, who did not even look up, though I could feel the resentment coming off her in waves. No doubt, by the end of the morning, we would have one of our now weekly face-offs. Unfortunately, our relationship had not seen any of the changes that I'd had with the others.

"So, you're finished with your degree and your move finally?" Patrice asked as she handed me a plate full of bacon and eggs. She was still concerned about my lack of appetite, although lately, that hadn't been as much of an issue.

"Yes, thank goodness. Not that I'm ever going to get to use my degree now." I shrugged as I made this comment, and Alana snorted derisively across from me before pushing away from the table, letting her chair scrape loudly across the floor before she stomped out of the room. Everyone else acted as though nothing had happened. The conversations around me continued, although Sam shot me a grin across the table. He had a prickly relationship with Alana as well.

"I was hoping to talk to you sometime today about what you were going to be doing now. Come to my rooms later on today, and we can have a chat."

Patrice excused herself then, and I was left wondering what else in my life was about to change.

A few hours later, I found myself sitting across from Patrice and Damon. I was suddenly nervous. The meeting felt very official, with them both sitting side by side.

"Now that you've finished your degree and worked out your living arrangements, it has been discussed, and I think you should start to actively take part in the group. A large part of being a member of our family is protecting humanity from vampires. You have been doing your research, so you know this has been a fight we have been waging for centuries, but so far, you've been shielded from what is ultimately your birthright.

"Now that the last of your previous life commitments are done with, we see no reason why you cannot be out there, fighting the fight with the rest of us. You are still a target, but the prophecy does say that you will be the one to turn the fight back in our favour, so although we will still be protecting you, we're going to stop shielding you as we have been." This was the most I'd ever heard Damon speak, and I could hear Liam's words come back to haunt me; *I'm of the belief that you need to face up to reality and accept that this is your destiny, and I refuse to play game*s. I felt like I was being told off, yet I had never asked anyone to protect me. I just didn't want to live this life they had all forced upon me.

Patrice could see that this approach was not the way to go. She placed a hand gently on Damon's arm, and after a moment of hesitation, he excused himself.

"I know that Damon is rather blunt, and I know that you didn't ask to be coddled, but we thought, now that you were no longer attending classes and preoccupied with your living arrangements, that you would like to finally get out there in the field and experience the real deal. You and Liam have been training hard, and we think you are more than ready for it." I took this all in and realised that I had not actually said a word since I sat down.

"So, where will I be going?" Although I had read all the histories and I had been training with Liam, I didn't have the confidence in my abilities that the others seemed to have. However, I also knew that they would not be letting me do this if there was any danger that I might not come back in one piece. I was too valuable to them. At least, that's what I told myself.

"You, Liam and Alana will be checking out a nest of vampires that Alana found last night when she was... when she was out." There was something that Patrice was leaving out, but I let it go, as there was something else that she had said that I was more concerned with.

"Alana? On my first night out? Who came up with that idea?" I was not impressed, and Patrice could tell.

"It was my idea. I thought it was time for the pair of you to get over your differences and learn that you are on the same team." She said this pointedly, and I opened my mouth to state that it was not me with the problem, but it was Liam who spoke up behind me from the open doorway.

"I honestly don't know if that's such a good idea, Patrice." I wasn't sure which part of the grouping he had a problem with, but I didn't want to get into it with Patrice around.

"Well, it's been decided now, so you'll all just have to make the best of a bad situation." I could tell from her tone that Patrice was done with the conversation, so I let myself out, careful not to brush against Liam as I stepped around him while he remained standing in the doorway. Clearly, he was not done with the conversation. He shut the door behind me, but I lingered in the hallway, waiting to see if he could persuade her not to put Alana and me together. It was Patrice who spoke first, though.

"Do you want to explain to me exactly what happened last night?" There was an edge to Patrice's voice that made it clear that she knew what had happened between Liam and me the night before.

Seriously, is there anything these people don't know?!

"It was a slip-up. It won't happen again." Liam knew I was still there, and I could just imagine how uncomfortable this all was for him.

"I know it won't. You know what that young woman has been through and what she means to our cause. And for Alana to be the one to witness it all. You've certainly gotten yourself into a bit of a mess, Liam." Patrice had gone into mum mode again, and I had a mental image of Liam with his head bowed, possibly even scuffing his feet like a little boy who was being told off. I heard Liam cover a small laugh with a cough and knew he had seen my mental image as well. Whilst he was older than Patrice, she was like a mother to all of us, and I knew she worried about the impact a relationship between myself and Liam would have, not just on us but on the rest of the Order as well.

I decided to leave them to it, not wanting to hear anything further and went off to do some practice in the gym. Not long afterwards, Liam joined me. Neither of us brought up the night before or his conversation with Patrice but settled into our workouts in companionable silence.

But now everything was different. I caught him shooting me an appreciative look as I started punching and kicking the punching bag in front of me, attempting to make my transitions as smooth as possible. Realising I had seen him, he turned back to his own workout, rolling his head from side to side, trying to shake it off. Something unsaid hung over both of us, and I had to force myself not to be distracted by the sight of Liam as he shed his shirt and started doing chin-ups. The smirk on his face let me know he could hear my thoughts, and I started to think about mundane things to try and keep the sexual tension under control.

But it wasn't easy to control your thoughts when the object of your lust was nearby without a shirt on. As he'd only ever worn long sleeve shirts around me, even when I'd seen him in his sleeping clothes, I was surprised at the presence of a large tattoo that covered his left arm from the elbow up to his shoulder and onto his chest. It was an intricate tattoo featuring elaborate Celtic knotwork, a sundial of some kind with glyphs that I didn't recognise, flowing into a dragon's head, stopping just over his heart. I had never cared for tattoos in the past, but the one adorning Liam's body instantly quickened my pulse. I had to turn my back on him then, for both our sakes, and I didn't envy Alana for having to deal with the pair of us tonight. I knew it would be hard for her, knowing her feelings for Liam and her dislike of me. It was going to be an interesting night.

Just before dusk, armed with only the stakes that were strapped to my thighs and in my pockets, I found myself alone in a car with Liam and Alana. I had an earpiece in one ear and was wearing a tiny, hi-tech camera attached to the puffy vest I wore. I felt like I was on some sort of SWAT team. Which, I guess, was close to the truth. The tension in the air was so thick I could almost see the knife that was stuck in it, a mental image that again had Liam smothering a laugh with a cough. None of us had uttered a word since we had left the Manor, and we had been driving for twenty minutes. I recognised the streets we were winding through and realised that this nest was definitely an issue, as it was only moments from my new place, as well as my parents and a few of my sisters. I also had an unsettling feeling that it might be the nest where Will was living now. I had not expected to come face-to-face with him on my first night out, and I found myself shaking at the thought.

I noticed Liam watching me and shaking his head, reassuring me that this was not the nest that Will now called home. Alana saw this exchange from the back seat, and I could tell that this all just made her even angrier. We really needed to stop pissing her off, or one of us was going to end up dead tonight. Liam rolled the car to a stop, and my heart began to race. I started to realise I wasn't ready for this. Liam turned to me, just looking me in the eyes, letting me know I could do this. From the backseat, Alana cleared her throat loudly.

"Sorry to interrupt yet another lover's moment, but would the pair of you kindly tear yourselves away from each other for one moment so that we can discuss strategy?" The venom in her voice was so evident that I was convinced that one of us would be going home injured, at the very least. This was not a good start.

Five minutes later, I stood at the back of the house, Liam a few feet behind me, his attention split between watching the house and monitoring how I was faring. Alana had taken point and moved into the house as the sun was setting. Nervously, I watched as the first vampire burst from the house and hung back as Liam quickly dispatched her as another raced past them. I moved forward, prepared to take him on. The adrenaline had kicked at the moment I had stepped from the car, and it felt good to unleash the first punch. My opponent was momentarily knocked back, stunned. He righted himself, getting a good look at my face, and I could tell he recognised me as his lips curled up into a sneer.

"So, they've finally let her out of her gilded cage." His eyes flicked towards where Liam was fighting a third vampire, though I knew he was aware of my every move. "But her knight in shining armour is ever-present."

"You talk too much." I stepped forward and punched him in the face, frustrated that he seemed to know all about me. I heard something crunch, and he reeled back, clutching his nose. I didn't allow him to speak any further, going after him and pummelling him in the chest with both fists, driving him further back until he was pressed back against the wall of the house. I pinned him there with my left forearm and yanked out the stake that was in my right pocket, plunging it hard into his heart. I knew I'd hit my mark as he twitched and the glow of his blue eyes faded out.

As his body slid down the wall, I stepped back. I had lost track of what was going on behind me and was startled as an arm wrapped around my chest. My attacker pulled me hard against his chest and attempted to yank my head to the side to get at my neck. I brought my right foot down sharply to crush his foot, and he let out a grunt of pain, momentarily distracted from trying to bite me. I used that split second to my advantage and grabbed the arm across my chest, leaning forward and pulling down at the same time, propelling him over my head. He crashed forward and landed on his back, staring up at me in shock. I didn't give him a chance to get his bearings as I held him down with my knee and used my stake once again, driving it deep into his heart with both hands.

"Isolde!" I jumped up and spun around as Liam called out, seeing another vampire running towards me. Liam was squaring off with another of their coven, and I was grateful he'd allowed himself that brief moment of distraction to alert me. These two appeared to be the last, as Alana had appeared behind them in the doorway and watched as I spun on the spot and connected with the woman's face as she rushed at me. Her head snapped back as she flew through the air, and I tried not to allow myself to be distracted by the strength that I had used in order to make a fully-grown vampire fly.

Distantly, I was aware that Liam had dispatched the vampire he'd been fighting, and both he and Alana were holding back to watch as I fought the last of them. My opponent was back on her feet, and her face twisted with rage as she charged towards me again. I took on a fighter's stance, my left foot forward and both fists raised as if preparing to punch her. But as she reached me, I feinted left, spinning myself as she lost her balance, passing the space I'd previously stood. Now behind her, as she tipped forward slightly, I unleashed a flying kick that sent her sprawling forward onto the ground. As she attempted to flip herself over, I was beside her in an instant, and as she rolled onto her back, I brought my stake down and slammed it into her chest. She let out a scream, but it cut out, and I watched with satisfaction as the glow of her eyes faded.

The silence around me was deafening, and I raised my head slowly to find both Liam and Alana watching me closely. Liam's face shone with both pride and awe, as though I'd surprised him with my abilities. Alana looked surprised at first before something else flashed across her face. I wasn't entirely sure, but I got the distinct impression that she was angry. Had she wanted me to fail?

We encountered no further nightwalkers, and by around 2 am, I sat on the large, four-poster bed in my room at the Manor, listening as Liam and Patrice talked outside my door. I had my legs curled up beneath me, a mug of hot chocolate clutched between both my hands. I was staring ahead of myself, unable to believe what had taken place earlier.

"There was no touching her. It was as if she was the most experienced fighter there. I've been training with her for months, and I knew she was good, but I had no idea she was going to be that good." I could hear Liam pacing backwards and forwards in the hall. "No other Protector has been that confident on their first time out, Patrice. It was like.." He trailed off.

"It was like watching you fight, Liam." Alana's voice sounded from further away, and I realised she must have come from her own room, further down the other end of the hall. She had practically fled away from us once we returned to the Manor, unable to handle spending any further time in our presence.

"It must be one of her abilities coming out. The prophecy did say that she would have powers we'd never come across before." There was an edge to Patrice's voice, and I wondered if her mind was racing as fast as mine was. Well, if this was an ability that no one understood, I liked this one, but I was still going to need to adjust to suddenly possessing skills that even a ninja would envy.

Whilst Liam and Patrice continued to talk in the hall, I stared off into space, not realising at first what I was doing, until I noticed that the vase of fake flowers on the chest of drawers across the room from me was trembling. I had been staring directly at it intently.

Am I doing that?

I rolled my head from side to side, the residual adrenaline from the night's events still rolling off me in waves, and I was finding it hard to stay still. I focused on the vase, attempting to channel my nervous energy into getting it to move.

"I don't think even I could take her, Patrice. This changes everything." I was distracted from my musings as I realised that Liam was thinking that I may not need the round-the-clock protection detail anymore. I agreed with him, but I worried this meant I wouldn't see him as much anymore. I had become so used to having him close by that the thought of being alone again scared me more than I was willing to admit.

"I don't know. I certainly don't feel like testing her new abilities too much. We will just continue on the way we have been going for now. Let her adjust to her newfound strength." I tuned them out now, focusing on taking deep, calming breaths. I needed to find some way to work off all this leftover energy.

Patrice checked in on me again before heading downstairs, and Liam entered the room to sit beside me on the bed.

"How are you doing?" He asked needlessly, as he could no doubt hear the freaked-out thoughts going through my head.

"Um... yeah... I'll have to get back to you on that." I tried to laugh off my fear, but he simply looked at me. He knew me well, and not just because he could read my thoughts. I felt myself being drawn closer to him, but I jumped up suddenly, stepping away from the bed. Being on a bed with him was not a good idea right now.

"I'm going to have a shower." I nodded towards the bathroom connected to my room. He stood as well, nodding.

"I'll leave you to it." He moved quickly towards the door as I headed for the bathroom, closing the door behind me and leaning against it, staring up at the ceiling. Jumping his bones probably wasn't the best way to burn off these feelings, but that knowledge didn't make it any less appealing.

Chapter Fourteen

A FTER THE LONGEST SHOWER of my life, I dressed in loose black pants and a white cropped shirt that left my stomach exposed. I stood in front of the bedroom mirror and breathed in deeply. With my eyes closed, I focused on each breath, my chest rising and falling rhythmically as I did so. I was trying to use the mind-clearing techniques that Liam had taught me, but without the flame to focus on, I was struggling. When I reached twenty, I gave up and opened my eyes. The shower had done nothing to ease the adrenaline of the night I'd had, along with the tension that had been rolling off the pair of us in waves.

Ever since my birthday, I'd had a high libido, something that Will had commented on enthusiastically and used to his advantage. At the time, I had put this down to the excitement of being an engaged woman. After Will's death, I'd been too numb to everything except grief and anger, but as the fog of grief had begun to lift, I'd been noticing my sex drive kicking in once again. The past few days had not been helping either.

I looked in the mirror now, taking in my reflection. Through the thin material of my clothes, I took note of the changes that had slowly been occurring in my body since I'd started training with Liam daily. Muscles I had never noticed before were now defined, and I wasn't unhappy to see how strong I had become.

Remembering the sexually charged intensity between myself and Liam in the gym earlier in the day, I shut my eyes and counted again, continuing to focus on my breathing as I attempted to get my feelings under control. I was very aware that Liam would no doubt be able to hear my thoughts, and I struggled to shut down my train of thought. Without realising it, Will's role in my fantasies had slowly been replaced by someone else, and I had always had a very vivid imagination.

I imagined the feel of his hands on my body, of his mouth on mine. I could practically feel the sensation now as his fingers ran through my hair before wrapping it around his fist as he pulled my head back.

Lost in my overactive imagination of how he would make my body sing in ways it hadn't done in months, it took a moment for me to note the sound of heavy breathing other than my own.

Liam's heavy breathing.

I slowly opened my eyes and met his gaze in the mirror as he stood at the door to my bedroom. He must have left the door partially open when he had left, causing the door to swing silently open when he knocked. His hands grasped the top of the door frame as he stretched up, surveying every inch of my body like he could see through the very thin clothing I wore. He was wearing only his grey sweatpants, having just finished in the shower himself.

From the heated look he gave me, he'd heard every thought going through my mind in the last twenty minutes. I couldn't keep myself from admiring him. The fact that he was the most beautiful man I'd ever seen was sending my overactive libido into overdrive. I felt my gaze drift to the tattoo on his left arm and chest once more, eyeing it hungrily in the mirror as he continued watching the reflection of my face. He cleared his throat.

"I thought I'd try and help you with the mind-clearing again." He nodded towards the low table where we had sat days earlier when I had played with the flames. I felt like I was playing with a different kind of fire now, in this moment.

I nodded at him, unable to speak, and turned to face him finally. He hesitated for a moment, almost as though he was afraid to step into the room. That was understandable, given the thoughts I was struggling to keep a grip on. It was a dangerous line we were walking right now, one that, if crossed, may have repercussions we weren't yet ready to face. He finally crossed the threshold, but instead of going over to the table, he came towards where I still stood, watching his every movement. Until now, I'd never really appreciated how gracefully he walked. His movements were so fluid, no doubt from the centuries of martial arts training that had honed that beautiful physique.

He came to a stop in front of me, looking down as he studied my face closely, as though trying to work out the answer to a puzzle. Whenever we stood this close to each other, I was afraid I would get lost in those eyes. I forced myself to look away, still trying to get a lock on the swirling emotions inside of me. Instead, I focused on the details of his tattoo, which was now at my eye level. Mesmerised, I traced a finger around the swirls on the dragon's head and neck, noticing as he tensed beneath my touch, but he didn't move, holding himself perfectly still as I traced every swirl over his heart. I noticed the goosebumps that appeared on his skin.

"This is beautiful," I whispered, still refusing to look up at him. He brought his hand up to cover mine, forcing me to stop moving my finger over his skin.

"Perhaps some Tai Chi would be better than mind-clearing right now. Probably shouldn't be playing with any flames at the moment." He had a point there. The last time I'd attempted mind-clearing when my emotions were this heightened, two nights ago, I'd nearly set fire to the table. The ball of fire had grown so large while I stared at it that it had been like a miniature sun, and I'd struggled to control it. Liam had been shaken then, and if something managed to rattle Liam, I didn't want to be messing around with it.

He lowered my hand slowly before placing both of his on my shoulders and turned me back around to face the mirror. I still couldn't bring myself to look at him, even if it was only in the mirror, and I could feel my heart racing as he stood close behind me. For someone who was meant to be trying to help me clear my mind, he was doing a terrible job with all this close contact.

I had thought that he would step back then, hearing the dangerous train of thought that was plaguing me, imagining all the ways he could use those hands on my skin to help me find the release that I so desperately craved. Instead, he moved even closer until his body was pressed up against my back, and I was unable to hide the gasp that escaped me.

"You are so beautiful, Isolde.' His voice was low and husky, and something told me that I wasn't the only one having trouble concentrating on clearing their mind. My gaze met his in the mirror finally, and his eyes remained locked on mine with every movement. Neither of us seemed capable of looking away.

'You think I'm beautiful?" My voice was barely louder than a whisper.

"You know I do." His hands were still on my shoulders, and I watched his face as he began massaging my neck and shoulders. I sighed as he worked each knot out slowly, continuing to watch my face in the mirror, gauging my reactions. Eventually, I let my head fall back against his chest. This is what I wanted. Not mind-clearing. Not Tai Chi. What I needed was his hands on my body. He pressed himself harder against my back, bringing his mouth to my ear, and I shivered at the feel of his breath on my skin.

"What do you need, Isolde? I need to hear the words out loud," he whispered in my ear.

Slowly, I reached down and took his hand, guiding it to my right breast. I let out a sigh as he squeezed it gently.

"I want your hands on me," I whispered, and his breath hitched slightly as he moved his hand to slide slowly under my loose top. He cupped my breast briefly before moving to roll my nipple between his fingers. A low moan escaped my lips as I watched him. His touch was firm and warm, and I could feel the strength in his hands, the kind of hands that could crush you if they wanted to. Or provide the lightest touch. I shivered as he ran his other hand along my ribs before moving it up to cover my other breast.

"Like this?" He whispered, cupping my breasts gently in his hands. I nodded, my eyes closing, enjoying the feeling of his hands on my body.

"No, don't close your eyes. Look at me." I opened my eyes, my gaze finding his once again in the mirror. Both of us tracked the path of his hand that slid slowly down my stomach. I shivered as he began tracing a circle around my belly button.

His other hand moved to the opposite breast, massaging it as he used his arm to hold me tightly to him. His gaze returned to my face, drawing my eyes to his once more, and I felt his hand move lower, pushing below the band of my pants that hung loosely on my hips, tracing a path down my lower abdomen until he finally found that bundle of nerves. I drew in a sharp breath as he drew circles around it with his forefinger, and I moaned softly, my hips moving against him, as I bit down on my lip.

"Just like that? Is that helping?" He asked, his voice still low and husky, as we continued to hold eye contact in the mirror. I spread my legs even wider, inviting him to explore further. He did just that as he slowly slipped a finger between my folds. I was so turned on, and he could tell from how wet I was as he worked his finger inside of me. His thumb replaced his finger on the most sensitive part of my body and began to stroke firmly.

"Yes." I breathed out huskily as I watched him. I felt the warmth exuding from my body, the goosebumps all over my skin. "Please don't stop." Slowly, he used his body against my back to gently urge me to ride his hand, rocking me back and forth in a slow rhythm.

"That's it. Just like that, Isolde." I felt myself becoming more and more aroused as he whispered the words in my ear, working his finger in and out in a steady rhythm as his thumb continued stroking. I tried to control my breathing, trying not to come too quickly.

I reached my hand up and gripped the back of his head as he pressed light kisses to my neck before gently taking my ear lobe between his teeth, never taking his eyes from mine in the mirror. My hips were moving on their own now, and I continued riding his hand as he worked a second finger inside me. I could feel the pressure building inside me, knowing I was moments from coming. I attempted to slow my breathing, trying to control my body as I could feel my orgasm building. I needed this to last after weeks of the build-up. Liam began working his hand faster, and I whimpered. I felt my body tighten as my breaths started to come faster. I could feel how hard he was against my back, and he continued to hold me tightly against him, pinching my nipple with the hand that had continued teasing my breast.

"Oh, God, I'm coming, I'm coming," I chanted in a whisper, and my hips took off against his hand, bucking and twitching in time with my gasping breaths. The building pleasure finally exploded, sending shock waves of euphoria through my body. I felt every single one of those waves crashing over me, one after another, my breathing remaining heavy as I collapsed against his chest. He held me tightly as I rode out the orgasm, his fingers still buried inside of me. As I worked to get my breath back under control, he slowly removed his hand and moved to step back. I grabbed his hand.

"I want you. Right here, right now," I said, my voice cracking. His eyes gleamed with lust as we stared at each other in the mirror. I turned to face him, and he cleared his throat. I could tell he was battling an internal war between what he *should* do and what he *wanted* to do. His hand shook slightly as he raised my hand to his lips, turning it over to kiss my palm.

"You should get some sleep. It's been a long night." His voice wavered as he spoke quietly.

Without thinking, I leaned into him, and he put his arms around me tightly, holding me close as I processed everything. He was right; it had been a long night. However, that didn't stop me from wanting Liam, and I knew he felt it as well, especially after what we had just done.

I leaned back to look up at him and found him already looking down at me. Rising onto my toes, I kissed him hungrily, trying to get as close to him as I could. He held me close, and our bodies pressed together. Stepping forwards, he pushed me back against the mirror, and I gasped as my back met the cold glass, and we continued to kiss with growing intensity, months of frustration flowing through us both. He had his hand under my top, his fingers digging into my back. I wrapped my leg around him, urging him to keep exploring. A knock sounded at the door, and we stopped suddenly, both looking over to see the door handle moving.

"Isolde?" Patrice's voice called through the door, and it started to open slowly. Liam was away from me in an instant, and by the time Patrice had the door fully open, he was seated on the other side of the room, looking as casual as ever. Patrice took in his shirtless appearance and my flushed face as she surveyed the scene before her.

"Are you sure you're okay to go home tonight? You still look a little..." She couldn't think of what to say, but I nodded.

"Yes, I'll be fine. I think I'll head off now." I looked at Liam, who nodded. There were so many reasons why we shouldn't do what we had nearly done, and I knew I needed to get home and be away from him.

I had a cold shower when I got home, hoping that would help, as they always talked about those in the movies. However, it only made me shiver uncontrollably, and I tossed and turned for the remainder of the night, unable to forget the feeling of Liam's body pressed against mine, his fingers moving inside of me. Of his intense gaze in the mirror as he made my body sing. And no matter how much I knew we shouldn't have crossed that line, I wished like crazy that Patrice had not come to check on me.

Chapter Fifteen

Early the next morning, after only a couple of hours of fitful sleep, I arrived at the Manor to find everyone rushing around frantically. Patrice noticed my arrival and rushed towards me.

"What's going on?" I questioned Patrice. I tried not to react as Liam appeared at my side.

"Alana and a few others went out last night on another hunting mission, but not one we knew about." Patrice's face was tear-stained, and I knew instantly that this was not going to end well.

"Who's missing?" Although I didn't like Alana, I still didn't want anything to happen to her.

"Alana is missing... The others... There were no other survivors." Liam answered from beside me, his voice almost wooden, and I could feel him blaming himself. He had been too distracted by everything that had happened with me.

"Who was with her?" I asked, scared to hear the response. Liam looked as though he was struggling to answer, so I looked to Patrice, who swallowed hard before responding.

"Omari, Kazeem..." She began listing names of some of the newer Protectors that were close to Alana and had kept their distance from me, but my blood went cold as she stumbled over the last two names. "Sam... and Katyana." I felt myself starting to tear up as she named the two Order members that I had started to become closest to. Beside me, Liam had balled his hands into fists, and I could see him struggling to keep his emotions in check. With tears rolling down my cheeks, I placed a hand on his arm, bringing his gaze to me. His eyes were shining with unshed tears.

"This isn't your fault, Liam. You couldn't have done anything." Though he may have been able to hear what they were planning, it was not his responsibility to police the actions of the others.

"Isolde is right, Liam. This wasn't your fault." Patrice stated as she handed Liam a set of car keys.

"We still don't know why they went there. You need to go back and see what you can find out." With a nod, Liam turned to walk back out the door, but Patrice stopped him with a hand on his arm.

"Take Isolde with you." It was a simple command, but I couldn't understand why it was being given. Why should I go with him? Surely, it would be better to have a more experienced member of the Order partner with him. Without saying a word, Liam nodded and took me by the hand, towing me along behind him. I looked back at Patrice, who nodded at me with a knowing look.

"Why did she ask you to bring me along?" I asked Liam's back as he led me into the elevator that led down to the basement car park. The car that we climbed into was a tank. The majority of the Orders cars were bulletproof, but this one looked like it could withstand anything, including a bomb going off underneath it.

"Patrice thought it would be good for you to come along and see if you can pick anything up that I can't." This line of thought confused me.

"I don't understand. What do you mean by 'pick anything up'?"

"We're still yet to fully test your abilities. Patrice wants to explore if you may have any psychic abilities. A few of the others have them, and as your powers are meant to be the strongest, the elders are eager to explore what else you can do." Liam had still been refusing to make eye contact with me. I had come to know Liam pretty well over the past few months, and I knew that he was blaming himself, no doubt believing that if we hadn't been together last night, he would have been able to prevent what had happened.

I touched the hand that he rested on the gearshift, giving it a squeeze.

"Hey. Don't do this. I know that you are blaming yourself for what Alana did, but she obviously kept you out of it for a reason. You saw how she was after what happened when we were all together last night." I had been so focused on my newfound ninja skills and crazy sexual tension that I was only just realising that Alana had been acting strangely when we returned to the Manor. No doubt jealous of my abilities and the attention that others had been giving me.

"That doesn't excuse the fact that I was so distracted that I didn't know what was going on."

"You can't save everyone, Liam. Especially when they don't want to be saved." Liam remained silent, and I finally gave up, staring out the window. Now that I was no longer trying to convince Liam that he wasn't responsible, I struggled with the realisation that Katyana and Sam were now gone. I tried to push away the grief that was threatening to overwhelm me, knowing that I couldn't afford to fall apart just yet.

We arrived at the address that Patrice gave us, an unused warehouse in the northern suburbs on the outskirts of the city limits. It had all the signs of having fallen into disrepair, with broken windows and graffiti on the walls. It also had a strong sense of foreboding around it.

"That feeling that you're having right now is exactly the sort of thing Patrice is hoping for," Liam said as we climbed out of the car, and I looked over at him apprehensively as I shut the door.

"I still don't know how I feel about everyone just waiting for me to develop magical powers." I stopped as Liam handed me a stake, still not really looking at me as he scanned the area. "What exactly are you expecting to find here? Wouldn't the vampires that attacked them all be gone by now?"

"We cleared the area earlier, but we still need to be careful." Liam led the way as we did an entire loop of the building, and I followed behind as he looked through the broken windows, checking to ensure that we were indeed alone. I followed behind, checking doors for any way inside. I was overwhelmed by the strong sense that something bad had happened here.

"How did everyone know what happened if no one knew about this mission?" Liam turned to look at me properly finally.

"We have a team of seers in our London location, and one of them contacted Patrice about 5 hours ago. Unfortunately, the team had already left, and by the time I got here with Daniel and Celeste, it was too late." Although he delivered the information very matter-of-factly, I could see the emotion in his eyes, the guilt he harboured for not knowing about what was happening beforehand. I realised that the team must have been gathering whilst he and I were preoccupied last night. I swallowed hard, nodding at him, and he continued moving on.

When we returned to the back of the building, I placed my hand on the door handle, as I had done with all the others. This time, however, a flash of images hit me, and I was nearly knocked off my feet.

I wrenched the door open, and we raced inside, expecting to have the element of surprise. But, we were met by a small army of vampires, and they moved tightly around the five of us, sealing off our escape. We hadn't expected so many. It was unheard of to have this many nightwalkers gathered in one place.

To my right, I saw Adam step forward and grasp Sam by the neck with one hand, lifting him off the ground. His toes scraped the ground as Adam held him there for a moment, choking the life out of him before snapping his neck with a flick of his wrist. I felt terror build up inside me as Katyana cried out, struggling against the nightwalker who had grabbed her from behind. He bit into her neck and fed off her with such aggression that he eventually ripped her head from her shoulders. To my left, Omari and Kazeem managed to hold their own for a little longer, but I was held in place by several nightwalkers, forced to watch as everyone that I had led here was ripped apart.

I was forced to kneel before Adam, who stepped forward and wrenched my head to the side. As his teeth bit into my neck, I knew at that moment that my death would be different to the others, and I felt fear I had never felt before as I realised that my fate was sealed.

"Isolde?" Liam shook me back to reality, and I looked up, realising that the force of the vision had knocked me to the ground. "Are you okay?" He had been watching me with concern, and that had distracted him from being able to see into my mind properly. I slowly climbed to my feet.

"No..." I was struggling to piece my words together, reeling from everything I had just seen, watching people I had come to consider friends die in such brutal ways. I didn't even bother trying to stop the tears that rolled down my face. And experiencing what had happened to Alana... I felt nausea rolling through me, and I bent forward, retching. Liam moved forward to hold my hair back while I emptied the contents of my stomach. I eventually stood up straight again, still feeling hot and clammy.

"I just saw... I was inside Alana's head as... They turned her, Liam. The entire group of vampires that were here drained, Alana. They took her with them and left everyone else. Why?" Liam could see the confusion in my eyes, the sadness. I hadn't liked Alana, but after seeing her death flash before my eyes, I felt her loss keenly.

"I don't know. I don't even know why they came here. This wasn't a nest." Liam returned to the car to grab me a towel to wipe my mouth with. I followed close behind him as he moved back to the door. I let him open the door this time and lead the way inside, hesitant to touch the door again in case the vision reappeared. I led Liam to the spot where I had seen Alana killed. He knelt and touched the ground, brushing the blood-stained concrete with his fingertips, his eyes briefly taking on a far-away look before he looked back up at me.

"How much did you see?" I reluctantly replayed the vision in my mind again, allowing Liam to see everything I had seen. Revisiting it all was like ripping a wound open over and over again. Once I had finished, I opened my eyes to find he was looking at me with surprise. His gaze returned to the blood on the concrete.

"Your visions are the same as the ones I see when I'm..." He trailed off, almost as though he realised he had said too much.

"What do you mean, the same as yours? You have psychic abilities as well?" I don't know why I was surprised. With his mind-reading abilities, it made sense.

"My visions are the same as yours, experienced from the perspective of the person involved. The others that have some psychic ability just get fragments or, in some cases, just an impression of what occurred." He looked thoughtful for a moment.

"Liam?"

"Hm?" He looked at me after a brief moment, his mind elsewhere.

"How do you get visions?" Something about the way he'd looked down at the blood had me intrigued.

"What do you mean?" He was stalling now, and he could tell that I knew that.

"What triggers them for you? For me, it must be touching something that they did, like the door handle that Alana touched. What triggers them for you?" He looked at me for a moment, clearly wondering how much to tell me. After a moment, he nodded, resigning himself to the truth.

"I get my visions from blood."

I recalled how he had just brushed the blood-stain with his fingertips, his eyes losing focus briefly.

"So, when you touch blood?"

"Not just touching." This was the first time we'd ever come close to speaking about his... eating habits. He usually avoided any discussion with me about his vampiric side.

"So... when you're..."

"Feeding. Yes." He looked uncomfortable, but I pushed on.

"You told me once that daywalkers only fed off the blood of animals." I found myself wrapping my arms around myself unconsciously, and I stopped, not wanting to appear apprehensive. Liam was watching me, clearly hearing my racing thoughts.

"What I said was we could survive off the blood of animals. That they could quench our thirst."

"But you also drink human blood?" I didn't know why I wanted to know... Then again, maybe I did.

"Sometimes, yes."

"When?" Liam was growing more and more uncomfortable. He ran a hand over his face.

"Isolde, do we really need to..." He looked at me, almost pleading with me to drop it. Unfortunately, I had reached the point where I needed to know.

"When do you feed from humans, Liam?" He sighed, shoving his hands in his pockets.

"When they let me." He looked straight at me, deciding to just go with brutal honesty.

"What do you mean when they let you? Who has let you?" I tried to keep the dismay from my voice, but it was there. I couldn't fathom the appeal of having someone bite me after seeing the brutality when the nightwalkers fed. Liam continued looking into my eyes before answering.

"Alana has before. And there have been others over the centuries." I felt myself draw back, away from him.

"Alana?" I was shocked at this turn in the conversation. I couldn't take it all in. However, Liam had clearly decided that I was going to hear it all now that I had pushed it this far.

"Yes. About thirty years ago, Alana and I had a brief dalliance. I have been around for centuries, Isolde. There have been women in my life along the way."

"But you said that you'd made it clear to Alana that you weren't interested in her that way." I was trying not to be hurt by this, to appreciate the honesty. But I was losing.

"No, I was never in love with her, not in a way that meant anything at least, and when I'd realised the depth of her feelings for me, I ended the sexual side of our relationship."

"So, what's been going on with us? Am I just the next one to come along in a long line of women that you've cast aside once they fall in love with you?" I didn't care if he knew how I was feeling anymore. I was hurt, unable to believe I'd almost allowed myself to be used in such a way. Liam moved towards me, shaking his head, but I stepped back, refusing to allow him to touch me. He let the hand he'd raised to touch my cheek fall to his side.

"No. I could never have done that to you."

"Because I'm the chosen one? Because everyone treats me like I'm about to break?" I was angry now, tired of being treated with such fragility, ready to break at the slightest movement.

"Because I have been with you every day of your life since you were born. I have been protecting you, watching over you. When Will died, I felt that grief with you. Although you only met me five months ago, I have known you your entire life. And lately." His words trailed off for a moment. "How I feel about you now... I've never felt that for anyone before." His words were angry like he didn't want to admit to either himself or to me that he had developed feelings for me.

"So, my entire life, you've watched me?" I'd known this, yet discussing it now, I didn't know how to feel about it. I hadn't truly allowed myself to think of him standing in the dark each night for twenty-five years, watching over me from the time I was a baby until now.

"Not in the creepy way you make it sound. I needed to keep you safe."

"So, I'm just a job to you?" He groaned, shaking his head in frustration as he turned away.

"Now you're just trying to pick a fight with me." He led the way to the car, and I trailed behind him, unsure of what to make of everything we had just discussed.

"No, I really want to know." I reached for the passenger door. He was behind me in an instant, moving at the uncanny speed that I'd seen him do so many times now, turning me to face him. He moved closer, pressing me back against the car.

"As I've come to know you properly, to develop a connection with you..." His voice trailed off as he gazed into my eyes. He cleared his throat, gathering his thoughts. "I have never wanted to keep anyone alive more in my entire existence. It is the hardest thing I have ever done. You are not a job to me, Isolde. You have become my reason for existing. I need to keep you safe because the idea of anything happening to you terrifies the shit out of me. And it's got nothing to do with prophecies or your destiny or what you mean to the fucking Order." He gripped my chin, forcing me to hold his gaze. "For twenty-five years, keeping you safe has been my sole purpose. And these past few months..." His eyes stared intently into my own, and his body pressed hard against mine. I could feel his heart beating against my chest. I knew my own was beating fast, processing everything he was confessing. "If anything happened to you, I would burn the world to the ground." He held me in his gaze for what felt like an eternity before stepping back and going around to the other side of the car.

I stood still for a moment, attempting to pull myself back together, trying to take in every word he had just said and the three words that he had left unsaid. Silently, I climbed into the car. Neither of us said a word as we drove back to the Manor.

Once we returned, everyone gathered in the communications room to discuss what had been discovered so far.

"The seers contacted us at 3 am. They had only just seen what was happening, and there was not enough time for us to save anyone. We arrived at the warehouse to find a bloodbath. We found no nightwalkers, though, just bodies." Celeste started going through everything that they had seen when they arrived at the warehouse earlier that morning. Celeste and Daniel were the head of most missions, in charge of the teams who went out each night. Celeste normally remained at command, running point, but not this morning. They had grabbed Liam as he was getting ready to head to my house to take up his usual guarding duty. It was decided that he would be needed more on this mission. Their sole purpose on the initial mission had been to clear the area before anyone else, such as the police, arrived. But when they came across the scene, that mission changed to returning with the bodies of our fallen team members. Once the sun was up, the elders sent Liam back to get the full story of what had occurred, aware of his psychic abilities. I was just thrown in as a training exercise.

"Does anyone know why they were there?" Patrice looked around the table, but everyone shook their heads.

"Isolde did have a vision while we were there. It appears that Alana has been turned." Liam filled everyone in on what we had both seen.

"And you say that Adam was there?" Patrice looked over at me. I nodded in the affirmative.

"Yeah, I didn't recognise any of the others, though. Will wasn't there, from what I could tell." Patrice nodded, looking stressed.

"If Adam is involved, then it can't have been a coincidence that many vampires were together. No doubt Connor has something brewing," Liam stated, and I looked over at him, wondering who Connor was.

"Agreed. We are going to have to step up our patrols. Something is coming. I can feel it." I shivered at Patrice's words, not liking the sound of what she said but sensing the same foreboding that she did.

Chapter Sixteen

THE FOLLOWING DAYS WERE spent attempting to determine why the team had left that night and where they may have taken Alana's body while she transitioned. From what we could tell, Alana had been jealous of the attention I received on my first mission out and had decided to take on Adam to win favour with the elders.

Liam avoided being alone with me, and I couldn't tell if this was because he was still punishing himself for being distracted or if he didn't want to explore what had been developing between us. For my part, I was trying to deal with the grief of losing yet more people who meant something to me. Katyana had been such a massive presence in the Manor, and I felt her absence every time I walked through the door. Sam had been the closest in age to me amongst the Order, and I missed the way we both joked about the older generation around us. Hell, I even missed the daily arguments with Alana.

I wished I'd been given the chance to get to know Kazeem and Omari. There were so few Order members these days that to lose even one was tragic. Losing five at once was devastating, and I could see its impact on the others. Celeste had lost her best friend when Katyana died, and she was struggling to focus, torn between needing to find Alana's body and wanting to break down and mourn the loss of her friend. Due to how long they all lived and the fact that our jobs were so dangerous, I somehow believed that they were immune to grief. It was only through watching them all now that I realised how very wrong I had been. When they'd said that they understood my grief when Will died, I had been so wrapped up in my depression that I'd failed to put that connection together. Something I was deeply ashamed of now. When you lived for centuries, death was more brutal to bear.

Time was ticking by, and we knew that Alana would be awakening in two days if we didn't find her beforehand to halt the transition. Every waking hour was consumed by our attempts to find answers, but we were coming up short and now relying on the seers in London to try and find her location. I needed to get away from the stress for a few hours, and after letting Patrice know where I was going, I climbed into my car and headed home.

I drove in a dream state, and I marvelled at the fact that I had not killed others, or myself, in a car accident, as I rarely remembered getting to destinations in my car these days, just arriving wherever I was headed in one piece. At least, on the rare occasions I was alone in my car. I had become so used to Liam's presence that I struggled to remember the last time I had driven without him. However, tonight I made a conscious effort to pay attention to getting home. For some reason, I felt something in the air, like something was about to happen, and it was with a sense of foreboding that I realised this something couldn't be good, given all that I had learnt since Will's death. Well, apparent death... Could you consider someone dead if their body was still walking around, determined to bring about your demise?

Failing to pay attention on the drive home, I found myself sitting in front of my house, the engine ticking as it cooled down... How long had I been sitting here? I needed to start paying attention to what was happening around me. The park across the road stood empty and foreboding like each tree hid an invisible enemy.

Suddenly, I was knocked from my internal musings by the sudden movement of my car. I jumped in my seat and looked around to see what had forced my car to rock violently. Maybe I had just imagined it. It was possible but seemed unlikely. My senses were suddenly on high alert, and I could feel my heart begin to race. Everything was still for a moment, and I was grateful that I now always drove with all my car doors locked. Too many stories about women being carjacked scared me into the habit. That and my first face-to-face encounter with Will as a vampire when Liam had yanked me from the car.

But it was no crazed carjacker that was attempting to rip me from my car two seconds later. I screamed as I saw the face of the man I once loved appear next to my window, twisted in fury as he attempted to rip the driver's door off the car. From what Liam had told me of vampire strength, he should have succeeded, and yet my door held fast. I didn't allow myself time to think about why as I used the extra time to crawl over to the passenger seat. I wasn't sure what good I thought this would do me, but thankfully, I didn't have the chance to find out. There was a blur of movement outside. Then Will was knocked to the ground. I couldn't see where he had gone, which scared me even more. Two blurred figures appeared in front of the car, and I watched with terrified fascination as they danced around each other. I realised that Liam had once again come to my aid. Will had the strength of a new vampire on his side, but Liam had the advantage of years of training on his... Well, centuries.

I wanted to hide behind my hands until it was over like I used to while watching horror movies. A fast-forward button would be handy right now. But unfortunately, neither of these things was an option. I could not hide because if Liam lost, Will would come after me next. And there was no way I wanted to fast-forward to that. Despite my newly developed vampire-fighting skills, I was still uncertain that I had the mental strength to kill the man I had loved for over a decade. I held my breath as the two lunged at each other in mid-air. Liam kicked Will in the head, and they both landed hard. I leaned forward to see better and dug my nails into the dash as Will jumped to his feet and took on a fighter's stance, ready for the next round, but Liam was already moving again.

I didn't see what happened next as they moved at lightning speed, but the next thing I knew, Will was gone, and Liam was leaning heavily against the side of my car. With trembling hands, I unlocked my door and climbed out, shaking so hard I could barely walk. Liam was by my side instantly, all signs of fatigue gone as he raced me to the front door. I had my keys gripped in my hand, and he took them from me as I was shaking too hard to unlock the door. Once through the door, I was so grateful that Aurora wasn't home, yet at the same time, I was terrified because she wasn't. I couldn't guarantee her safety if she wasn't within these walls.

I realised after a moment that I was sobbing uncontrollably, and this was causing the shaking. Liam held me tightly as I struggled to get myself under control. After the past few days, it was all a bit too much for me to handle, although I could pull myself together much quicker than I had after my past freakouts.

'Are you okay?' I asked Liam hoarsely after a moment, my forehead pressed against his shoulder, working to get my emotions back under control.

'Fine.' He answered shortly, and I looked up at him. He was looking at me with concern. 'I think I should be the one asking you that.'

I took a deep breath and then let it out again. "How did he find me? I thought the Order had the house cloaked from nightwalkers?"

"He saw you drive through an intersection near here and followed you. He can't get in and won't be able to find this place again on his own." Liam looked at me, still concerned, as I was swaying slightly. "You're safe, Isolde."

'I'll be okay. I just need to sit down for a minute.' I allowed him to guide me to the couch, and we sat down. I couldn't let go of him, and he held me in his lap as I took deep breaths. He held me tightly, and as I gained more control over myself, I realised how close we were to each other. I shifted to look up at him, and we gazed at each other momentarily.

"I thought it had been decided that you didn't need to guard me anymore?" I whispered, moving so that our foreheads met. He let out a ragged breath and closed his eyes.

"I couldn't stay away." He spoke so softly that I could barely hear him.

I sat back slightly, and he opened his eyes. I reached up and ran a hand through his hair before bringing my lips to press gently against his. He kissed me back softly as he wove his fingers through my hair with one hand whilst pulling me closer to him with the other. I moved so that I was straddling his lap, and he ran his hands down to my hips, deepening the kiss, as he pulled me forward so that my chest was pressed against his. He gripped my hips and rocked my pelvis against him as he trailed kisses down my neck. I moaned and continued rocking my hips as he lifted my sweater and shirt over my head, and I undid my bra, sliding it down both arms and tossing it onto the floor behind me as he moved his lips to my right breast and began sucking hard. I gasped as his hand returned to my hip and continued rocking me against him, and I felt how hard he was already rubbing against the seam of my jeans. He moaned along with me as I rocked faster, moving his mouth to my other breast. I arched into him, urging him to suck harder.

"Fuck, Isolde." He lifted me off him and looked up at me as he began slowly undoing the button on my jeans, then dragged the fly down one agonising tooth at a time, smirking up at me as I panted with need. Sliding my jeans down my legs and moving to sit on the edge of the couch, he pressed a kiss against my abdomen, and I ran my fingers through his hair as he trailed kisses along the lace edge of my underwear before sliding them down. Pausing, he looked up at me with questioning eyes. Asking for consent. I nodded, my hair spilling over my shoulder and breast.

Taking his time, Liam ran his hand up the inside of my leg, and I tipped my head back with a sigh as he used a finger to start circling the bundle of nerves at the apex of my thighs with a feather-light touch, surrendering myself to his caress. He worked me up gently, and I moaned softly, then gasped as his tongue replaced his finger. Feeling myself sway a little, I was grateful when he pulled me closer and held me in place with one hand as he moved the other between my legs, sliding a finger inside me, and his tongue and finger began to work in tandem to bring me to the edge. My breathing became ragged as I moaned and writhed against him, riding his tongue and finger together.

"Oh God, Liam, I'm coming." I cried out, and he sucked harder as he sped his hand up, and I came hard, my legs giving out from under my body, and he caught me, keeping me from falling to the floor. He lowered me to sit across him before gently guiding me to lay back on the couch, continuing to work me up slowly to a second, intense orgasm with his hand as I writhed in his lap. My vision blurred as I came again with a hoarse cry.

"I could watch that all night." He breathed, slowly taking my hand and pressing a kiss to my palm, his eyes on mine as I breathed heavily, waiting for the stars to clear from my vision. I took my hand from his lips and ran my fingers through his hair as I sat up and kissed him. He palmed my breast with one hand as he used the other to tangle his fingers through my hair.

"I want you, Liam," I whispered against his lips before rising to my feet, pulling him up and leading him into my room. There would be no one to interrupt us tonight, as Aurora and Jacob were away for the weekend, staying down the Gold Coast to attend a wedding. Liam closed the door behind him, and I leaned into him as he stood with his back against the door. I wound my arms around his neck, kissing him hard before I stepped back to pull his shirt over his head.

"You have far too many clothes on. Let me help you fix that." He watched as I stepped back slightly to admire him, and he gave me an amused smirk as I ran my hand down his chest and over his toned abs. Centuries of kicking ass had caused him to develop muscles in all the right places. With a single finger, I traced each detail of his tattoo, and he shivered when I reached the head of the dragon, coming to a stop at the edge of its nose, right over his heart. I looked into his eyes then, as my hands moved slowly down to the buckle on his belt, and his breath became uneven.

He made no move to help me, allowing me to take my time and set the pace. It took all my self-restraint not to jump on him and devour him right there. I moved forward and planted a kiss over his heart, and he let out a long breath as I moved slowly down his body, planting soft kisses as I went, finally managing to undo his belt. I knelt to remove his jeans and boxers until he stood before me, as naked as I was. I looked up at him from where I knelt before him and watched as he let his head fall back against the door as I ran my hand over his erection. He moaned and closed his eyes as I took him in my mouth and ran my tongue over the tip, working my hands and mouth together. He tangled his hand in my hair, looking down at me and slowly rocking his hips in time with my head bobs, his gaze full of lust.

Growing impatient, it wasn't long before he pulled me off him and raised me to my feet before hoisting me up. Grabbing my thighs and urging me to wrap my legs around his waist as he kissed me hard, his hands gripped my butt as he carried me slowly towards the bed. He turned so that he sat on the edge, and I straddled his lap again. I raised myself onto my knees, watching his face as I lowered myself down onto him. We both moaned together as I took him inside slowly, inch by glorious inch.

He framed my cheeks with his hands and pulled my face gently down to his, our foreheads touching as I began to rock slowly, my arms wrapped around his neck and back. Moving his hands away from my face, he slid one behind my neck and wrapped my hair around his fist gently whilst the other gripped my hip, guiding me up and down.

"God, Isolde, you're so perfect," He whispered, trailing kisses down my neck as he pulled my hair gently back so that he could gain better access to my breasts. He took my right nipple in his mouth and sucked hard as I continued rocking harder and harder against him. I could feel another orgasm growing, and he let go of my hip, reaching between us to help me along with his fingers.

"Fuck, Liam. Oh, God!" I cried out as I came, his mouth still at my breast and his hand rubbing furiously, causing yet another orgasm to follow immediately after. My legs started to give out, and I slowed down, the pleasure running through me, making it difficult to move.

He lifted me off him, turning to lay me down on my back and pressed a kiss to my belly before sliding up my body and bringing his lips to mine. Easing back inside, our eyes locked as he started to rock his hips slowly. We moved together like this for what could have been minutes or hours, the chorus of our moans and sighs filling the room until I began to feel another orgasm building. He picked up his pace as my inner walls tightened around him, and pleasure shot through me once again as I cried out. He kissed me gently, and I struggled to breathe as the aftershocks rippled through me.

Slowing his pace once again, he allowed me the chance to get my breath back but continued to keep me on edge, little shock waves continuing to cause me to shudder. Once I gained control of myself again, I wrapped my legs around his hips as he pulled himself upright. As he rocked his hips back and forth at increasing speed, he ran his hands up and down the front of my thighs. I could feel him getting closer to coming himself as he reached down and rubbed my most sensitive spot once again.

"Come with me, Isolde," he said, and my back arched off the bed with his words as we came together in one last powerful thrust. He lowered himself on top of me as I kept my legs wrapped around him, holding him close in my arms as we breathed heavily together.

Not long after, I lay wrapped in Liam's arms; his chest pressed to my back as I fought off the sleep I knew would inevitably come. I was afraid to fall asleep, knowing that everything would have changed when I woke, and I worried about the consequences of crossing the line we had just set ablaze. Because although I knew that his feelings were as intense as my own, I was very aware that he didn't need much sleep. This gave him plenty of time to think about this change in our relationship. Now, we had gone way past complicated. I turned in his arms to face him and traced a finger across his lips, and he kissed it softly.

"You should get some sleep," he said quietly, raising his hand to push my hair behind my ear before running it gently down my back.

"I'm scared to fall asleep," I whispered, and he looked at me thoughtfully for a moment before nodding.

"You think I won't be here when you wake up?" He continued moving his hand up and down my back as he spoke, and I snuggled closer into him.

"You are notorious for overthinking things," I mumbled, resting my forehead against his. He kissed me softly for a moment and then pulled me in tighter.

"How about if I promise to be here when you open your eyes? Will that help?"

"That depends. Are you planning to talk yourself out of this while I'm sleeping?" I struggled to fight off sleep, but I was slowly losing the battle.

"I can't fight this anymore. Now go to sleep." Comforted by his words, I snuggled into him and allowed sleep to take over finally.

Chapter Seventeen

A BEAM OF SUNLIGHT lay across my face, and my first thought was that I had forgotten to shut the curtains. My second, panicked thought was of Liam, and I turned my head so quickly that I wrenched my neck. I let out a yelp before finally noticing the arm that was wrapped around my waist and the body pressed up against my back. Liam raised himself up on his elbow and looked down at me with a smirk before moving his hand to massage my sore neck.

"I gave you my word, and you still didn't trust me to be here in the morning?" I blushed a little, but he laughed, a laugh that was so relaxed and normal. I loved seeing this side of him. I rolled to face him, and he rearranged us so that I lay on top of him. He guided my face to his and kissed me softly.

"Good morning." I gazed down at him as he ran his fingers through my hair and lightly down my back, which sent a shiver down my spine. I loved it when he played with my hair.

"Good morning." He smiled at me with a knowing smile. I kissed him again, harder this time and let myself get lost in this perfect moment.

Hours later, I emerged from my room, unsure of the reception I would be receiving from Aurora, as I'd heard her and Jacob come home earlier. Liam was in my shower, and Aurora entered the kitchen, stopping when she saw me, surprised.

"Oh, I thought you were in the shower. Who's in there?" From the look on her face, she already knew the answer to that question.

"Liam." I didn't bother explaining, knowing Aurora was a big enough girl to work it out on her own. Jacob came in behind her and was equally surprised to see me.

"Liam's in the shower," Aurora told Jacob, who raised an eyebrow before snagging an apple from the fruit bowl.

"I'm gonna leave you two ladies to it. No doubt you're both about to start yelling." He backed out of the room, hands in the air, before all but fleeing back to their room. Smart man.

"Well, go on, let it out. I know you're dying to give me your opinion." I continued to make breakfast for myself and Liam, my back to my sister, knowing the look that she was giving me was no doubt full of judgement.

"So much for 'we're just friends' then, huh?"

"Looks like it." I was purposely being aloof, and I could tell it was pissing Aurora off.

"So, you're a couple now, is that it? I can't believe you got over Will so quickly." I turned toward her, doing nothing to hide the anger that I knew was written all over my face. As I did so, something caught Aurora's eye, and I saw her look at my wrist as I pushed my hair back. Too late, I realised that I was not wearing a jumper, which I had taken to wearing to hide my tattoo.

"And when the hell did you get a tattoo?!" I disregarded the question, still focused on her last statement.

"You know nothing about how I grieved him or what I've been through. I will always love Will, he was my first love, and if he were still alive, I would be marrying him soon. I have forgotten nothing." I spat the words at her, and she recoiled, stunned by my anger. I never spoke to her like this. "But I have to move on with my life, and I have chosen to do so with Liam, who is a kind and caring man. You should be happy for me instead of expecting me to wallow in self-pity for the rest of my life." I was fuming, and Aurora finally saw how she was hurting me, backing down slightly.

"I'm sorry. I guess I was just thrown by the fact that you found someone else so quickly. You loved him so much... I guess I just expected you to take years to get over him..." She had run out of things to say. I angrily wiped away a tear, annoyed that I had started to cry. This conversation was ruining the great mood I had woken up in.

"Well, I have found someone, and you're just going to have to deal with that." I took the two plates of toast and brushed past her as she remained leaning against the bench before heading back into my room. Liam was sitting on my bed, a towel wrapped around his waist, with one eyebrow raised.

"Don't ask." I could not help but admire him, eyes drawn once again to his amazing chest and the tattoo. I felt the corners of my mouth raise as my eyes drifted over his abs, and he smirked at me.

"Stop that. You'll make me blush." I knew he was in my head, and I put the plates down on the bedside table. I headed towards my open bathroom door, slowly unbuttoning my pyjama top. As I reached the door, I looked back over my shoulder.

"Well, aren't you coming?" I giggled as he came after me in one fluid movement, lifting me so I could wrap my legs around his waist, and he walked us into the bathroom, kissing me as we went.

As the morning grew later, I knew that we should head for the Manor, but I could not bring myself to leave the comfort of my bed and Liam's arms. I lay on my stomach, propped up on my elbows, as I looked down at Liam, who was playing with a few strands of my hair.

"Are you happy?" I asked quietly. He let the strands of my hair fall through his fingers as he reached up to stroke my face gently.

"In all my existence, I don't think I've ever been happier... With you, it is as if I forget about all of the supernatural parts of the world and can just feel human for a while. I'm back to being the twenty-five-year-old man I was all those years ago." I smiled and kissed him softly before fixing him with a playful grin.

"So, all of those women who came before me... You never felt this way for any of them?" Although I tried to sound casual, he knew it was something I was genuinely concerned about. He looked up at me thoughtfully. "Okay, you're taking way too long to answer. Now I'm worried." Liam put a finger to my lips and smiled reassuringly.

"I'm just trying to think of what I can say that will make you see that those women were nothing more than passing phases without making me sound like a complete cad."

"A cad? I keep forgetting how old you are until you use terms like that... That's something that I've only ever heard my grandfather say." I grinned, and Liam rolled his eyes.

"Ha ha." He said drily. "In all seriousness though... Remember when I told you that I had to give up my role in the Church once my brother disappeared? And that the idea of taking a wife, of tying myself to someone, was not something I had ever wanted for myself? I meant that. Until you entered my life, I'd never met anyone that I could imagine wanting to spend a lifetime with. Many lifetimes." I was speechless for a moment, trying to work out how to respond to this. After a moment, I sat up, trying to gather my thoughts.

"Why me? What's so special about me?" I couldn't fathom how someone who had been alive for so long, who had experienced so many lives and seen so much, could feel so strongly for someone like me, who had experienced nothing of life in comparison. It was like comparing a toddler to a great-great-grandfather. Liam sat up beside me, gently bringing his hand to my chin and urging me to bring my gaze to his.

"Why not you?" He asked, looking me in the eye. "Although you believe you're so young, look at all you have been through. You are an old soul, wise beyond your years." He pushed my hair back behind my ear and leaned in close. "You're beautiful." He gently kissed my forehead. "Sexy." Kissed my nose. "And never before in my life have I ever met someone so determined and self-aware. You intoxicate me." He kissed my lips softly. "I have protected a lot of people in my life, but never before have I wanted to keep someone safe as badly as I do you." He kissed me again, and I kissed him back hungrily but pulled back after a moment to look at him again.

"So, you think I need to be kept safe? Is that why I appeal to you so much, because I play the damsel in distress so well?" Liam groaned and flopped back into the pillows, pulling me on top of him.

"Believe me, Isolde, I know you are more than capable of holding your own. Everything I do is driven by a need to protect you. To keep you safe and shield you from further heartbreak. However, at the same time, the things that you have been through... They've made you who you are." He stated this so simply, and yet I felt as though he had just given a rousing speech, much like you see in the movies. I searched his face, knowing that he would truly do anything to keep me safe.

"Thank you." I kissed him softly again. His hands began stroking up and down my back as the kiss grew, and he grabbed my hips, starting to rock them against his. Just as I started to trail kisses down his chest, we were interrupted by the sound of Liam's mobile ringing. He groaned as I reluctantly rolled off him, and he grabbed it from the bedside table.

"Hello?" I headed for the bathroom as he took the call, figuring that I would have to leave the safety of my room now. Sure enough, when I emerged a few moments later, it was to find Liam sitting on the bed, already wearing his jeans.

"They need us at the Manor," he said, looking up at me as I stood in front of him and absently ran my fingers through his hair.

"Of course they do." I sighed, pushing my hair out of my face to pull it back into a messy bun on top of my head.

"So..."

"So, what?" I asked, leaning into him as he wrapped his arms around my waist.

"So, I'm going to need my shirt back." He tugged at the hem of the shirt I was wearing. His shirt. Which I had pulled on as I headed to the bathroom. It was all that I was wearing.

"Really? Are you sure? I think you look great without it." I smirked, and he laughed.

"I'm just going to have to take it off you; you realise that, don't you?"

"You can try." I darted out of his arms and attempted to run for the door, but he caught me in his arms, turned me to face him and kissed me. Within a second, I was naked once again, and he was fully clothed, his lips pressed to mine as he held me close to him. He pulled away with a cheeky grin, and I loved seeing him this relaxed... So free.

"That's playing dirty." He sat back down, watching me appreciatively as I walked to my dresser and started digging through it to find something to wear.

"I know, but it was fun." I threw a shirt at his head.

Half an hour later, we entered the Manor hand in hand, figuring there was no point in being secretive. Gerard was the first person to see us as we walked through the door, and he raised an eyebrow but refrained from commenting. Patrice, however, was not so stoic.

"Is there something the two of you would like to share?" She asked, an edge to her voice, but Liam simply shrugged, letting me take this one as he went off in search of Celeste. But not before giving me a brief kiss on the lips and exchanging a look with Patrice.

"Not really. I'm not sure why we need to keep everyone informed of our relationship status." I followed Patrice into the kitchen, in desperate need of coffee.

"I know that you are new to this life, Isolde, but there are certain ways of going about things. You're being in a relationship with Liam was not part of your destiny." I hadn't noticed Damon as he followed us in as well, and I rolled my eyes. All Damon ever did was lecture me about my destiny and my duty. I had had enough, and Patrice could see I had reached the end of my tether.

"I've already had a similar conversation to this one this morning, so I'll make it quick. What I do and whom I do those things with is not a topic of discussion amongst the elders. I did not ask for this life, and I am more than happy to walk away from it the first chance I get, so just keep trying to control me, Damon, and you will see how serious I am about that." I put a hand up as he opened his mouth to protest, stopping him in his tracks. After a look from Patrice, he stopped himself from commenting, leaning back against the bench and crossing his arms as I continued. "Now, I understand your concern, and while I appreciate it, my relationship with Liam is our business alone," I swear I saw a glimmer of respect in Patrice's eye as I gave my little speech.

For his part, Damon continued to look pissed, but he must have realised that I truly had no issues with walking away from this life. As it was, I had no qualms about walking away from this conversation. I moved to leave the room before turning back to say one final thing. "And not a word to Liam about this. I don't want to hear that you've been lecturing him about how I need to be protected and how we shouldn't be together. We are two consenting adults, and if we want to be together, then you are all just going to have to deal with it."

I found Liam in the Intel room with Celeste and Daniel. They didn't seem to care about the fact that Liam and I were now an item, and I figured that they had had to deal with their fair share of crap from the elders regarding their relationship. If it were up to the elders, we would all be celibate. Liam stifled a laugh as I leaned against the table beside him, no doubt having heard my rant at Damon.

"What have I missed?"

"Celeste was just going through what they found last night."

"Catch me up?" I looked at Celeste expectantly. She looked briefly taken aback by my take-charge approach before getting down to business.

"We managed to track the vampires that took Alana." She nodded towards the map on the large TV screens on the walls. A red beacon was blipping away in the middle of what appeared to be a satellite image.

"Where is that?" I was no good with maps if they didn't have suburbs and street names written on them. I saw a look exchanged between the other three and began to realise that I probably didn't want to know. Liam was the one to answer me.

"It's your old house." Yep, I was right. I didn't want to know.

"You mean the townhouse? The one that you convinced me not to burn to the ground?" I crossed my arms over my chest, leaning my hip against the desk next to me as I surveyed the three of them.

"Yes. We know that Will had full access to the house while you were living there, but when it was sold to the new owners, we figured he would no longer have any interest in it. That has usually been the case in the past." As Celeste spoke, I could feel Liam watching me, waiting for my reaction.

"So now he's killed off the new owners, and they are using it as a base." Celeste and Daniel exchanged a thoughtful look as I summed up what they were avoiding saying out loud.

"That certainly looks like what's happened," Daniel said to Celeste, who nodded.

"We'll look into this further. Looks like you guys might be off on a mission tonight." They both turned back to the monitors, pretty much dismissing us. This was their department, planning the missions while we were the muscle. Liam led the way out of the room and down the hall to the training room.

"I don't think you should come tonight." I turned to face Liam in surprise, from where I'd started to wrap my hands to prepare to start taking my frustration out on one of the many punching bags.

"What? Why?"

"Because when it comes to Will, you freeze. Any other vampire nest, I would not have any hesitation to have you at my side, especially with your abilities. However, one where he might be... Not to mention that these vampires are the ones gunning for you." What he said made sense, and yet, I was still fuming at the amount of people trying to tell me what to do today.

Liam was clearly in my head and ready for my argument as he came towards me and wrapped his arms around my waist, pulling me to him. "How about this, you stay here, logged into the comms, and that way, it's like you being there?" I felt like I was a child, being placated with a lollipop. Liam smiled down at me. "Your mental images are some of the most imaginative and entertaining I've ever seen." I smacked his shoulder.

"Shut up!" I think I just successfully disproved his theory this morning of having an old soul with that one little outburst. However, he contented himself to know he had won this round for the time being as he pulled me back in for a kiss. Sighing, I had to admit that he was right. When it came to Will, I did freeze. And we could not afford that sort of mistake.

I helped the others prepare, watching as Daniel, Dylan, Yumi, Edward, Colin and Zuri strapped themselves with various weapons. As usual, Liam was armed only with a stake that he had strapped to his thigh. I briefly kissed Liam goodbye and watched them leave, ignoring the pang of discomfort at being the one left behind.

Once they had departed, I headed back into the intelligence room where Celeste sat, watching as the GPS trackers on the cars allowed us to track their route to my old home. Patrice sat cross-legged on a table in the corner of the room, surrounded by candles. I sat down at the computer that

Celeste had assigned me, attaching a communications device to my ear. On the monitor in front of me, I could see the back of the first car as I watched the world through Liam's eyes, or rather, through the camera attached to his black, padded vest. Each of the team wore one, and the images were filtered onto one massive screen on the wall.

Celeste had assigned me to Liam whilst she and a few others monitored everyone else. I gratefully took the coffee that Barbara handed me as she walked past on her way to her monitor. I had already decided that I did not enjoy being on this side of an operation. Although I could see everything, I was powerless to do anything.

"Can you hear me?" I said into my headset.

"Loud and clear." Liam's voice came back to me.

"Well, at least for once, you can only hear what I'm saying." I mused. I stayed silent for the remainder of their drive as the team discussed tactics amongst themselves. Whilst everyone else was to deal with any vampires they came across, it was Liam's job to find Alana. As the cars rounded the corner into my old street, my heart rate increased. I wasn't sure what to expect once they entered the property, and I was not looking forward to seeing my old home being used as a vampire nest.

Once they arrived, the team fanned out around the property, intending to enter simultaneously through the back and front doors, as well as through the windows at both sides of the house. Across the room from me, I saw Patrice begin to perform a cloaking spell to prevent civilians from witnessing the breaking and entering that was about to occur. The last thing we needed was for the police to show up.

I had watched Patrice perform several spells over the past few months and admired the fluid and graceful movements as she used her entire body, the chants almost sounding like a song as she uttered the words to bring a cloak of silence and invisibility over the exterior of the house, coming down behind the team. As soon as Patrice completed the spell, she nodded at Celeste, who simply said, "Go!" into her headset.

Then all hell broke loose. As one, the entire unit moved into the house. It was like watching some cop movie on mute, as not a single sound was made. I watched as Liam entered the home, proof enough that there were no living residents remaining. I had provided everyone with a detailed description of the layout of the house, advising Liam that the master bedroom was upstairs, at the back of the house. I had surmised that it would be the most likely place that they had left Alana. Not only was it the largest room, but it also got the least amount of sunlight. Liam followed my directions towards the stairs at the back of the house. Ahead of him, I saw Daniel take down the first vampire that they had come across.

Liam continued through the house, yet to come across any resistance. It didn't look like there were many vampires there, which was good but surprising. It didn't make Liam's ultimate job any easier, though. He came to the top of the stairs, throwing a small female vampire down the stairs when she attempted to attack him. I couldn't see what became of her, but I imagined one of the others downstairs dealt with her after that. A larger vampire stood in front of the bedroom door, guarding it. In life, he could have been a rugby player and built like a small mountain. I watched, not realising I was holding my breath, as Liam took him out with ease, staking him in the heart before the vampire had so much as moved.

Then he opened the door, and I fought back a wave of guilt. The new owners lay dead in a heap in the corner of the room, their necks twisted at an odd angle, their eyes staring vacantly at a world they could no longer see. I attempted to swallow the lump in my throat, knowing now was not the time.

"We should have burned it to the ground," I said bitterly.

"Don't blame yourself, Isolde. We had no way of knowing this would happen," Liam said, as beside me, Celeste put her hand over mine. Her eyes were still focused on the progress of the rest of the team, who were spread throughout the house, most of them taking out at least one vampire each.

I returned my gaze to the screen in front of me to see that Liam knelt next to the bed, where Alana's body lay. She certainly looked dead, and it was hard to believe, as we looked down at her, that she was being bombarded with the blood memories of the entire coven. Including the same blood memories that had coursed through Will all those months ago, turning him into the soulless being he had become.

I watched as Liam's hand gently brushed a strand of hair away from Alana's face, and I felt a wave of sadness for him. I knew that although Liam had no romantic feelings for Alana, he still cared for her deeply, and what he was about to do was going to be incredibly hard for him. I had tears in my eyes as I watched Liam's hand raise the stake above Alana's chest before plunging it deep into her heart.

I jumped back as Alana's eyes flew open, no longer brown, having already turned to the tell-tale piercing blue. They were glazed over, unseeing. Then, slowly, her body disintegrated into dust, which took me by surprise. I looked at Celeste with a raised eyebrow.

"That's normal. When they are in the process of turning, it's like the body doesn't know what to do, so it simply disintegrates into nothing," she said, and I swallowed hard as Liam took Alana's necklace from the dust and placed it into his pocket. All that remained of her.

The team arrived back an hour later, having disposed of the bodies of all of the vampires. They were subdued, sadness coming off each of them in waves, pained by the task that they had to perform. I realised that although Alana had not been nice to me, she had been a much-loved member of the Order. Now that they were no longer preoccupied with the task of finding her before she turned, I was a witness to their mourning.

They were now able to grieve the deaths of all the Protectors that had been killed on the ill-fated raid. It scared me how the deaths had diminished the ranks of the Order. I wasn't sure how much more death and loss I could handle, and it made me fear becoming too close to anyone else. Because letting people close to my heart made it easier to lose another piece of it when they were ultimately ripped from me. And yet, I found myself clinging tighter to Liam as he walked through the door, and we drew strength from each other as we held one another amongst the heavy cloud of grief.

Chapter Eighteen

S EVERAL DAYS LATER, I sat beside Liam, holding his hand as we went through the process of saying goodbye to our fallen friends. I was surprised to discover that a small section of the Toowong Cemetery was cloaked to hide a burial plot for the Order. I had come across dates going back to the settlement of Brisbane in the early nineteenth century, though most were recent, from when the official branch had taken up residence here when I was born.

Liam squeezed my hand, and I returned my thoughts to the present to see that Sam's was the latest coffin being lowered into the ground, and I immediately felt my stomach clench. A tear began to form in the corner of my eye, and I swallowed hard. I had already watched the Priestess perform the death rites for Omari and Kazeem, and I felt as though I was engulfed in a cloud of grief. Mostly, though, I felt like an intruder. I did not feel as though I should be here. Some of those buried had been as old as one hundred, but I had only known them for a few months.

Liam let go of my hand and put his arm around me, pulling me closer, and I realised he had heard my thoughts. I knew he was also drawing his own comfort from my presence, and I gripped his hand as Katyana's coffin was lowered next, blinking back the tears that were starting to sting my eyes.

The final coffin was for Alana. Without a body to bury, they had instead placed a small urn inside that contained her necklace. I felt my throat constrict with emotion, and the tears finally started to track down my face. I had witnessed too much death over the past few months and was unsure how much more I could take.

As the group slowly dispersed, I stood before the headstone erected in Katyana's memory, a single rose in my hand. I couldn't bring myself to leave, and Liam stood speaking to Patrice for a while before coming to stand beside me. Neither of us spoke as we stood looking at the headstone. This was not how it was meant to end for her. To end a life like ours, alone and interred in the ground. To eventually be forgotten... Liam put his arm around me again as tears slid down my cheek.

"I feel as though all I've done these past six months is cry," I said sadly as Liam kissed the top of my head and pulled me close to his side.

"I've buried a lot of people in my time... And it never gets any easier. However, you were wrong about one thing. They are never forgotten." And I realised he was right. With the slow ageing and having Liam around, they weren't forgotten. It was a small glimmer of happiness in an otherwise bleak moment.

Liam stepped away from me, going to talk to the Priestess who had presided over the ceremonies. I walked amongst the headstones, reading the names of the fallen. As I read the name "Isabel King 25.10.1870 – 28.11.1994", which was relatively young for a member of the Order, a movement out of the corner of my eye caused me to look up. I froze, sure that I must be seeing things.

Alana stood a few feet from me, her eyes wide as she stared intently at me, her hand raised, as she beckoned me towards her. I looked around, hoping that someone else could see her as well. However, no one was looking in her direction other than me.

I must be going insane.

Her lips moved, but I heard nothing.

"I can't hear you…" I strained for any trace of a sound as her lips stopped moving, and she lowered her hand.

"Liam?" I said his name quietly, looking back at where he stood a few feet away. He excused himself from the conversation with the Priestess and came to join me. I looked back to where I had seen Alana, but she was gone.

"Are you okay? You look like you've seen a ghost."

"I think I may have," I said, staring at the spot Alana had stood moments ago.

"What do you mean?" Liam looked confused.

"I just saw Alana standing right there. She was reaching out to me, and I think she was trying to tell me something, but I couldn't hear her." Now Liam's expression turned to one of concern.

"You saw her?"

"Yes… Is that something unusual? I'm never sure what's weird and what's normal anymore." Liam scanned the group as I spoke, looking for someone. He spotted Patrice and signalled her over.

"Is everything okay?" Patrice came to join us, looking down at the headstone of Isabel King, assuming it must be something to do with our location.

"Isolde just saw Alana," Liam said, and Patrice looked up at me sharply.

"What did she say?" This line of enquiry took me aback. There was no question of my sanity nor any doubt of what I had seen.

"Um… Her lips were moving, but I couldn't hear her," I said, and Patrice looked crestfallen. "I don't understand; why am I seeing her ghost?" I figured if she were going to appear to anyone, it certainly would not be me.

"Ghosts generally appear to people they have a message for."

"Why would she have a message for me?" I asked, confused. Patrice looked at Liam, who shrugged, shaking his head.

"I don't know." It was puzzling, and we headed for the cars when it looked like Alana would not reappear. I kept looking back over my shoulder at the spot where I had seen her, all the while wondering why on earth Alana would have a message for me.

A few nights later, I sat on my bed. It was the first time I had been truly alone in months, having forced Liam to stay at the Manor and Aurora and Jacob were away for the weekend. With the magical wards over the house, the elders had agreed that there was no point in having someone watching over me when no vampire could cross the transom. I told him that I just wanted some me time. Which was true, but I did not intend to stay home to do it.

There was something that I needed to do. And I needed to do it alone. My phone had been blowing up with unread messages from friends and family, each reaching out in their own way. I had become so distant from everyone that I doubted anyone would be surprised by my silence on today, of all days.

It was meant to be my wedding day.

I sat on that bed for hours, going through photo albums that had been packed in a box since we had moved from the townhouse. Before all the craziness had happened in my life, I was known for taking photos to document every occasion, and as a result, I had thousands of happy snaps. Most of them were photos of myself and Will over the years. It was the first time I had been able to bring myself to look at them since Will had died, and going through them all now brought tears to my eyes. Things had been simple back then.

I saw a photo of the two of us at a friend's wedding eighteen months ago. There was a twinkle in Will's eye, and I knew now, looking at this photo, that it was at this time that he had decided it was time to propose to me. In the picture, I stared at him as he looked at the photographer, toasting the camera. The look of devotion on my face sent a shiver down my spine. My world, indeed, had revolved around him.

Why had no one told me I was almost unnaturally devoted to him? For someone who claimed to be an independent woman, my entire life had been about him. I had been in love with him from age ten when I stopped seeing him as someone with boy germs. I had even come home early from the trip of my dreams because I couldn't bear to be away from him. Yet, when he was no longer in my life, I had moved on quicker than anyone had believed possible, including myself, if I was honest. I had never doubted anything in my relationship with Will and could never fault his devotion to me.

But on meeting Liam, it was as if I was seeing everything more clearly. My life with Will had been an illusion—a fairy tale. With Liam, he indeed saw me. He saw the good, the bad... everything. He didn't just expect me to be in love with him; he questioned it daily, even though he could read my mind. Will had just taken my devotion to him for granted. And why wouldn't he have? I followed him around for more than half of our lives. However, he had never followed me.

I tucked the photo away in my pocket and closed the last of the photo albums. I was finished with them and knew I would never look at them again. I couldn't bring myself to destroy them, though. Some part of me needed to keep that part of my life alive. I didn't want to lose touch with the people who remained around me. However, I was moving on.

After midnight, I left my house and headed towards my former home with Will. I drove through the streets of Bulimba, which lay silent in the darkness. Pulling up across the road from the complex where we once lived, I took out a book I had smuggled out amongst my belongings that morning when I left the Manor. Having witnessed Patrice perform the cloaking spell several times, I was confident I could do it, even if only for a few minutes. A few minutes was all that I needed.

Now that I'd worked out that I didn't need chants to harness my power, I wondered if I even needed the book, but I couldn't risk anyone seeing what I was about to do until I was ready. After familiarising myself with what I needed to understand about the spell in order to cloak the house against prying eyes and ears, I fearlessly stepped out of the car. I didn't envy any vampire who tried to cross me tonight.

Coming to a standstill in my old driveway, I surveyed the remains of the crime scene tape hanging from the door frame, fluttering in the breeze.

After the team had removed all the vampires from the house, we had put in an anonymous call to the police to let them know of the fate of the new owners. There was an ongoing investigation, but no solid leads. There were now whispers of gang activity, and the police were searching for a connection between Will's death and the current occupants' grizzly demise. The theory was that I had been the target. Our connections inside the police force were working on drug-related theories, keeping the truth firmly hidden, as usual.

I entered the house and shut the door softly behind me. After checking for any remaining vampires and ensuring that I was alone, I took out the candles from my backpack and set them up in a circle before stepping inside. I sat on the ground with my legs crossed.

The concept of the spell was simple. Chant the words, and a cloak would come down over the area I envisioned in my head, creating an illusion that any passers-by would see nothing but an empty house, and no noise would be detected outside the barrier. But, because I was doing it without the chanting or the actual spell, I hoped that envisioning the barrier would be enough. I took a deep breath and focused on the candle directly before me.

Light.

I smiled as all the candles lit at once. At least I knew I could still do that little bit of magic. Now to work out the barrier... I closed my eyes and tried to imagine a barrier encircling the house, and I felt a calm fall over me that I'd not felt in a long time. I focused on my breathing and ignored any other sounds, bringing all my senses down to the rhythmic inhale and exhale.

Barrier.

Nothing happened. I tried not to let the disappointment cause me to lose focus, but I opened my eyes to stare at the flame again. As much as it seemed incredible to be able to do magic without spells or chants, it was rather inconvenient not knowing what to say to get the larger magical enchantments to work.

I first focused on the magic that I had perfected with the flames and spent a few minutes spinning the balls of light in the air. I'd been practising this daily since I'd done it the first night with Liam. I could now make them all go in multiple directions simultaneously before coming together to form a giant ball of light, like a miniature sun hanging in the air. Once I'd reminded myself that I was competent at something, at least, I returned each flame to the candles and closed my eyes again.

Hide and protect me.

Instantly, I felt a power run through me as the air around me began to pop and crackle. I knew without a doubt that it had worked, as I looked out the window to see that a shimmering haze now surrounded the house, my car just a blur on the driveway. I probably should have included my car in that thought...

I stepped out of the circle and went to where I had left my backpack by the door. Kneeling to unzip it, I pulled out two fuel cans. I was about to do something that I never thought I would do in my life. And something I should have done months ago.

As I walked through the vacant rooms, I approached our old bedroom. Before entering, I took a deep breath and attempted to suppress the disturbing memories of the previous occupants' tragic fate. Upon entering, I took a moment to survey the space and deliberately concentrated on the happy memories it held. Every laugh we'd shared while lying in bed. Every kiss and touch. I tried not to tear up at the memory of the room lit up and covered in flower petals.

At last, I took a deep breath and slowly poured the fuel out in a line until I found myself at the front door again. The smell of petrol was strong now, and after gathering my belongings, I opened the door to stand on the front step. Making sure I had no petrol on myself, I held a single candle and willed it to light again. I focused on the flame and took a deep breath, working up the courage to do what needed to be done.

I raised the flame and stared at it briefly before slowly lowering it to the ground before me. And watched as the line of petrol lit up. Watching as the fire ran the length of the hall and up the stairs, I took the photo of Will and me out of my pocket, placing it into the fire. Then I turned and walked away.

As I sat in my car, I watched as the house was engulfed in flames. Once the deafening roar of the fire reached me, I lifted the cloaking enchantment from the property. I applied it to my car, ensuring that the containment enchantment remained intact to avoid any harm to nearby homes. Onlookers emerged from their houses as the blaze grew, stunned by the spectacle. I called the fire department using a prepaid phone I had purchased earlier in the day, and soon after, I heard the sound of a siren in the distance. With my car still shielded by the second cloaking spell, I drove away unnoticed.

As I was too wired to return home or to the Manor, I drove the streets for a while, not comprehending where I was going until I found myself at the top of Bartley's Hill in Ascot. Although it was across the river from Bulimba, I could see the smoke from my arson attack, and I let what I had done truly sink in. In setting my former home ablaze, I had let go of the past. I hoped I could now face Will without being bombarded by memories of what we'd shared. The Will I knew was dead, and I had to stop allowing myself to see him in the creature that he had become.

I watched the sunrise from the lookout, but exhaustion soon set in. Unsure of how my return would be received, I quietly returned to the Manor. The rest of the Order were asleep when I let myself in through the front door and headed to Liam's room. He was sleeping peacefully, and I slipped out of my jeans before snuggling beside him. Resting my head on the pillow, I closed my eyes and drifted off to sleep, feeling content and happy to be there.

When I awoke hours later, I rolled over to find Liam watching me, a small smile playing on his lips. He had been up for a while and was fully clothed, sitting in the armchair next to my side of the bed.

He reached over and pushed aside the lock of my hair that lay across my cheek.

"Anything you want to tell me about last night?" I could tell he already knew everything I'd done in the early morning hours.

"It was just something I had to do," I said, my voice thick with sleep. He lifted the covers and slid into bed beside me, pulling me close, and we lay facing each other, our noses almost touching.

"I know." He kissed me then, and I lost myself in the moment with him, allowing everything else to fall away.

No one else seemed to know what I'd done, and when Liam didn't say anything to Patrice, I wondered, not for the first time, why there were things that he didn't share with the elders.

"Do you not trust the Order, Liam?" I asked later that afternoon as I wrapped my hands, preparing for another sparring session. Liam moved to help me, his hands gently cradling mine as he secured the wraps. Once he was done, he pulled me close and rested his chin on my head. I clung to him, unsure whether I should be concerned or not.

"I just have this feeling that there is more going on than what we're being told. It's not that I don't trust the Order, but I definitely don't trust Damon. From the few conversations I've seen between them, he's been putting a lot of pressure on Patrice. There is something slightly erratic about Damon's behaviour when it comes to your powers, and I don't think we should be giving away too much about your abilities until we know more." I pulled back slightly to look up at him. Although I'd asked, I hadn't expected him to share that he had doubts about the group he had been a part of for over five hundred years. But I also had suspicions about Damon, and it made me feel better to know that they weren't entirely unfounded. After a few more moments of scanning his face, I nodded.

"Okay. I'll follow your lead then. We're a team, right?" He lowered his lips to mine, kissing me softly. I felt my heart skip a beat as he rested his forehead against mine, the tenderness evident on his face.

"It's you and me, Isolde. Always."

The next few days were uneventful. Almost scarily so.

After yet another quiet night, I returned to the Manor along with Daniel. We had checked out a few places in Fortitude Valley which were common feeding grounds for nightwalkers, but had come across nothing more than a few drunks stumbling home after a big night. It was making me edgy.

I dropped my stuff in my bedroom and changed into a sweater dress before searching for Liam, who'd been out with Gerard and a few others in the city. According to the chatter through my earpiece, their night had been as quiet as mine. I found him sitting behind his large desk, a massive pile of books before him.

"Hey," I said, sitting on the bed behind him. He swivelled his chair around to face me.

"Hey. You had a slow night as well, I gather?" He already knew the answer, although I nodded anyway.

"Yeah. It's starting to freak me out a little."

"It's not a good sign, especially because they were active only a week ago. Something is coming." I was not comforted by this line of conversation. I indicated towards the pile of books, eager to change the subject before the troublesome thoughts consumed me.

"Just catching up on some light reading?" I asked, and Liam laughed.

"Hardly. I'm reading through the histories to see if there is anything in here that could tell us what we might be about to come up against."

"How would the histories help you? Wouldn't it be better to read books from the prophecy section?" I raised an eyebrow, and he shrugged.

"I've never been all that good with prophecies. The thing with the prophecy section is that all the books there seem to be written in tongues."

"Huh?"

"They're incredibly hard to understand." He translated.

"Even for you, who's been around forever?" I had assumed that Liam knew everything, and this conversation confused me.

"Usually, the only person who can understand the prophecy is the person who made it, to be perfectly honest." Liam didn't acknowledge the jibe about his age, though he did smirk slightly. I got to my feet with a sigh.

"Well, it can't hurt to look, right?" I had never looked at any prophecy books and realised, with a jolt, that I'd never even read the prophecy about myself. Liam raised an eyebrow.

"Be my guest. I'll stick with these." He tapped the nearest book. His attitude was not giving me any confidence that I would find anything useful, but I figured doing something was better than sitting back and waiting.

I went down to the library, wondering where to start. After perusing the shelves for a while, I came across the section I sought. Selecting a few books at random seemed to be the way to go. However, as I started to pull books from the shelves, I came across one that caught my eye. THE GEMINI PROPHECY.

Being a twin, I was immediately drawn to the title of the slender book. It looked much newer than the ones around it and was tucked away, almost as though it wasn't meant to be seen. I set aside my other books and brought them to the closest armchair to read.

In the dark of night, when the moon is high,
Two sets of twins, born of different time.
One set of boys, one set of girls,

Destined to face off in a battle that twirls.

The long-running war, ancient and dark,

In a struggle for power, a vicious shark.

Two twins were chosen, one from each set,

To lead their side and never forget.

The last of the girls will be the missing piece,

Of a puzzle that will not cease.

Their fates are sealed, and their tasks defined,

To fight to the end, and never mind.

One twin from each set will stand strong,

For good or evil, right or wrong.

The balance of power rests in their hands,

To bring peace to the land, regardless of the order's demands.

With strength and courage, they'll face their fear,

The fate of all mankind on their shoulders to bear.

But with unwavering will and steadfast hearts,

They'll win the war and never depart.

Rivers will rise, and rain will fall,

The earth will become a danger to all.

And at that time,

The horsemen will begin their ride.

Thus the prophecy foretells,

Of the twins who rose, as on a spell.

Heroes of a vampire war,

It shall come to pass at New Years Dawn.

"What?" I spoke the words out loud, even though no one was around to answer the burning questions that this raised. I could now understand what Liam meant about them not making sense, but I knew without a doubt that there was something about this prophecy I should know about.

This couldn't be the prophecy that everyone had been talking about. And the horsemen will begin their ride? As in, the horsemen of the Apocalypse? I didn't know much about the Bible, having been raised without any real dedication to any religion. Still, I knew enough about the last book of the Bible, Revelations, to remember that it mentioned the four horsemen who would see the beginning of the Apocalypse... No one had said anything to me about the end of the world. With shaking hands, I put the book aside, not wanting to read anymore. The idea of the end of the world was not something I could deal with at the moment... or ever...

When sleep finally claimed me that night, images of fire and a river of blood plagued my dreams. I decided I didn't like prophecies...

Chapter Nineteen

T HE NEXT DAY I invited Celeste to join me for coffee. I was hoping to take a break from the vampire world and have some female bonding time, having realised how much I missed my close friendships before joining the Order. But my life had drastically changed, which made it harder to maintain the friendships that had previously meant the world to me. I found it challenging to discuss my current life and evade the truth, despite Aurora's constant – and judgmental - reminders. Thus, avoiding them all together seemed like the easiest option.

We bought drinks from a local cafe and wandered from the Manor down to New Farm Park, finding a spot on the grass near the rose garden under a large tree. We contented ourselves with a spot of people watching while we sat in companionable silence at first, just soaking up the fresh air and the chance not to have to think too much.

"How are you holding up?" Celeste finally broke the silence, sipping her coffee as she turned to look at me.

"I think I'm handling everything a lot better now. I don't think I've thought about how insane we must be for at least a week now, so that's an improvement." I smiled at her, and she laughed.

"Honestly, I've been in this life for nearly sixty years now, and it still strikes me as strange now and again. Thank goodness for Daniel." She smiled as she mentioned her husband's name, and it was nice to see her take a moment to appreciate having someone to share the insanity with.

"How long have you two been married?" Although we had been making small steps towards a friendship, I still didn't know much about her life before meeting her, and I thought it was time I started to change that. Her smile grew, appreciating the hand of friendship that I was extending.

"We've been married for fifty-four years. Daniel was already in the Order when I turned twenty-five. At first, it was just flirting, but one day, he saved me from a nightwalker attack, and after that, it just all fell into place for us. No one talks about it much, but it is rare for Order members to marry. So what we have is something we work hard not to take for granted." I nodded, having observed that most of the other Order members avoided developing romantic entanglements with others.

"Is there a reason why others tend to avoid becoming involved? I would have thought it would be easier than developing relationships outside of the Order. Especially with our longer life spans and all the secrets we keep?" It was the first time I'd had a chance to ask someone these questions, and I wondered if Celeste had ever discussed her relationship with Katyana through their many years of friendship. I tried not to focus on the tightness in my chest at the memory of our friend, the pain of her loss still raw.

"Honestly, I think it's because they are scared that if the relationship ends, it's a long time to live alongside that person. And with our heightened sex drives, quite a few prefer not to form attachments and focus on the physical aspect." She shrugged, but something she said caught my attention as I nodded.

"When you say we have heightened sex drives..." I had never really been one to discuss my sex life in depth with friends, but her words had touched on a subject that had been in the back of my mind for months.

"Ah, so you've noticed that, huh?" She said with a bit of a smirk, and I blushed. She reached over and squeezed my knee. "I didn't understand what was happening at first, but in my first few years within the Order, my sex drive rocketed, and Daniel and I were at it like rabbits. Even now, after fifty-plus years of marriage, I still can't get enough of that man."

"Why is that? The high sex drive, I mean?" She took another sip of coffee before answering my tentative question.

"The theory is that it's because of the magic that runs through each of us in different ways and our connection to it. Sex, at its basic level, is all about furthering the human race, and our role in the Order is to protect humanity. But honestly, I think it's because sex is all about pleasure, and the magic in our blood heightens so many of our senses, so why not that as well?" I let her words sink in. It made sense, and it felt good to have some answers as to why I couldn't get enough when I was with Liam.

"So, is that why I seem so much more... receptive..." I didn't know how to talk about this easily, and Celeste laughed now, seeing my discomfort.

"You mean, is that why you can have so many orgasms in one session that you feel like you might combust?" She had no such issue with putting into words how my body was put through the wringer each time I was with Liam. I nodded, taking a quick mouthful of coffee to hide my embarrassment. "Well, Liam's exquisite looks and amazing body aside, yes, that is why you're able to orgasm at the lightest touch. Sometimes, I'm convinced all it would take is a certain look from Daniel, and I'll explode. It also helps that Liam has had so many years to truly hone his craft." She grinned, and I huffed a little. I didn't need to be reminded how many women he had undoubtedly been with over the centuries. She gave my knee another squeeze.

Even without the ability to read my mind, I sensed that she understood my feelings on the matter.

"You've known Liam a long time. Has he ever..." I wasn't sure what I wanted to ask, and it felt like I was betraying Liam just having this conversation. Celeste noted my hesitation and cocked her head to the side.

"I've known Liam for a long time. Almost an entire lifetime, really. And in that time, I have *never* seen him like this. Even when he had that brief dalliance with Alana, he has always been all about the job. He has friendships with us all, but since you've become a part of the family, it's like it's awakened something inside him. And I love that he has found that with you. You both deserve happiness after the grief you've both experienced." I felt something inside of me uncoil at her words, as though I'd been holding on to a fear that what was developing between myself and Liam was just a passing phase for him. I blinked back a tear and smiled at Celeste.

"Thank you... I hadn't realised how much I needed to hear that." She reached over and gave me a one-armed hug.

"You've been through a lot in your short life, Isolde. And we have no idea what this life has in store for any of us. You have a lot of responsibility that has been put on your shoulders, but don't forget to allow yourself to have moments of joy. It's those moments that make the hard times worth it. It's all we can try to strive for. Hold on to those beautiful moments. It's what will get you through the tough ones." Her words hit hard, and without thinking, I turned to her and wrapped her in a tight hug.

"Thank you," I whispered, and she squeezed me back.

"Any time, Isolde. We are all here for you, don't forget that. You just need to let us in."

We passed another hour chatting about everything and nothing all at once, and I felt lighter than I had in months when I returned to the Manor. Almost as though I was finding myself once again. And I liked that feeling very much.

That night, I sat in my meditation corner and began clearing my mind, staring at the flame once more. I'd decided to step up the exploration of my abilities, and Liam sat quietly in the armchair near the bed, reading a book, although I wasn't sure how much he was taking in, as I could feel his eyes on me constantly. I'd told him I wanted to attempt to connect with the blossoming telekinetic abilities I'd noticed in brief moments where my emotions were heightened. This had sparked his own interest as well, but now I was finding that interest distracting.

"It's tough to concentrate when you keep staring at me all the time." I continued to stare at the flame as I spoke, and he closed the book, getting to his feet.

"Do you want me to go?"

"No. I want you to come closer." I didn't know what made me say that, but I smiled as he walked over, sitting behind me. He reached forward and lifted me into his lap, and I laughed as he nuzzled my neck.

"Is this close enough, Isolde?" His breath tickled my neck as he whispered in my ear, and I pushed aside the wave of arousal that threatened to overwhelm me. Any time we were close like this, I found it difficult to resist him.

"Perfect. Now be quiet." I tried to speak authoritatively, and he kissed my neck softly before running his hands down my sides, circling my waist, and holding me close. When I was confident that he would behave himself, I returned my concentration to the flame before me, and eventually, our breathing settled into an identical rhythm. I willed every candle in the room to light up and worked on bringing the flames together, practising the magic that I had perfected now before willing them back to their respective candles. Liam remained still, allowing me to play with my power without distraction, offering me the support of his presence and nothing more. Taking a deep breath, I turned my focus now to the book that Liam had left on the chair across the room. At first, nothing happened. But I was learning that I needed to find the correct commands within myself to give direction to the magic that flowed through me.

Perhaps reading my thoughts and intentions, Liam gently ran his hand down my arm, taking my hand and raising it. He held both our arms outstretched, reaching towards the book, which began to move in place a little. I felt power begin to tingle through me, almost as though it flowed from his body into mine. Closing my eyes, I followed his silent direction, keeping my arm outstretched towards the chair.

Rise.

I felt Liam's intake of breath, his chest pressed hard against my back, and I opened my eyes slowly. The magic flowed through both of us as though we were one body and mind, and I could feel it crackling through the air around us. From how Liam was tensing behind me, I could tell that he felt it too. The book had risen in the air and was lazily turning clockwise. Together, almost as though we could anticipate each other's movements, we slowly turned our hands and beckoned the book closer. I watched with fascination as it floated gently towards us before finally lowering into my lap. Liam returned his arm to my waist and squeezed me tightly as I stared at the book in amazement. I could still feel the air humming with the shared power that flowed through us both.

"Is this normal?" I could barely utter the words, as I feared it would shatter the energy that bound us together. He reached around and gently placed his hand on my chin, tilting my head, and I twisted slowly in his lap until I could look into his eyes.

"That was the first time I've been able to tap into any physical power. I've never felt an energy like this before," he whispered, his words filled with awe. I leaned into him, pressing my lips softly to his. I was afraid to make sudden movements, not wanting this feeling to end. I could tell that Liam felt the same way, as his actions remained slow and gentle, sliding his other hand up my back and tangling his fingers in my hair, holding my head there as we continued the kiss. This wasn't about sex, I realised. It was about the feelings that had been building for months, and I allowed myself to get lost in this perfect moment, simply enjoying the closeness and the power that swirled around us. I'd never felt so connected to another person; it was like a drug. I could get used to this.

Moving at a snail's pace, I turned myself until I straddled his lap, my dress riding up my thighs. Slowly, he ran his hands down my back until both rested on my hips, and I allowed him to pull me closer. I expected the magic to disappear entirely as clothes were shed and we brought our bodies together. Instead, the magic flowed back and forth between us, shattering through our bodies over and over as we moved against each other. It was a long time before either of us was able to move afterwards, our bodies depleted by both the magic and the pleasure that had rippled through us so intensely.

Eventually, we gathered our strengths and dressed once more, but I felt more aware of him than ever, and I could tell he felt the same. It was like he had become my other half, and I was aware of every breath and heartbeat that flowed through him. It was hours before the sensation dissipated, and I wondered what it all meant.

Chapter Twenty

A FEW WEEKS PASSED, and before I'd realised, it was a week from Christmas. Time had begun to move so quickly that I hadn't even known it was the holiday season. Christmas in my family was usually a huge family gathering, generally at New Farm Park, as none of our homes were big enough to accommodate a family of our size. When I had mentioned the holiday to Liam, he'd looked surprised, evidently having forgotten about it himself.

"What do you normally do?" I asked him as I settled on my bed at home, surrounded by the presents I had just bought on my frantic shopping trip. He stood in the doorway, staring at the mountain of gifts in amazement.

"Um... it's not usually a big thing amongst the Order. We might have lunch or something, but it's just another day for us." He shrugged, and I looked at him in surprise.

"We don't celebrate Christmas?!" I was alarmed. Coming from a big family with children around all the time, Christmas was my favourite time of the year. Discovering that I was expected to spend the next few centuries amongst people who barely acknowledged it was pretty disheartening.

"I guess when you see as many Christmases as we do, you just get over it after a while." He said it so flippantly, and I felt my heart sink momentarily before shaking my head firmly.

"Well, this year, we are celebrating Christmas. God knows we need some cheer with all the crap we've been through lately." I went back to my task of wrapping the gifts before me. Liam sat down in my overstuffed armchair, shaking his head, obviously thinking I would have no luck getting everyone to join in.

But I proved him wrong. The following day, I approached Patrice with my plan for a giant Christmas feast, and her face lit up with excitement as she agreed it was just what we needed.

"I'll organise everything! Leave it to me." I was relieved to hear her say that. After my initial announcement, I hadn't been entirely sure of how I would pull off arranging something at such short notice. I had come to the realisation that I would need to make an appearance at four separate Christmas celebrations. Between my immediate and extended family, seeing Will's parents, and now gathering with the Order, that was a lot of Christmas Cheer to spread around.

I roped Liam into staying at my parents' house on Christmas Eve, figuring it was time for him to meet the rest of my family. I hadn't seen most of my sisters in months, which was something I'd realised with disbelief. Since finding out about my apparent destiny, I hadn't had much opportunity to spend time with them, something that they had all started to notice.

As I walked through the front door with Liam in tow, I was set upon by a gang of over-excited children, all under the age of six. Liam looked a little panicked at seeing this many children, but I gathered as many of them to me as possible in a giant group hug, overjoyed to see them all again. As the night wore on, I noticed how uncomfortable Liam was. I was so used to seeing him around the other members of the Order that I hadn't stopped to think about what it would be like to be surrounded by people he didn't know. As most of my family had never met him, and some did not even know of his existence, they were all a little taken aback by him, and Liam could no doubt hear the confusion in their thoughts. No one had expected me to move on from Will so quickly, and although they all tried to talk to and include him, it was a relief for both of us when we retired to my old room.

"I'm sorry," I said as he wrapped me in his arms once the door was closed. We leaned into the embrace, drawing comfort from each other.

"It's okay. I understand where they are all coming from." Liam rested his cheek against the top of my head. It was the first time in my whole life that I felt disconnected from my family, and I realised with a jolt that this was how it would be for the rest of my life. At least whilst my family was still around. It was something I had avoided thinking about until now. I would outlive the rest of my family... Unless I were killed in some violent way first, I would watch as my family grew old without me... It was not a very comforting thought.

By the time Christmas Day drew to a close, I felt emotionally drained. Breakfast with my family had been just as strained as the night before. So much so that I let Liam off the hook with the extended family in the afternoon, and he returned to the Manor with relief.

Lunch with Will's family only lasted an hour and a half as an air of despair hung over everyone. We all felt Will's absence, and I hated that I knew what he had become whilst they believed he was buried in the ground. His parents and sister didn't mention my new boyfriend once, but I could feel the judgement, and it was a relief to leave. Something else to feel guilty about, even though I knew I had done nothing wrong.

The family BBQ, which I usually looked forward to, made me feel like a stranger amongst people I had known my entire life. I realised everything was different now. No one else had changed; it was just me. I felt as though I was acting out a part in a play. I knew all the lines by heart, but there was no feeling behind it anymore.

I pulled my car into the underground garage of the Manor and sat for a moment, listening as the engine ticked away, cooling down. After the day's strain, the last thing I felt like was another gathering of people, and I wish I hadn't thought to suggest it. I dragged my feet as I stepped into the elevator, but when the doors opened, I gaped in shock at the scene before me. It looked as though Christmas had blown up in the front foyer. It was covered in decorations that put Santa and his elves to shame. A tree stood from floor to ceiling, and the lights twinkled prettily from amongst its branches.

I stood staring at it all in wonder as Liam appeared at my side, a broad grin on his face as he took in my expression.

"Did Patrice do all of this?" I found I was unable to tear my eyes away from the decorations.

"We all did. After everything last night and this morning, I thought you could use a bit of Christmas cheer, and Patrice was already organising a 'feast to die for', as she describes it, so we thought we would get into the Christmas Spirit. Hence the snow." He pointed upwards, and my mouth fell open to see snow falling, though it disappeared before it reached us. I looked at Liam in stunned silence, unable to take it all in.

"Most of us come from the northern hemisphere. We prefer a white Christmas to the searing heat," Celeste remarked as she came down the stairs. She was dressed in a beautiful red and white dress, and I looked down at my shorts and t-shirt, suddenly very aware of how under-dressed I was.

"If you go to your room, you'll find something that will make you feel less conspicuous." Celeste smiled warmly, and I grinned back in appreciation. I was so grateful for the friendship that had developed between us, and I hugged her quickly. I headed to my room and gaped at the beautiful dress and matching shoes that were laid out on the bed. Liam came into the room behind me and wrapped his arms around my waist. I turned in his arms and hugged him hard as tears welled in my eyes.

"Thank you so much for all of this," I whispered into his chest, overwhelmed.

"You're welcome," he whispered back, kissing the top of my head. He left me to get ready, and I sat on the bed, staring at the dress. It was an ice blue and white, one-shoulder number in a shimmery material. The lengths that had been taken to ensure that I had at least one happy moment at

Christmas made me realise something. Although I felt disconnected from the family I had been born to, I had a new family now. One that I didn't have to lie to or keep secrets from. It made me realise that I was truly home.

After a quick shower and slipping into the dress, I entered the dining room downstairs. The lights had been switched off, and candles illuminated the room. The table was laid out beautifully, and I felt a lump form in my throat as I looked around the room, taking it all in. I slid into the chair next to Liam, and he sat back in his seat, slinging his arm casually along the back of mine. There was an air of excitement in the room as everyone gathered around, and it was so lovely to share this moment with them all.

That night, after several hours of laughter and great food, I slept in Liam's arms in my bed at the Manor for the first time. The dinner had been perfect, and it had had the effect that Patrice had desired, a much-needed tender moment amongst all the grief we'd been feeling lately.

Initially, my sleep was dreamless, a first for a long time.

Then Alana appeared. Looking around, I realised we were back in the abandoned warehouse. This time, when her lips moved, I could hear her.

"Isolde, I have to tell you something," she said urgently, and I searched her face for any of the hate that used to be there. All I could see was fear.

"Alana, what is it? Why did you come here that day?" I motioned to our setting. In the back of my mind, I knew it was a dream, but it seemed so real. Alana's skin was deathly pale, with dark rings around her sunken eyes.

"Something is coming. And it's not good. You will not be safe. No one will be."

"Alana, you're not making any sense. What do you know?" Alana looked frustrated.

"You're not listening! Something is coming!" She snapped, and I saw a flash of the Alana that I used to know. "It is not just you that they want. And you won't be able to save your sister." She started to fade before me.

"Wait! Which sister?! Why do they want one of my sisters?!" I rushed towards her as if grabbing her would make her stay solid, to keep her from fading away further. My hand went straight through her as I grabbed for her wrist. Before she disappeared completely, her lips moved again, and I strained to hear her whisper... And then I woke up, sitting bolt upright in bed.

"Hey, hey. Isolde, it's okay!" I realised I had yelled Alana's name as I had woken abruptly, and Liam sat up next to me as I tried to stop myself from hyperventilating.

"Did you see her?!" I asked stupidly before remembering that Alana had been in my dream, not reality. Liam surprised me, however, when he nodded. "Were you in my dream too?" I didn't remember seeing him there.

"No, I could see it in your mind, the same as your thoughts."

"What do you think she meant?" I asked, already on my feet. We both threw our clothes on haphazardly.

"I'm not sure. I wish she hadn't been so cryptic." Liam followed me downstairs to the communications room, where, as usual, Patrice was in discussions with some of the Elders in various locations worldwide via the computer.

"Isolde? Liam?" Patrice jumped as she turned off the monitor abruptly, which struck me as odd, but I had more important matters to consider.

We filled Patrice in on Alana's message, and she looked at me with great concern.

"Do you know why she knew where to find Adam?" Patrice asked, and both Liam and I shook our heads.

"I asked her, but she just said something was coming." I could feel myself becoming more and more frustrated by the whole situation. Liam touched my shoulder and squeezed it reassuringly from behind me.

"It will be okay. We'll work it out, won't we?" He looked at Patrice pointedly, and she nodded distractedly.

"Of course... Of course, we will! We've already got people watching your family, keeping them safe."

Patrice hugged me, no doubt attempting to offer some reassurance. However, something felt wrong. Why did it feel like more was happening here than what I was being told?

Chapter Twenty-One

OVER THE NEXT SEVERAL days, I went through the motions of what had become my life. By day, I continued privately working on my abilities and training with Liam. In the evenings, I was a part of the various teams dispatched to keep order in the supernatural world. Sleep was often a last priority when I fell into bed, tangled in the sheets with Liam, either at home or in one of our rooms at the Manor.

However, things had changed over the past few months. Since my fighting abilities had become so much more advanced than all the others, I was no longer just one of the team. I was the main fighter. For the first time, my abilities were being utilised, and sometimes I was separated from Liam, each being sent off on different missions where our abilities were more helpful. I found it disconcerting on the missions where we were separated, as I had grown so used to his constant presence, and I missed him, even though we were only apart for a few hours.

On New Year's Eve, I was sent out with one of the teams tasked with monitoring the crowds at South Bank. Because it was expected to be so busy, our numbers had been doubled, and for the first time, I learnt that not all members of the Order of the Dragon were seventh sons and daughters. Because numbers in the recent decades had started to dwindle, they had decided to start using outsiders as well; those who, due to their encounters with the supernatural, chose to fight alongside us. I discovered that Megan, the real estate agent that Aurora and I had dealt with, was one of these people. I had been surprised when she had come forward and sheepishly shook my hand again, apologising for her part in the deception at the time. Although these people were aware of our dangerous world, they did not live as we did, usually living relatively everyday lives, helping only when necessary. It felt strange to be discussing the realm of the supernatural with people who had not been forced into it as I had been. I envied their freedom to choose. Even though I had accepted this life for myself finally, I still envied others for their freedom to live under the illusion of normalcy.

I mingled with the crowds at South Bank as the time drew closer to midnight. The worst year of my life was ending, and I was happy to see the back of it. Liam was also stationed somewhere else in the crowd, and I wished he was nearby. So far, there had been no sightings of any vampires, and I hoped it would be an uneventful evening. Moving along with the flow of the crowd, I eventually found myself on the spot where Will and I had shared our first kiss. It had taken me a little while to understand why I had a strange sense of déjà vu, and once I had put the connection together, I wished I hadn't. In my mind, I was swept back to that night. It had been a much quieter night, and it had been just the two of us, sitting on the garden wall, watching as the City Cats came and went from the ferry terminal. Everything about that night had been perfect, as most of our relationship had appeared to be, and being forced to remember it was painful. As I was lost in my memories, I didn't realise the countdown to midnight had started. The next thing I knew, the people around me were joyfully exchanging New Year's greetings as the fireworks began. With tears in my eyes, I watched the impressive display above me as couples all around shared their first kisses of the new year. I tried to imagine that Liam was standing beside me, wrapping his arms around me in his usual way, keeping me safe. A tap on my shoulder brought a smile to my lips, and I turned, expecting to see Liam.

"Happy New Year, Isolde." Will looked so much like his former self that, for a moment, I was speechless. He made no goading comments or nasty remarks. He just stood before me, his crooked half-smile playing over his lips.

Then he kissed me. At first, I kissed him back out of habit and a longing for the past. But then reality set in. I used my extra strength and shoved him away, and he groaned as I glared at him.

"Get the hell away from me," I hissed, trying to sound like I was not being torn apart inside.

"And here I thought we were sharing a moment. It's not nice to lead boys on, Isolde." And there it was, the creature that Will had become, which made it much easier to do what I did next. I brought my knee up sharply between his legs, momentarily stunning him. By this time, Liam had joined me. Not far behind him, I saw Daniel and Megan shoving their way through the crowd.

As Will straightened up again, a few people around us started to notice the commotion and were watching us rather than the fireworks. There was nothing we could do but glare at each other, as Will appeared to be alone, and we couldn't draw attention to ourselves any more than we already had. Will growled and faded back into the crowd, and I felt my legs start to give way under me as Daniel and Megan trailed after him to ensure no harm came to anyone in the crowd.

It was the first time I had come face to face with Will since he had followed me home that night, and although I'd moved on with Liam, it was still heart-wrenching to see the creature he had become. Liam guided me to a nearby bench, which had been recently vacated so that the former occupants could get a better view of the fireworks. I cursed my weakness when it came to Will. I could stake any other vampire without a second glance, but when confronted with Will, I froze.

"Are you okay?" Liam held my face in his hands, inspecting me as though he thought I was about to pass out. I looked up at him for a moment before answering.

"I am now." He breathed out, pulling me into a tight embrace, almost like he feared losing me. And I realised that was precisely what he was feeling. He had heard everything going on in my mind and had no doubt seen the kiss. I knew it would have hurt him. The idea of losing me was one of his deepest fears, and seeing me kissing Will, even if it was just a momentary slip, would have just about killed him.

"I'm so sorry," I whispered into his ear, and he held me tighter. After a moment, he drew back and looked down at me.

"I'm just sorry that he was the one who kissed you at midnight and not me," he said, attempting to push it all aside. I knew it was an act but decided to play along for now.

"I'm sure it's midnight somewhere in the world right now." I leaned into him, and he kissed me hungrily. There was something more intense about this kiss than any we had shared before. Almost as though he was trying to erase any memory of the earlier kiss with Will and compete with the past.

Later that night, as we drove back to the Manor along with the rest of the team, I stared silently out the window, trying not to be affected by the events of the evening. Everything in my head was a mess, and I knew that Liam was trying not to hear what I was thinking, as thrown by his intense reaction as I was. So many times in the past few weeks, things had shifted between us. We were relaxed, at peace with each other. We had enjoyed the quiet times and spent many a morning lying in each other's arms. However, there had been brief moments when things had been so intense that I had almost feared how we hungered for each other, especially after evenings spent hunting for nightwalkers, adrenaline coursing through us. In all my years with Will, we had never had a passion like that, and I was unsure how to handle it. I had never envied those women who seemed almost addicted to their partners, preferring the ease of my relationship with Will. They fought so passionately and often would be sent on massive crying jags that I could not handle watching, believing their relationships to be toxic and unhealthy. But I had come to understand that I had been playing it safe with Will. I had loved him with all my heart, but it was only now that I realised something was missing. Something I didn't even know that I had wanted.

After the teams debriefed, I made my way up to my room alone, hoping that a warm shower would calm the turmoil in my mind.

As I came out of the bathroom wrapped in a towel, I wasn't surprised to find Liam sitting on the edge of the bed, staring at his hands. I stopped a few feet from him, waiting for him to speak first.

"I'm sorry," he said quietly, still not looking up at me. "I don't know what I was thinking."

"I'm sorry that I made you feel that way," I said, knowing that my actions tonight were not blameless. No matter what occurred after, I still allowed Will to kiss me, even if just for a moment. Liam looked up at that quickly, the hurt and even a little anger evident in his eyes.

"Seeing you kissing him... It hurt. And I know you're not over him, and maybe you never will be." He looked down at his hands again, and I moved closer to him now, though still out of his immediate reach.

"A part of me will always belong to him. He was my first love. He was safe, the sort of man most parents dream their daughters will end up with." I watched as Liam tightened his hand reflexively into a fist, still not looking up at me. "However, I never would have had a life with Will. I see that now in a way that I never saw before." I waited for Liam to look up at me again, and he eventually did so, reluctantly. "I'm never going to be safe. The life that I was born for doesn't leave room for safe. No matter what happened to Will, I never would have been able to marry him, to live the life I had believed I wanted. I was always destined for this life of constant chaos and danger. He could never have known me the way that you do." As I said this, I moved to stand immediately in front of Liam, and he began tracing his fingers over the pattern of my towel along my hip.

"I love you." He gripped my hip at those words, and I heard his sharp intake of breath, causing me to repeat them before I continued. "I love you. In a way that is so different to how I loved him that I know this is the reality. The life that I had with him was just an illusion." It was the first time that either of us had said the words to each other, and I felt my heart beat hard in my chest as I waited for his response.

In one swift movement, he pulled me forward so that I straddled his lap and kissed me fiercely, pulling my towel off me in the process. I kissed him back just as hungrily, wanting him more than ever. He began moving me fast against him, and the desire to be closer to each other was overriding everything else. I felt how hard he was against me, and I quickly undid his fly while he worked his fingers inside of me, readying me for him. He hissed as I moved his hand away, lowering myself onto him and rocking my hips, taking him all in.

"I love you too, Isolde." I ground myself against him as he breathed the words, revelling in hearing them said out loud. As he kissed my neck, I found that I craved something more from him. Following the direction of my thoughts, he pulled back, surprised. I moved my hair to the side and almost unconsciously tilted my head.

Yes. The consent that I gave him through my thoughts was all the invitation that he needed, and I gasped with unexpected pain, quickly giving way to pleasure, as he bit into my neck. It was unlike anything I had ever imagined, and I lost myself in the moment, understanding now why others had asked for this. Perhaps even begged for it.

Moving quickly against him, his hands guiding me up and down, with his mouth at my throat, I felt the most explosive orgasm of my life shatter through me, taking him over the edge as well, and we collapsed back on the bed together, completely spent.

Later, as we lay naked beside each other, our legs tangled together, I sensed a sadness in Liam as he stroked his hand gently up and down my back. I raised myself onto my elbow, looking into his eyes as I wondered at the melancholy behind them.

"I had a vision." He brushed my hair back over my shoulder, his fingers tracing lightly over the bite mark on my neck, knowing I had been about to ask what was wrong.

"From my blood?" I hadn't thought about that in the moment, having been so lost in the act of loving him. He nodded. "What did you see?" I wasn't sure I wanted an answer, knowing it likely wasn't good.

"I saw your future." I felt a shudder go down my spine, and he pulled me closer to him. "You were a vampire." I realised that I wasn't surprised by this, almost as though a part of me had expected that, at some stage, I would become a vampire.

"Was I a nightwalker or a daywalker?"

"You were kissing Will, so I'm guessing you were a nightwalker." He couldn't bring himself to look at me, and I knew that, for some reason, he was blaming himself. I placed a hand on the side of his face.

"Hey. Look at me." He did, slowly. "Just because you had a vision, it doesn't mean that it's going to be true. We are forewarned now so that we can stop it." I could sense his disbelief as he surveyed my face.

"That's not how it works." He gazed into my eyes sadly.

"Have all of your visions come true in the past?" I was a little thrown by the resignation in his eyes.

"Most of them have, yes."

"Most, but not all of them, right?" I was clinging to that little glimmer of hope.

"We have managed to change the outcome of a few, but that chance is scarce. And we don't know the circumstances of how you change. I can't guarantee I can save you when I don't know what will happen." I looked down at him, concerned at how he always took the world on his shoulders.

"Liam, I have faith in you. I know that we will stop this. But, if a time ever comes when it looks like that might be my future, I want you to promise me something." He looked almost fearful. As if he knew what I was about to ask, which he probably did. "I want you to promise that if I am bitten, and it looks as though I am going to become a nightwalker, I want you to be the one who makes sure that I come back as a daywalker... or not at all." Liam started shaking his head, but I stilled it with my hand on his chin. "Promise me."

"Isolde, you don't know what you're asking me to do." His voice shook, but I held his gaze.

"Promise me." Holding my gaze for the longest time, clearly wrestling with his thoughts, it was a long time before he breathed.

"I promise." His words were barely a whisper, and I knew that promising either to turn me or end my life was killing him, but I needed to ensure that I would not become a monster. I bent to kiss him softly, and he pulled me on top of him, needing to hold me close, knowing that, at least for the moment, now was not the time to worry about the future.

The next day, I decided to make an appearance at home, if for no other reason than to get some clothes. I hadn't spoken to Aurora properly in weeks and I missed my sister. I hated the way things had become so strained between us. Where once we had told each other everything, now there was silence in our home, when I bothered to be there at all.

I let myself in the front door, before coming to a stop on the threshold, surprised to see a suitcase beside the couch.

"What's going on?" I asked as Aurora came down the hall.

"I've got that conference in Sydney to organise," Aurora replied, and I looked at her questioningly. She laughed bitterly.

"Of course, you wouldn't remember." She rolled her eyes. "I told you about this months ago. Work is sending me to run a conference between our offices here and the ones in the US." I remembered now. Aurora had been so excited when she told me, having been given an opportunity that could very well see her get a promotion at the company where she worked as an events coordinator. I kicked myself mentally for forgetting that it was in January. She was due to get back the day before our birthday. I felt my heart begin to race as panic set in.

"When do you leave?"

"I'm leaving now. So, sorry you forgot. I know how much you would have loved to have come and seen me off on what could be the biggest opportunity of my career," she said sarcastically, and I bit back a retort. There was no use in allowing her to get to me, to let her see how much the deterioration of our relationship was upsetting me.

"Well, have a safe trip." I brushed past her, but she caught my arm, sighing.

"I'm sorry, that was mean and uncalled for." I looked at her momentarily, waiting to see where this was going.

"After Jacob picks me up next week, we should go out. I know Ainslie has been dying for a catch-up, and it would be good to do things like we used to... I've missed you," she said sadly, and I smiled.

"That sounds really good. I've missed you too." I hugged her tightly as a tear slipped down my cheek. I knew she was crying too, and we both laughed.

"So soppy." She kissed me on the cheek. "See you in ten days."

I waved goodbye as Jacob backed out of the driveway, watching Aurora wave back from the passenger seat. As soon as they were out of sight, I rang the Manor and was reassured by Celeste that Colin was already on it. At least they hadn't forgotten that Aurora was leaving town for a few days.

Somehow, my involvement in the fire at my old townhouse had finally been discovered. I knew the balance of power in the Order was shifting, with myself slowly rising to the top. As far as they were aware, though, I had used the spell book that I had taken from the Manor. My use of magic that night had everyone on edge around me—everyone except Liam.

Patrice pulled me aside when I left Liam's room the following day.

"You should not have performed magic without the proper training, Isolde. Don't you realise the danger you put yourself in?" The concern in her eyes was tinged with fear, though I did not know if it was *for* me or *of* me. The powers everyone had expected of me had been slow to arrive, but now that they were starting to present themselves, people were beginning to question whether it was a good thing. I learnt that no one else had been able to use magic as quickly as I had, having gone through years of training to perform simple glamours. To perform cloaking and containment spells with the power I had done and control them was unheard of. And that was without them being aware of my fire abilities.

For his part, Liam just went on as usual. He had known this was coming, had seen it in his visions as he had fed on me several times while we had sex. Neither of us had shared the knowledge of these visions or my growing powers with the rest of the Order, the doubts about their intentions still holding us back. And I had to admit; it felt good to be the one with the knowledge for once.

Chapter Twenty-Two

THE DAY AURORA WAS due back, I headed home in the afternoon, expecting to find Aurora and Jacob. I had been waiting to hear from Aurora since she had left, but there had been silence, although Jacob had received text messages sporadically. I had hoped she was just busy and worked hard to convince myself that we would have heard if anything bad had happened.

I unlocked the door and dropped my bag on the floor. Liam remained in the car, having just taken a call from Celeste as we pulled up.

"Aura? Jacob? You guys here?"

"Hey." Jacob walked out of the kitchen, freshly made sandwich in hand.

"Where's Aurora?" I realised it was just the two of us at home. Jacob looked at me in surprise.

"What do you mean? You were meant to pick her up." Jacob looked at me, confused.

"No, she told me you were picking her up," I said slowly, and he shook his head.

"She texted me this morning saying she'd asked you to pick her up. Something about wanting some girl time." He shrugged.

"Jacob... Aurora never texted me. We haven't had girl time in a long time." I was worried now, though I tried not to show it. I grabbed my bag and rummaged around for my mobile as Jacob looked on in confusion.

"Yeah, I thought that was weird too." I started dialling Aurora's number. It went straight to voicemail. "Maybe her flight was delayed, and she's still on the plane?" Jacob was trying to sound optimistic whilst I was starting to lean towards blind panic.

"Yeah, maybe..." I walked back out the front, already dialling the Manor's number. As I raised the phone to my ear, Liam appeared at my side, no doubt alerted by my frantic thoughts. I hit the red button on my phone as I took in the worried look on his face.

"Have they heard anything from Colin?" I asked Liam in a low voice as I heard Jacob leaving a voicemail for Aurora in the other room. Colin was the Protector assigned to follow Aurora on her trip to Sydney.

"No... And they're worried." I could feel panic rising, and Liam placed a steadying hand on my shoulder, squeezing gently.

"Hey... She'll be okay." I wasn't convinced, and he knew it.

"Jacob, I'm going to the airport." I grabbed a copy of Aurora's itinerary from the coffee table. I wrote her flight number on my hand, struggling to ignore the million and one scenarios going through my head, primarily so Liam wouldn't hear. Car keys still in hand, Liam laced his fingers through mine, bringing my hand to his lips as we headed out the door.

"Wait, I'm coming too." Already at the car, we both turned to see Jacob closing the door behind him before jogging down the stairs. I exchanged a worried glance with Liam, but we couldn't think of a good enough reason to tell him why he shouldn't join us without raising suspicion.

As Liam drove, I sat silently in the front passenger seat, every possible scenario going through my head. Liam reached over and squeezed my hand again. No doubt, Jacob thought I was overreacting. And maybe I was. However, if Jacob knew what I knew, he would be freaking out too. Liam put his foot on the brake as the light turned red, just as my phone rang, and I jumped before ripping it out of my pocket. The number was blocked. I prayed it was my twin.

"Aurora?"

"Hey, sorry. My phone died." Relief flooded through me.

"That's okay. Who is meant to be picking you up?" I shot the guys a thumbs up, and Jacob fell back against the back seat with a relieved sigh.

"Well, I was going to text you and ask, but my phone died, and I missed my flight. I figure this is all a sign to stay down here a couple more days. Sarah and Ian broke up, and she desperately needs some girl time." It seemed like a typical Aurora thing to do, but something nagged at me. The light turned green, and Liam started to change direction before we got stuck on the bridge over the river with no way to turn around.

"Are you sure?"

"Yeah, I'll be home Monday. I'll text you my flight details, although Jacob should be able to pick me up." After another few moments of conversation, I passed the phone back to Jacob and breathed out, willing myself to relax. The nagging feeling in the back of my mind was still there. Something wasn't right. Aurora hadn't even mentioned the fact that by delaying her trip, we'd be spending our birthday apart for the first time in our lives.

"She'll be fine, Isolde." Liam looked at me earnestly as Jacob spoke to Aurora. I wondered if Jacob had noticed that Liam had not looked at the road once since she rang.

"I'll feel better once she's home." I stopped talking as Jacob returned my phone to me, and that was all we could say on the topic.

"You had me freaking out, Isolde! Don't do that again," Jacob said angrily from the backseat, and I absently apologised, not even really listening.

"Well, I guess it's just you and Ainslie tonight." Jacob's words drifted through my reverie.

"Huh? Oh, yeah. I guess so. That's okay. I'm sure we can still get up to enough mischief without Aurora." I grinned at Liam, who rolled his eyes. He had yet to meet Ainslie, but he'd seen me the night before my twenty-fifth birthday and knew my intoxicated state was partly due to Ainslie's influence. Mostly her influence, really. She did like to party.

I am going to try Colin again as soon as I get her home. Something isn't right.

Upon hearing this, I looked sharply over at Liam, only to discover that he hadn't spoken. I stared at him, unable to understand what had just happened... Had I imagined those words?

Why is she staring at me like that? Liam looked at me searchingly, and I felt my mouth drop open. The stricken look on my face concerned him even further.

Because I've just heard everything you were thinking! I almost screamed this aloud, though I knew the yelling in my head was enough for Liam. For his part, Liam did well not to drive off the road.

"Jacob, I'm going to head to Liam's for a bit. I'll see you later," I said as calmly as possible as Liam pulled up out the front of the house. I was unable to take my eyes off him, and the calm facade fell away once Jacob was inside.

"How the hell am I hearing your thoughts suddenly?" I knew it was pointless to have this conversation aloud, but I was desperately clinging to normal right now. Well, normal for us. "And hey, you were just telling me

everything was fine, but then you were thinking you need to call Colin!"
Liam pulled away from the curb.

"I don't know why you're suddenly hearing my thoughts... And you
can't get mad at me for agreeing with you!" Liam looked as freaked out as
I felt, so I forced myself to wait until we reached the Manor before asking
any more questions. It was tough not to respond to the questions Liam was
asking himself, and I admired that he got us back to the Manor without
crashing, as every thought he had caused him to look sheepishly at me.

"Is this what it's like to be you?" I asked, frustrated. I didn't like having someone else's thoughts in my head. Dealing with my own was hard
enough. Although I suppose it could be helpful when I didn't know what
he was thinking.

"No poking around up here." Liam tapped his temple.

"Hey! Now you know how it feels."

"I spend most of the time attempting to block out your thoughts to
respect your privacy." I shot him a shrewd look.

Yeah, right.

Liam laughed, shaking his head. We pulled into the basement car park
and headed into the house. I prepared myself for the onslaught of thoughts
as I entered. But it didn't come. The only thoughts in my head, other than
my own, were Liam's. I raised an eyebrow at him questioningly, but he
looked as confused as I felt, and his thoughts confirmed that he truly had
no answer as to what was going on between us.

"Isolde? I thought you headed home for the night?" Patrice came out of
the kitchen, her face showing her concern.

"We've got a bit of a problem... Potentially. And it would also seem that
another ability has emerged, though it's confusing." Liam trailed off, but I
could hear his train of thought continue. *Have we formed a bond?*

It was my turn to look confused. *Bond?*

"Come into the comms room." Patrice led us down the hall.

"Okay. The problem first." Patrice indicated that I should sit down at the large table in the middle of the room, but I was too agitated and started pacing instead.

"Apparently, no one has heard from Colin. Is that true?" Patrice looked concerned, though not surprised.

"Yes, it's true. We sent James to follow him up. Strangely, we haven't heard anything from him yet either, but he only left yesterday."

"Well, Aurora missed her flight. She texted Jacob to say I would pick her up from the airport, but I never spoke to her about it. Then she rang when we were on the way to the airport to say her phone had died." As I said it, I could tell I sounded crazy, but that didn't stop the nagging feeling.

"How did she sound? Did she say anything was wrong?" Patrice asked calmly, her tone of voice shifting to one of comfort.

"No... She said she missed her flight, which is unlike Aurora, and that her friend down there had broken up with her boyfriend and needed some girl time."

"And does that sound like Aurora?" Patrice's voice was kind, and I could tell she thought I was worrying too much.

"I guess... I just have this nagging feeling that something is wrong." I shrugged, unable to explain anything more than that. Put it down to twin intuition.

"I'm sure everything is okay. I will admit that it is strange that we've not heard from Colin, but James will let us know what he finds in Sydney. I promise to let you know if there is anything to worry about." I supposed that was the best I could hope for without sufficient evidence, so I nodded. It wasn't lost on me that they hadn't seen fit to inform me that they had lost contact with Colin in the first place.

"Now, this new ability?" Patrice raised an eyebrow at Liam.

"Well... It would appear that Isolde is now hearing thoughts." Patrice looked surprised.

"That's not the best part... It would seem I'm only hearing one person's thoughts." I looked sideways at Liam as he started thinking about the bond again.

"Yours?" Patrice looked at him again, not sounding the least bit surprised. Both Liam and I looked at her, confused.

"You were expecting this." Liam was clearly in Patrice's head, which I found frustrating.

"Why were you expecting this?" I almost felt like stamping my foot, and Liam grinned, amused by my mental tantrum.

"It's just a theory, but I've noticed how attuned you are to Liam and his abilities. Your fighting abilities, for one. They appeared when you were fighting alongside each other. Your ability to sense vampires is also a stronger form of one of Liam's natural daywalker abilities, not to mention your stronger visions... I don't know why you can only hear Liam's thoughts, though." This took me aback. I had not put this together before. I realised that this also explained so much more about the abilities that we were still yet to share with the Order. I noticed as Liam shifted beside me, prompting me to turn and study his face. He appeared to be focused on Patrice, deliberately avoiding making eye contact with me.

"I think I know why she can only hear me. I have heard of this connection amongst daywalkers. I met a couple about a century ago. They were connected in a way that I never thought possible. They were completely bonded, psychically. They could sense everything with each other, read each other's thoughts, often over great distances and even experience things through each other."

I looked at him searchingly.

"What formed that bond?"

"They had the bond before he turned... They believed they were soul-mates..." I noticed absently as Patrice slipped out of the room to give us some privacy while I processed this information.

"Soulmates... Is that even possible?" This threw me. Soulmates were not something I'd given much thought to before now.

"I don't know. But this does explain why I have a harder time tuning you out, unlike with everyone else." Liam leaned back against the table, crossing his arms, and looked at me searchingly.

"I just... Do you believe it now?" I didn't know why this affected me, and I could tell Liam was unsure of how to take my reaction.

"I know I love you. I don't know anything other than how I feel about you," he said, and I realised how my hesitation must look to him. I moved to stand in front of him and touched the side of his face.

"I love you too. I think a part of me always has. You've been in my dreams my whole life." I kissed him softly, and he pulled me closer, wrapping his arms around me as I melted into him, surrendering myself to him and his words in my mind.

I love you, too – more than I ever thought possible.

It's strange hearing your voice in my head while I'm kissing you...

Welcome to my world.

Later that evening, I sat at a table at the restaurant as I waited for Ainslie and played nervously with my water glass.

Okay, so, girl's night with Ainslie. I can't tell her anything about my life these days, and I suck at lying to her. We're going to have heaps to talk about.
I shot a sarcastic thumbs up at Liam, who sat at the bar with a book,

remaining in my line of sight as I sat waiting for Ainslie to show up. Liam held my gaze for a moment, a small smile playing across his lips.

Well, you know I will be around, so at least that's something...

This is distracting. I still haven't worked out how to get you out of my head.

Do you want to? I thought you enjoyed knowing what I was thinking for a change. I looked towards the door, making a show of waiting for Ainslie to appear. I could hear the teasing in his tone, but I had to admit that he had a point. That still didn't make it any less frustrating. I looked back at Liam, who was smirking, and I rolled my eyes.

"Hey!" I jumped as Ainslie appeared in front of me.

"Hey yourself!" I leapt up to hug her. "It's so good to see you!" I felt tears well in my eyes and blinked quickly, trying to keep my emotions in check. I hadn't seen Ainslie in months, which felt so strange. I used to spend all my time with Ainslie, Alex and Will, but ever since Will died and my world had gone topsy-turvey, I had seen Ainslie only a handful of times. She didn't even know about Liam. I really had become a terrible friend.

"I know. I can't believe how much we haven't seen each other. I was only saying to Alex how much I missed you the other day, and I thought, screw it, make a plan and force you to come! And then you called anyway!" It was such a typical Ainslie statement, and just like that, it was as if no time had passed between us.

We chatted easily over dinner, keeping the topic on Ainslie and her exploits. Then the waitress appeared with the cocktail menu.

"So, what about you?" Ainslie asked after we'd ordered (Pina Colada for me, Cosmo for Ainslie, just like always).

Crap. "What about me?" I drank the last mouthful of my wine, left over from my dinner, and hoped I sounded casual. My palms had started sweating.

"Well, we've talked about me for over an hour now. As much as I enjoy the time in the spotlight, we didn't come here just to talk about my fabulous life. So, spill, what have you been up to that's kept you so busy?"

Fighting vampires, regular battles with my undead fiancé, discovering that I'm destined to end a war that has been raging for millennia? I shot a glance at Liam as the answers I couldn't give raced through my mind, and he smiled back sympathetically.

"Um, nothing much. Working a lot?"

"I went into Opalescence about a month ago, and they said you'd quit not long after everything happened last year. Are you working somewhere new now?" Nothing was accusing about the questions, but I could feel my anxiety spike.

"Yeah, I started working as a research assistant at a place in the Valley," I blurted out without thinking, remembering the line I'd fed to my family months ago.

Nice. Liam looked impressed. He hadn't been there when I'd had that conversation with Aurora and my parents, and I hadn't thought about it in a long time.

Thanks, figured I'd stick with the original story.

I mean, it's sort of true... You do research a lot. He smirked, and I resisted the urge to roll my eyes.

"Cool! That sounds awesome! Researching what exactly?" I returned my attention to my friend.

"Just history stuff." I shrugged, hoping Ainslie, who had never been even slightly interested in history, wouldn't ask any further questions.

"So, is that where you met your boyfriend?" Ainslie asked casually, and I must have looked surprised because she grinned as I searched for a response.

"How did you – What boyfriend?" Too late. Ainslie laughed.

"Come on, Is. I know there's a guy. I do still see Aurora at parties, at the very least." I grimaced, and Ainslie patted my hand. "Don't worry; she only said good things."

Huh, that would have been interesting to hear. I had to agree with Liam's cynical comment there.

"Well, Aurora doesn't approve."

"Oh, bully to her. So, who is he?" Ainslie settled back in her seat, fishing for gossip.

"His name is Liam. He's Irish. We met at Uni." Might as well stick with the original lie.

"Cool. What's he like?" I knew we had Liam's full attention now as I saw him sit up straighter in his seat, listening intently for my response.

"Well, obviously, he's a great guy, or I wouldn't be with him." Ainslie nodded.

"And? Come on. I need more details than that, babe. How do I know this guy is good enough for my best friend?" I had forgotten how details-based Ainslie was.

"Like what?"

"Is he hot? Does he give you the warm fuzzies? You gotta give me something, woman." I laughed.

"Well, hot is an understatement. He is probably the hottest guy I have ever laid eyes on." I smiled, purposely not looking at Liam as I continued. "Very caring and protective. He's got the charm going, that's for sure. And definitely an old soul."

"Do you love him?" Ainslie asked quietly, almost sadly.

"Yes. Yes, I do love him. I didn't think I would find someone else after what happened with Will. But it's almost like I have known Liam my whole life. It's hard to explain."

I love you too. I must have looked lost in thought as I smiled at Liam over her shoulder because Ainslie reached across the table, holding my hand.

"I can't wait to meet him. He sounds like a special guy..."

"He is. He is incredibly protective. I feel safe with him."

"I guess with everything that has happened, that is very important." I smiled sadly at her words, struggling to keep my emotions in check once again.

"I never thought about it that way, but you're right." I pushed my chair back and stood up. "I'm just going to duck into the ladies. I'll be back in a second."

"Oh, hon, I'm sorry! I've put my foot in it, haven't I?" Ainslie looked stricken, but I waved her away.

"Don't be silly. Nature calls, that's all." I excused myself and wove through the tables to the hall leading to the bathrooms. I rounded the corner and walked straight into Liam, who folded me into his arms.

"Hi." It was all I needed to help me feel better, although something in the back of my mind caused me to feel slightly off. I pushed it aside, surrendering myself to the hug.

"Hi." I smiled up at him and raised myself onto my toes to kiss him. Alarm bells started going off in my head as he kissed me back.

"Just thought I'd make sure you were okay." As he said this, I heard his voice in my head.

Isolde... who are you talking to?

I gasped sharply as I realised the man before me was not Liam... The man with deep brown, almost black, eyes. I stepped back and his expression turned predatory.

You failed to mention that your brother is your identical twin, Liam.

Chapter Twenty-Three

I SOMEHOW MANAGED TO keep my face neutral, as Liam appeared at my side, wrenching me out of his brother's arms.

"Stay the hell away from her, Connor," Liam growled, and I pressed myself against the wall behind him, unsure of who I was more afraid of at this point.

So, this was Connor—Liam's 'older' brother. Older by mere minutes, it would seem.

"Hello, Liam, brother dear. How are you?" Connor asked with a smile, which sent shivers down my spine. The smile was cold and calculating, like a cat playing with a mouse before it swallows it whole.

"What are you doing here?" Liam hissed, keeping me firmly between himself and the wall, shielding me from Connor. I prayed that no unsuspecting patron would round the corner.

"Just checking up on my baby brother. Dear William told me you had finally settled down after all these centuries. And with his fiancee, no less. I had to meet the young woman who has so many of my people worked up." Connor ran his eyes over what little he could see of me from behind Liam as if appraising livestock. I moved closer to Liam's back, feeling a strong urge to get as far away from Connor as possible. "She is beautiful... You've done well. Pity you will have to watch her become one of us, Liam. You know how much it pains me to see you hurting." I could feel Liam's muscles become even more tense, and resisted the urge to shiver again.

"Isolde... Go back to the table. Keep Ainslie safe." I was surprised by this direction. Usually, Liam wouldn't let me out of his sight in such circumstances. Heeding his words, I slipped away from the pair and headed back to Ainslie, my legs barely holding me up.

"Hey, are you okay?" Ainslie asked me, concerned, as I sat down shakily.

"Fine, fine... Just ran into someone that I know in the bathroom." I tried to sound as if nothing was wrong, but as I spoke, I spied a familiar face over Ainslie's shoulder and felt my blood run cold. Will sat directly behind her, waving at me, his face twisted into that now familiar smile that sent tremors through every inch of my body.

Liam... we have a serious problem.

"Isolde? You look like you've seen a ghost. Are you sure you're okay?" Ainslie glanced over her shoulder. At first, she didn't see Will, turning back to face me. Then realisation dawned on her face, and she turned back slowly, freezing as Will smiled at her.

"Hi, Ainslie. It's been a long-time... You look good." I fought the urge to be sick. Instead, I stood up, pulling Ainslie out of her seat and putting myself between them.

"Isolde... What's going on?" Ainslie's voice rose with fear as Will rose to his feet as well.

"Leave. Now." I ignored Ainslie as I spoke to Will. I looked around the restaurant, trying to ignore the panic I could feel rising within me. I needed to protect Ainslie and keep her from being caught in the middle of what was about to turn into an ugly confrontation.

"Isolde... What the hell is going on here?!" Ainslie gripped my hand tightly, her voice shaking. Will moved towards me in a blur before grabbing me roughly by the hair and pulling my face close to his.

"Oh, I'll leave Isolde. But I won't be leaving alone." Will kissed me hard, and I struggled against him, pushing him away with my free hand as I used the other to move Ainslie as I backed away.

"I'm not going anywhere with you, William," I said as Liam appeared at my shoulder and shoved Will away.

Isolde, Connor is still around the corner. We are going to have to fight our way out of here.

What about Ainslie? Will had stopped and was glaring at us angrily, seeing the two of us exchanging looks.

"So, it's true... You're able to read each other's minds." I felt Ainslie grip my hand tighter.

How the hell... I shot Liam a quick questioning look, and he shook his head ever so slightly.

I have no idea, but we will work on that once we are out of here.

"Will, we don't want a scene here." I thought that statement was a stretch on Liam's part, trying to negotiate with a pissed-off vampire. Then again, he was also a pissed-off vampire, so maybe he figured it might work.

"Oh, Liam, brother. I think a scene is exactly what we need." Connor appeared beside Will. Around us, the other diners were starting to rise to their feet, and I realised, with a sinking feeling, that we were in a restaurant full of nightwalkers.

Why couldn't I sense this? I practically screamed this at Liam in my head.

It was Connor. He cloaked their presence. I was too freaked out to unpack that particular piece of information. Until now, I thought nightwalkers weren't able to wield magic.

We have to get Ainslie out of here, Liam...

And then I felt all the air leave the room as the newest member of Adam's coven rounded the corner behind Connor and Liam with casual grace, the trademark cruel smile on her face. My face.

My hand went limp in Ainslie's vice-like grip.

Then my legs started to give way from under me, though Liam caught me before I collapsed.

"Aurora?" I breathed, my eyes welling up. Her new, piercing blue eyes bored into mine, sadistic pleasure written all over her face.

"Hiya, sis."

I felt the world start to spin, and I fought the urge to black out.

Isolde, come on. Get it together. We have to get ourselves out of here first. Then we can fall apart. I wasn't sure if it was Liam's voice or my own, but I followed the advice in my head and reeled myself back together. By this point, we had reached the door. I could see the car from where we stood and shoved Ainslie in that direction.

Unlock the car! As I sent that thought to Liam, I pointed Ainslie to the car, with its lights flashing to show that the central locking was released.

"Get in! Go!" I yelled as one of Connor's minions launched himself at me. Ainslie screamed and ran as Liam, and I started fighting them off. I snapped a kick to the nearest vampire's mid-section as I punched another in the face.

Get in the car! I am right behind you! Liam's voice commanded in my head, and I raced for the passenger side as Liam ran along behind me. He dived into the driver seat and locked us in, slamming his foot down on the accelerator as he threw the car into reverse, tearing out of the parking space and narrowly avoiding a collision with another car that slammed to a halt behind us. I struggled to comprehend what had just happened as we fled the scene. I could only see Aurora's face, that cruel smile and piercing blue eyes. It was all too much.

"Isolde... What is going on? Will... Aurora..." Ainslie's voice from the back seat brought me back to reality. I had forgotten she was even there. I looked over at Liam.

I have to tell her something.

Tell her. They can do a memory charm at the Manor. I let out a breath.

"Will didn't die last year... Well... actually, he did, but now he's a vampire. And now, apparently, so is Aurora." I choked out the words as Liam reached over to grip my hand tightly. Ainslie remained silent in the back seat, and I turned to look at her, noting the confusion and disbelief written all over her face.

"What?! Have you completely lost your mind?!" She cried, her voice wavering. I let out a hollow laugh, no doubt adding to Ainslie's belief that my sanity was hanging precariously by a thread.

"I wish! Think about it, Ainslie. Try and find a better explanation for what you've just witnessed. I've tried to come up with thousands, and none of them have come close to the truth." I couldn't deal with this right now. I just wanted to curl up and cry.

"Who are you? Where are we going?" Ainslie moved her attention to Liam as I turned to stare out the window.

"I'm Liam. Sorry we aren't meeting under better circumstances..." Liam glanced at Ainslie in the rear vision mirror and no doubt Ainslie was gaping back at him.

The rest of the short drive was silent, and I dragged myself back to the present as Liam was pulling the car into the basement of the Manor.

"Where are we?" Ainslie looked as though she was about to refuse to get out of the car, but the look on my face when I opened her door must have persuaded her otherwise.

"Mission control." I led the way upstairs and headed straight for the comms room, where a meeting was underway.

"Ah, Isolde, Liam, we were just... Who is this?" Gerard looked stunned as Ainslie trailed into the room behind us.

"A friend. We have a problem." I looked around the room, spying Celeste and Daniel sitting across the table. "Did you find Colin and James?" Celeste only shook her head, perhaps sensing that now was not the time to say too much.

"Figured. Well, you can stop trying to work out what happened to them. They are either dead or nightwalkers because they failed. Aurora is now a nightwalker." I stated angrily before storming out of the room. I headed up to my room and slammed the door behind me before throwing myself onto my bed and beginning to sob uncontrollably. A few moments later, Liam entered the room and sat behind me, unsure what to do. I turned to face him, and he lay down beside me, pulling me close and allowing me to sob into his chest, my tears staining his shirt for what felt like the thousandth time since we first met.

I am so sorry...

I awoke a few hours later after having fallen into a fitful sleep. I went back downstairs and found Liam now in the comms room with Patrice and a few others. He'd left me after I'd fallen asleep, and they were trying to put together a plan, from what I could tell.

"Isolde... You shouldn't be up." Patrice approached, attempting to hug me, but I stepped out of her reach.

"How did this happen? Everyone told me she was being given the highest protection available, yet here she is, a vampire." I was angry, and the others looked at me, unsure what to say. "How the hell do I explain this to my family? To Jacob? My parents shared a home with her; she can kill them anytime." I looked out the window, seeing that it was still dark outside. "She could be killing them right now." I spun on my heel and sprinted from the room. Liam was behind me in a split second, his hand gripping mine, preventing me from leaving.

"Isolde, you can't leave. It's too dangerous now." It was Patrice who spoke, but it was Liam who was looking at me pleadingly.

Isolde... Please...

"My parents are in danger. Do any of you understand that? Aurora has already been killed... I won't let the rest of my family be slaughtered." I tried to shake Liam's hand away, but he wouldn't let go.

"We have people at your parent's house already," Patrice said, and I scoffed.

"Forgive me, but that is not a comfort to me right now!"

Isolde, calm down. Stop attacking everyone. It is not their fault. I looked into Liam's sad eyes as angry tears poured down my face.

No... It's not... It's mine. Liam looked as though his heart was breaking.

"Let me go, Liam," I said aloud. Liam looked down with tears in his eyes. He took a deep breath and slowly removed his hand, letting me go. He let his breath out shakily as I turned and walked away.

Be careful.

I never looked back.

I jumped into one of the bulletproof four-wheel drives and gunned the engine, tearing out of the basement. According to the clock on the dashboard, it was after 3 am, so traffic wasn't an issue, and I arrived at my parents' house within ten minutes, breaking every road rule possible.

The house was shrouded in darkness as I exited the car, unsure of what I would say to my parents. How would I tell them that one of their daughters was a vampire? And that they would now need to move. I took a deep breath and started to walk up the footpath. I didn't get far.

"Isolde! What are you doing here?!" Celeste stepped out of the darkness, with Daniel two steps behind her, like always.

"Telling my parents that their daughter is dead," I said woodenly, angry at their inability to protect my sister, even though I knew logically that the blame did not lie with them.

"They're not here. We told them there was a gas leak, and we had to evacuate them." I took in their appearance for the first time, realising they were both dressed in emergency services uniforms.

"Why are you still here then? And where are they?"

"They are in the guest room of your house." I opened my mouth to protest, but Celeste talked over me. "It's a safe house, Aurora won't be able to find her way back there, and the same magic protects it as the Manor. Daniel and I left Gerard there and returned here in case Aurora did come to pay a visit." As she spoke, a movement out of the corner of my eye caused me to turn away.

When I looked back a split second later, Will stood behind Celeste, a hand on either side of her head. He snapped her neck with a crack, and I screamed as he let her fall to the ground at his feet. Behind him, Daniel struggled against Adam, whose face was contorted into the same feral visage that he had worn the night he turned Will. Daniel cried out as his wife's body lay lifeless on the ground, and this distraction was all that Adam needed to gain the upper hand. He wrenched Daniel's head to the side and savagely bit his neck.

I screamed again, moving to fight Adam off, but was stopped by a hand that snaked around from behind me and clamped itself over my mouth.

"Hello, sister dearest," Aurora hissed in my ear. "We've got some catching up to do." I struggled to free myself, but Aurora's grip on me was like a vice. Connor appeared before me, smiling pleasantly. Adam let Daniel fall to the ground, and I watched helplessly as he tried to drag himself one-handed to Celeste's side, blood pouring from the wound at his neck as he clamped his hand over it.

"I have been looking forward to this for a long time, Isolde." The last thing I saw was Connor reaching towards my forehead before everything went black.

Chapter Twenty-Four

*A*s I SAT IN *the bedroom that Will and I used to share, I noticed four small collections of gifts in front of me, all bearing my name as the giver. Each gift had a label indicating its intended recipient - one for Will, one for Aurora, one for Connor and one for Liam.*

I reached for the pile labelled Will. The first gift I opened was something I had never seen before. It was a glass sphere with what looked like sunlight glaring at me, blinding me with brilliance. Blinking away the bursts of colour in my vision, I put it aside, reaching for the next gift in the pile. It was an antique watch, like the ones men used to wear attached to their clothes. The hands spun around in a blur before suddenly stopping to show the time 9:43. The time he had been pronounced dead. My hand shook as I put that aside as well and reached for the final gift. The wrapping fell away, and I turned it over in my hands. It appeared to be a sign; its wooden letters looped together to form the word 'acceptance'.

Next, I reached for the pile marked with Aurora's name. The first gift was a snow globe, a photo placed at the bottom. When I shook it, the snowflakes swirled together, forming the word "forgiveness" when they fell back to the bottom. The photo within it was of the two of us, standing face to face, with Aurora kissing me on the forehead. The second was a single vial of blood with my name written on it. I stared at it for a long time, trying to understand its meaning.

When no answers came to me, I set it aside and moved along to the third group of gifts, the one marked for Connor. Curious, I reached for the first gift, able to tell from the shape and feel that it was a book. I pulled it from the wrapping and read the title 'Life is an Illusion'. Once again, I struggled to understand the meaning as I put it aside. The second was a mirror, and I held it up, expecting to see my face reflected back at me. Instead, my features were blurred, and the word 'sacrifices' shimmered over the top.

"Isolde!" Liam appeared behind me as I turned at the sound of his voice. I looked at him, then back at the pile with his name on it.

"Isolde, where are you? Where did they take you?" I ignored him, his words making no sense to me. I reached for the pile of gifts with his name on it.

The first gift was a framed photo of the two of us. Our faces were out of focus as we stood cheek to cheek, our eyes on our hands held before us, our fingers intertwined.

"Isolde, look at me. I need you to focus. Where have they taken you?" Liam came to stand before me and took my face in his hands, forcing me to look at him.

"I... don't know." I still didn't know what he was talking about, and a sinister laugh began echoing around us. Just like in my nightmares, two shadowy figures appeared nearby, moving closer to where we stood. This time, however, I was able to make out their faces and realised, with a jolt, that it was Connor and Aurora. The laughter was growing louder still, and I clamped my hands over my ears once again as the room around us began to change, and we now stood outside, standing in front of a dilapidated old house.

"I know this place. Is this where they've taken you?" *The laughter halted abruptly, and I surveyed the house.*

"We used to play here. Dad worked for the people who owned it." On the ground, something shiny caught my attention. I knelt to pick it up. It was a delicate ID bracelet with the words "Eternally Yours" engraved into it. I looked up at Liam.

"I love you. Do you know that? It's you. It was always meant to be you." *Liam gently touched my face as I spoke, stroking my cheek before kissing my forehead.*

"I love you too. And I'm coming for you." *He vanished, and suddenly I was all alone. I felt cold and rubbed my arms, looking up at the house, which stood cold and empty. A sense of foreboding sent a shiver up my spine.*

Before me, words began to drift across the breeze that lifted my hair gently, the words starting to swirl around me before coming up as though they were appearing on a giant TV screen.

> *In a world blemished by darkness and light,*
> *A young woman shall rise with power and might.*
> *Her destiny was foretold in a prophecy of old,*
> *To bring balance to the turmoil untold.*
> *Of seventh son and seventh daughter born,*
> *Her heart will be set to mourn.*
> *There will be trials that she must endure,*
> *Before she reaches the future so pure.*
> *Her power will be unmatched and rare,*
> *Her soul will be pure, her intentions fair.*
> *But to end the apocalypse, she must pay a cost,*
> *To sacrifice what she loves and lost.*
> *A decision she must make with a heavy heart,*

For she knows this is where her journey must start.
With tears in her eyes, she'll rise with grace,
To battle the evil she must face.
The fate of the world will rest upon her hand,
As she brings an end to the chaos of the land.
Her journey will end with a triumph so bright,
As she brings balance between the wrong and the right.

Something hard struck me across the face, and I reeled back as everything around me tilted slightly. I was struck hard again, and the scene around me faded. One more hard blow and I realised it was all a dream.

"Wake up!" A voice snarled at me. It was a voice I knew well.

Everything around me was turning red, and as I came to, I became aware of a throbbing pain in my head and a burning sensation across my left cheek.

I opened my eyes slowly, looking directly into Aurora's new piercing blue eyes. She smiled at me, her lips curled back to show her new, glistening fangs. I shuddered and leaned back, attempting to distance myself from her as much as possible, which was hard to do as I was sitting on a hard wooden chair, my hands tied to the two centre beams that ran up behind my back.

"Good morning, sleeping beauty." She reached over to ruffle my hair, but I jerked my head away, glaring at her.

"Stay the hell away from me," I spat out, and she laughed.

"Oh, dear. That's not nice at all." She slapped me across the face again, bringing tears to my eyes with the force of the blow.

"Do you recognise where we are? I thought it was the perfect setting for our little reunion." Aurora danced across the room to where Will sat sprawled on a dirty old couch, flicking through an ancient-looking book.

"Why is it perfect?" I asked, looking around, not seeing anything particularly interesting about our current location.

"Don't you remember? This is where we were the first time you started talking about vampires and secret orders..." She spread her arms wide, her smile sickly sweet.

"What are you talking about?" I looked at her, confused.

"Oh... whoops." Aurora giggled and looked over at Will, putting her finger to her lips. "Not supposed to tell." If I didn't know better, I would have thought she was drunk.

"No, you weren't, naughty girl." Will grinned back at her, tossing his book aside and getting to his feet.

"Did you know we'd had magic used on us as children? Bet your precious Protectors never told you about that," Aurora said tauntingly. I tried to look like I knew what she was talking about, but I was failing miserably. Will laughed as Aurora came forward again and straddled my lap, getting as close as she could to my face. She walked her fingers over my forehead.

"It's all locked away in here. A memory charm. Just like the one they no doubt used on poor Ainslie tonight." I tried to lean away from her touch, but Aurora gripped my face with one hand, forcing me to look at her.

"Seeing as you clearly don't remember, how about I enlighten you?" Still gripping my chin, she jerked my head painfully, forcing me to look over to where she pointed at one of the corners of the room. "It was right there. We were six. We were playing with Bianca while Dad worked up at the big house. We weren't supposed to come in here, everyone told us it wasn't safe because it was falling apart, but we snuck in anyway. And we disturbed a vampire while he was sleeping." I tried not to look like I cared about what she was saying. "When he got a good look at us, it was like Christmas had come early... The chosen ones..." My eyes widened. "You know the prophecy? The one that the Protectors told you all about?" Her eyes glistened with excitement, clearly enjoying her story's effect on me. "There are two prophecies. We both have a destiny. It's not all about you, for a change. It's about both of us. And Liam and Connor, of course. The identical twins. One set of men, one set of women... Eventually becoming daywalkers and nightwalkers... But now... You're the only human left..." She grinned evilly as Will came up behind her and nuzzled her neck. I looked away, unable to stomach the sight of them together. Aurora was silent for a while, and I turned back to see them kissing each other hungrily. I felt nauseous.

"So. Back to my story." They had moved away, and Will sat back down on the couch, pulling Aurora into his lap. "When the vampire realised who we were, he got excited. He had us both locked in the room with him, intending to keep us here until the sun went down. Remember how Bianca went missing all those years ago? And we were the last to have seen her, but we didn't know anything? He killed her right in front of us. It was a traumatic experience, especially for two little girls as sheltered as we were... Then He came. Your Knight in Shining Armour," she said with disgust, as though being rescued had been the greatest disaster in the world.

"Liam," I whispered, not intending to speak but forgetting myself. Will growled into Aurora's neck, causing her to giggle. The contents of my stomach were threatening to make a reappearance now.

"Yes, your precious Liam. He busted down that door and took that vampire out without a second glance. He had someone else with him, a woman. She performed the memory charm on us and took Bianca's body away. Protecting us, they said. We weren't meant to know any of this yet. It was not our time. Deciding what we should and shouldn't know, as if they were Gods, making decisions on behalf of others, without regard for what they want or truly need." It wasn't reassuring to hear any of this. Yet unsurprising, with everything that I had seen. The Order took it upon themselves to control the outcome of every situation they encountered, especially within my life.

"Oh, and here's the best part... The destiny they have been telling you about. The one with your magical powers... Well, they left out a part." Aurora smiled cruelly, enjoying every moment as she wielded the knowledge I had not been privy to.

"Let me guess. You and I are meant to be mortal enemies?" I was growing tired of this and willing Liam to hurry up.

"Well, that's a possibility... But it just depends on who gets to you first."

"What are you talking about?" It was Will's turn to laugh cruelly this time.

"God, I can't believe how much they haven't told you! This is awesome. And they think of themselves as being the white hats. All that is pure and good. Yet they haven't told you a single thing. Not what really matters. Guess they aren't as honest as they portray themselves." He laughed again. I was becoming incredibly pissed off as I struggled to release my hands from the ropes that itched at my wrists.

"If you know everything, then spill. What have they left out?" I knew I shouldn't give them the satisfaction of knowing they were getting to me, but I couldn't keep my curiosity to myself. Aurora rolled her eyes.

"Oh, fine, spoil my fun. She has always been good at that..." She crossed her arms, looking put out as she directed this comment to Will.

When did I ever spoil her fun?

"I thought we decided that was in the past?" They had started conversing between themselves, ignoring my obvious attempts to break free from the chair.

"What can I say? I'm tired of pretending that everything between you was this perfect love story when you and I both know there was more to it than that." They had my full attention now.

"What the hell are you talking about now?" I couldn't believe it, but Will actually looked at me with a guilty look on his face.

"Your perfect fiance failed to tell you something when you returned from London. While you were away, the two of us started seeing each other. We both said it was because we missed having you around. But when you came back, and he went running back to you, I realised that it wasn't simply that. I had fallen in love with him. And I have always been in love with him. And he still had feelings for me too. But it was always about you. I had to protect my perfect younger sister. Couldn't hurt Isolde." Aurora was beginning to work herself up into a real tizz, but I looked at Will, wanting answers.

"Is that true?" Yep, the guilt was there, alright. How was this possible? "Well, you got your wish Aurora. He's all yours now." I felt ill again.

"Oh, thanks so much for your permission."

"Oh, get the hell over yourself!" I'd had enough. "For the last few months, all you've done is bitch and whine at me!" It was pointless yelling at her. The woman before me was no longer my sister but a creature who wore her face. And that creature was enjoying all of this just a little too much.

"I still haven't gotten to the punch line of my joke. The joke that is your existence."

"Well, hop to it then. I know you're dying to tell me." All I wanted now was to hear Liam's voice telling me they were about to storm in.

"The Protectors left out the key part of the prophecy. It's not about a human woman." She paused for effect, and I couldn't help but look at her now.

"It's about a vampire. The last of the four twins to be turned. The prophecy says that you'll be the one to end it all. But, if we could get you first, and turn you into a nightwalker, then there's no risk of you winning, is there?" Although I picked up on some of her story, she was rambling, and I didn't fully understand what she was telling me.

"Speak plain English, would you?!"

"Fine! Your destiny is to become a vampire! It was both of our destinies! And the Order of the Dragon knew it all along!" That stopped me in my attempts to get my hands free.

"You're lying..." I said quietly.

"Am I? Think Isolde. Think really hard," she said with a cruel smile, not noticing as Connor entered the room silently behind her and took in the scene before him.

"What, pray tell, is going on?" He asked with a smile, but there was a dangerous look in his eye as he looked at Aurora, who was puffing away, her anger having worked her up too much.

"Aurora couldn't keep her mouth shut," a voice said from behind me, and I turned to see Adam, who must have been standing there all along, keeping a silent vigil.

"I gathered," Connor tsked at her, and I watched in disbelief as she cast her eyes down like a child being scolded. Connor came to stand immediately in front of me and lowered himself to look me right in the eye. I noted the colour of his eyes.

How could his eyes change colour when none of the other night-walkers did? Last night, they were a deep chocolate brown. The same eyes on the man I had seen at Uni all those months ago. It was then that I realised that it must have been Connor that I saw that day, which was why Liam was so confused every time I had ever brought it up. But now, they were the telltale blue that was the same as the other nightwalkers in the room. The same as his brother's.

He winked at me with a cocky grin and straightened up again.

"So, Isolde, now you know the truth that the Order has been keeping from you all this time. Although, my dear little brother was just as clueless as you about the Gemini Prophecy. The elders only told him about the prophecy about you, and there was no mention of you becoming a vampire." I glared at Connor through narrowed eyes.

"You're all lying. Trying to turn me against my people."

"Really? Is that what you really believe?" He asked quietly, walking towards me. "Maybe this will help." He touched my forehead, just as he had done outside my parents' house hours before.

Instead of passing out this time, an onslaught of memories hit me. I flashed back to an old memory, one that had been hidden from me.

Liam stood over me, and I looked up at him, terrified. Behind him, Bianca's lifeless body lay on the ground, her neck twisted at an awkward angle.

"Isolde. Look at me. It's going to be okay. It is not time for you to know any of this yet. It is too soon. You deserve to have a normal childhood. It's the least we can give you." He crouched before me, a grown man looking into the eyes of a terrified six-year-old. I looked at my sister, who sat crying in Patrice's lap in the corner. Patrice was hugging her closely with tears in her eyes as she performed the memory charm, whispering the words as she rocked her back and forth.

"Who are you?" I asked Liam, still afraid.

"I'm someone who will protect you."

Then the night in the alley, the eve of my twenty-fifth birthday.

"It's you... I remember you." I told Liam, who had appeared before me on the dance floor in the nightclub. He had simply looked at me before turning and walking away. And I had followed him drunkenly outside and into the alley between it and the hotel beside it.

"Wait. How do I know you?" Liam stopped and turned back to me.

"We've met before. In your dreams." I snorted, thinking it was some line. Except, I knew his face. I had seen it in my nightmares on and off over the years.

"How..."

"Everything in your life is about to change."

"What do you mean?" I had leaned back against the wall, struggling to keep the world from spinning in my drunken state.

"I can't tell you yet. You need to start remembering on your own. But know this. Things are about to get very bad. And I can't protect you anymore." With that, he turned and walked away. I stumbled back into the club and told Ainslie it was time to go home and that it wasn't safe.

Every time I'd come across Patrice and Damon conversing, and they'd immediately gone silent, flashed through my mind as Connor took his hand away, and I returned to the present, feeling sick to my stomach.

"So now you know the truth," Connor said as I struggled to keep myself from falling apart. How had I not noticed all of this before? How could I have believed that they had told me everything? How could I have trusted them all so completely?

My mind was reeling, but suddenly, we were all drawn to the sound of someone kicking the front door in, and we all looked towards the door. The sound of wood splintering and snapping was followed by complete chaos as the outer room filled with voices and the sounds of fighting. In my head, Liam was screaming at me to hold on, but I blocked him out.

This was how it was meant to be. It was always going to come down to this. Ever since Adam had turned Will and this nightmare had begun, it was always going to come down to all of us here in this room. I was ready to end this, finally.

Aurora and Connor had both turned their backs on me as the door to the room was flung open, not seeing me as a threat while I was still tied to the chair. Unaware of the abilities that I had been developing.

I concentrated all my energy on the ropes wrapped tightly around my wrists, imagining them coming undone, and eventually, I felt them slither off and hit the ground. Slowly, I rose to my feet and tapped Aurora on the shoulder. She turned, almost bemused, not expecting to see my fist flying into her face. Nor did Connor expect the roundhouse kick to the head. Unfortunately, this did not knock either of them out, but it allowed me to see what was happening in front of them.

Liam and Will circled each other whilst Patrice, David, and someone I didn't recognise had Adam pinned against the wall across the room. Gerard and another vampire were dancing around each other, trading blows. This still left me to deal with the other two alone. I could hear the sounds of fighting from the adjoining room and knew that the other Protectors were momentarily preoccupied. Realising this, Connor and Aurora turned to me at the same time. In the space of a heartbeat, they both had me pinned against the wall, and I gasped as the breath was knocked out of me.

"That wasn't very nice, sis. Sneaking up from behind, that's playing dirty." Aurora's words were a low whisper in my ear, and Connor grabbed her as she went to lean in to bite me.

"We do this together, little one." I couldn't believe they were arguing about who got to turn me into a vampire. I saw my opportunity and struggled to free myself, but Connor just looked amused, his grip tightening on my shoulder. Aurora nodded.

"Of course." And with the briefest of exchanged looks, they both turned on me, moving as one. I cried out in pain as they bit into either side of my neck. I tried to free myself, but that made them bite down harder, causing me to scream louder. Finally, Liam saw what was happening, and I heard him yell out from far away. I could hear the sounds of the fighting now as though it were in a far-off place, an annoying sound in the distance. I heard, more than felt, as both Aurora and Connor were pulled off me. I had no way of knowing who had won and who had lost. I just felt myself slipping into the darkness.

I kept wavering in and out, feeling myself being lifted from the ground and moving fast. What felt like hours later, I distantly felt the motion of a car being driven at high speed. I could hear arguing and Liam saying, "No, I won't do it." And Patrice yelled the words, "She's almost completely drained. I can't stop the bleeding. You've got to!"

I couldn't weigh in on this argument, did not even know what they were arguing about. I just wished they would all go away and let me sleep. I was seeing faces, so many faces. They were calling me to them. They had stories to tell me. I longed to hear those stories.

Then suddenly, Liam's voice was in my ear. The last thing I heard was his beautiful voice, whispering the words, "I'm sorry. Please forgive me."

Then there was another bite on my neck, though not as painful this time...

Eventually, darkness took over, and as I felt my last breath leave my body, I heard the sound of screeching tyres and crunching metal... Then the world went black.

Epilogue

LIAM

I OPENED MY EYES, briefly aware of the pounding in my head, before the pain dissipated, and I took in the room around me. I sat slumped in a chair in the corner of a vaguely familiar room. But I only cared about the body lying on the bed across from me. Isolde lay utterly still, her head propped up on a pillow with her eyes closed.

I leapt to my feet and crossed the room in two strides before stopping at the side of the bed, looking down at her. Remembering everything that had happened until someone crashed into us, I knew the transition had begun. I could hear my heart pounding in my ears, and I leaned down to push a lock of hair off her face, kissing her gently on the forehead. I could only pray now that I had gotten to her in time. We would have to wait for another seven days until we knew the truth.

Working to push my anxiety aside, I looked around the room again, trying to figure out where I was. Though the room itself was unfamiliar, the furniture I knew well, and I realised with anger who must have been responsible for the car accident that had knocked me out. I felt my fury growing, and I stalked over to the door. Glancing back over my shoulder to look at Isolde briefly, I wrenched the door open and let it slam against the wall as I entered the hallway. A door further down the hall opened, and a familiar figure stepped out, assessing me coolly.

"Where the fuck is she?" Ronson raised an eyebrow at me. A man of few words, he gestured towards the stairs, and I glared at him for a moment before going off in search of the one I knew would have all the answers—the source of centuries' worth of frustration.

"I see you've woken up." She stood in the centre of an elaborate library to the left of the bottom of the staircase. Her long black hair was hanging down her back, and she was wearing barely any clothes, as usual. She had always been aware of her beauty and wielded it like a weapon. I'd seen many men fall to their feet before her, though it had never had that effect on me, much to her annoyance.

"What the fuck, Eve?" I demanded of her, not even attempting to hide my anger at seeing her standing before me. Although she was small, barely coming to my shoulder, she exuded power.

"Careful, Liam. Your feelings are showing," she said with a smirk, her blue eyes holding my own as she stepped closer. I stayed perfectly still, watching her every move tensely. "Aren't you happy to see your family again?" She ran a hand down my left arm, and I gritted my teeth, refusing to play her games.

"Why are we here, Eve?" I glared at the woman who had changed my life five hundred years ago and noted the gleam in her eyes. Her lips curled into a delighted smile.

"Waiting for your young lover to wake up and for the madness to end finally, of course." She spread her arms wide as though I should know what the fuck she was talking about. I moved closer, raising my hands to grip her shoulders tightly, ignoring the fact that she most likely enjoyed this. She'd always enjoyed pain.

"Explain."

"All in good time, Liam dear." She patted one of my hands before stepping out of my grasp and moving to sit in one of the overstuffed armchairs. She waved at the one across from her.

"Take a seat, Liam." She was enjoying this far too much. Her lips curled into a smirk as her eyes danced with barely concealed glee. She knew how I felt about her and the world she'd dragged me into in 1510. When I was a man who had just turned twenty-five and thought I was accepting comforting words from a stranger within the walls of a darkened church. Instead, the stranger had taken my life from me and dragged me into this world without my consent, tying me to her for eternity. I hadn't seen her in twenty-six years, but I'd felt her presence over the years and knew she hadn't been far away. Her blood memories coursed through my veins, and blood called to blood, always. I grudgingly moved to sit across from her and crossed my arms over my chest.

"What now?" I asked my sire angrily, and she shrugged.

"Now we wait. Get comfortable, my love. It's all starting now." She gestured towards the television in the corner, and I noted for the first time that it showed images of the Wivenhoe Dam, the city's main water source. Its floodgates were open, and the banner down below announced that it had burst open without warning. The city was about to be covered in water with no way of stopping it.

Seven more days. And then we would know if I managed to keep my promise to Isolde or if I would be forced to kill the only woman I had ever loved.

I closed my eyes and leaned back to stare up at the ceiling as I let out a frustrated breath. The wait was going to be excruciating.

If you have a moment

PLEASE RATE OR REVIEW

Thank you for reading! I hope you enjoyed Illusions. Stay tuned for The Order of the Dragon – Book II which will be available later in 2023.

Please take a moment to leave a rating or review on the platform you purchased from or Goodreads. Every review helps in an incredible way.

About the Author

Allison A. Andrews is a wife and mother of one based in Brisbane, Australia.

Having always been an avid reader with an overactive imagination, when she isn't writing, she loves spending time with family and friends, travelling the world, and dreaming of the next story she can tell.

Website: https://www.allisonaandrews.com/